The two lives of Johnny Smith

The two lives of Johnny Smith

Ash Harris

B

First published by BlockPointPress 2023

01

www.blockpointpress.com

A CIP catalogue record for this book is available from the
British Library.

ISBN: 978-1-7393168-0-8 (hardcover)

Typeset in 18/11pt Minion.

Printed and bound in Great Britain by CPI Group (UK) Ltd.

For I, E, F & M, with love

1999

Fancied his mate more as it happens

What a fabulous day. The surf's well and truly up in downtown Pimlico and I really don't know which of us is looking the sexier: me in my dapper new suit and shades, or the long curvaceous bonnet and glorious styling of this the ground up rebuild that is my 1964 Aston Zagato.

Blondie: 'I told you I was going to stay out last night...'

Albeit, as I lean here basking in these late afternoon rays, why this ice-cold bottle of mineral water isn't quenching my thirst is beyond me.

Blondie: 'Not sure; somewhere near Victoria, I think.'

Damn, spilt some down my shirt. Still, it doesn't stop the babe wiping the pavement tables outside Jen's café giving me the eye up.

Blondie: 'I can't speak any louder, I'll wake him up.'

Nor throwing me a cheeky grin and displaying her curves in my direction either...

Marvellously.

Blondie: 'John, I think he said..., Johnny Smith.'

Only, where is that annoyingly familiar woman's voice coming from?

Blondie: 'Course it's his real name!'

Huh?

Blondie: 'Or at least I think it is...'

Ah...

Hmm.

That last night.

Blondie: 'With Shirley, in the Academia, off Old Street..., although dunno where she got off to.'

And that Shirley.., in that Academia.

Blondie: 'Yeah, he's alright. Bout twenty-one I'd guess.'

Humph.

Blondie: 'An estate agent, think he said. Or something like that anyway...'

If I can't presently feel my head, is it too much to hope I'm still asleep and dreaming?

Blondie: 'I can't really remember what he looks like, *exactly*... He's got one of those faces, y'know? I'll need to have another look in a minute!'

'It really won't make any difference Blondie, trust me.'

Blondie: 'Fancied his mate more as it happens; but I've been home with worse.'

Of all the beer joints, in all the boroughs, in all the world...

Blondie: 'Well, you did ask Mum!'

Mum?!
Fuck.
And I'm a child molester.

Although, hang on, she on the phone in the kitchen out there said she worked for a firm of solicitors, didn't she?

Blondie: 'Okay, yeah, I'll give you that...'

Which, notwithstanding what's left of my ego's opportunistic jibe at the resigned fatalist in me, would make her at least eighteen, wouldn't it?

Even if she does still live with her Mum?

Yikes, she's not the honeypot in a scam to blackmail me, is she?

I certainly wouldn't put anything past her solicitor bastards for bosses.

Blondie: 'Mmm, maybe I am, yeah...'

Yeah, exactly.

Exactly.

Only, if I really am awake, and really must accept looking nearly four years younger than I am and being in a career way too close to Estate Agency, what would be handy is if, contrary to the usual way of things on planet Smith, I could remember her my new intimate-friend-of-but-a-few-hours-ago's name sometime soon.
Please.

Blondie: 'Nah, think I'm gunna take a sicky.'

Not that either piece of information – or in my case the lack of it, or my ashamedness at such, or by extension my conscience – nor even the gorilla seemingly pinning us all face down to the bed, is in any way discouraging the one-eyed bystander in my boxers, obviously.
The irony of which isn't escaping one of us at least.

'Haven't you done enough already, you insur-erectionary bloody...?'
Unless the blood that's all too willingly disowned and abandoned the numb mush that is my brain has gone somewhere else entirely and I'm actually already dead and rigor mortis has set in: and that's not too much to hope for.

Hmm?

But, nope, there's no sign of any pearly gates on the immediate expanse of hazy white-sheet-ness stretching out from under my nose at any rate.

Actually, come to think of it, they should really be looming large in Mr Spence's room if there's any justice to it.

How could he have done this to me, the lanky streak of..?

I did tell us both it was only going to be a one-on-the-night-before-job-interview drink, didn't I? And so bleedin' what if we'd been invited to a bar opening in Hoxton for a one-on-the-way-home cocktail?

Blondie: 'Yeah, I'm gunna give Shirley a quick call, and then I think I'll go back to bed.'

What?!

But, surely, not this bed, though, right?

Blondie: 'Mu-um!!! You're not supposed to encourage me to do things like that, I'm your daughter, remember?!!'

Ackhh!

Fuck, if my head was going to jerk up from the bed primed for God knows what, it could have warned the rest of me, couldn't it?

Ouch.

I would expect my head to pound, but everywhere else as well?

Just what the hell did I physically do with her last night?

Humph.

And to think that, yesterday, I might well have been envious, quietly admiring even, of those able to seize the moment with a good-looking stranger – or, for that matter, even a half good-looking stranger – when all I should have been is grateful that such *opportunities* have not arisen much for me before.

This is what it must be like to wake up as the angst-ridden protagonist in some surreal Woody Allen lovefest.

I knew I should've stuck with Julia Hammond at school, no matter how fleeting and one-sided the reality.

Blondie: 'I *know* I'm not getting any younger, but I am still only twenty you know.'

Ah, great, twenty.

Or it would be great if twenty had a name I could remember.

'Come on, remember, damn it, you useless, good-for-nothing halfwit Smith...'

How can I face she of such familiar voice and lingering scent of perfume after doing what we did without knowing her name?

Blondie: 'Alright, I'll see what I can do, just for you Mum.'

'Fuck... But not here..., with me, though, err..., right?'

So what if it makes me a wimp, or crazy, or just downright negligent; further carnal relations with someone to whom my face is as forgettable as her name is to me would mean crossing a threshold of guilt even I'm not prepared to cross, however improbable the prospect in reality.

Particularly when she sees me again.

And even if she is, admittedly, very pretty, has a great bod, and isn't joking.

Or that the interview I've sought for so long, that will hopefully divert me off the tracks of my present, mundane existence, is at nine o'clock.

Hmm.

'Err, yes; that'd be nine o'clock this morning then, John.'

Pfft.

Surely only I could be this much of a fuck-up.

Yep.

The half-drunk and even-God-doesn't-know-how-old glass of water on the bedside table it'll have to be then.

If as much in punishment, and if I can somehow manage to direct its wildly oscillating contents into my mouth, that is.

Oh, and a mouth which now decides to be reticent and tight-lipped of course.

'Just several hours too bloody late, mate.'

Ugh-argh.

Ooh, that's better actually.

My tongue and senses are still working then.

Vaguely.

Even after the unexpected workout they had last night, the sex god impostor I am.

If a sex god impostor whose tenacity of erection may be more a measure of the tsunami swelling in his bladder than potency.

Well, this morning anyway.

And who, whether he now wants to or not, and impending nausea or no, had better get his potency to the en-suite toilet else turn the clock back twenty years.

Yes, fuck, and quickly.

Woah.

Blimey, is the room *actually* spinning?

Hang on, that's not the time is it?!

Really?! 08:05?!

Fuck, it really is five past eight; even my watch says so.

No, 08:06.

'Christ, give me a chance will you, you sodding alarm clock..., err, thing...'

Just because I ignored the glaring thing in my lustful haste last night, it's like it decided to hide deliberately at the back of the bedside table, carefully biding its time, literally, before taking its revenge.

Fuck, I might as well just fall back down onto the bed, be done with it all and have a heart attack.

'Harrumph.'

Blondie: 'Okay, Mum. Yeah, see ya later. Love ya too. Bye then.'

And while I'm lying here, can somebody, anybody, please tell me again why I ever bought this tangled absurdity that is my recycled-plastic-bottle-ceiling-lightshade-pendant-thing?

Anyone, anyone?

I must have too much of the money that I don't actually have.

Only, if I don't take another breath soon it really will be my last.

Nope, there goes the keypad on the flat phone again.

The torturer delays the executioner.

Blondie: 'Hi Shirl', it's me...'

Hmm.

Duly the indomitable Shirley, but what's me's name?

That would have been just too easy on me, evidently; no matter how oppressive the room already feels outside the duvet.

Only, name or no name, an ideal opportunity afforded by Shirl' or not, a bladder on the verge of capitulation or not – or that the shreds of my ego probably couldn't withstand listening to the rest of the conversation in any case – it really is now-or-never back up from the bed and out into it again.

Bracing for the worst this time.

Ackh...

Blimey.

And, unless I want to alert Blondie, quietly, and, highly preferably, without Elvis Presley-ing into anything.

Fuck!

Or stepping on anything.

Ye-owwww.
Who the fuck left whatever that was on the floor?
Humph.
Surging knob excepting, what a pathetic a physical state I've led myself into.
Still, if I can just close the bathroom door behind me – and, yep, slowly, to minimise the hinge squeak – salvation on both is nigh.
Yep.
There.
Right.
Now for the trickier bits...

Oops!

Oof.

Perhaps it would have been better to unbutton and drop my boxers before I sat-cum-fell down onto the toilet seat.

Nope, fuck, I'll just have to butt dance and wriggle them off from here...

Yikes, and sharpish.

Right, and, yep, now shuffle as far back on the seat as I can, yes; and, anatomically diabolically but unavoidably, gently or forcibly aim rigid knob down inside the rim...

And, lastly, identify and release the correct muscle in the general numbness down there to yes..., ackh..., no..., hang on..., yes..., successfully open my bladder.

Yes.

And, ahh, umm, thank Christ, the Devil or whoever else for this.

Relief in far more ways than one.

Including not having to face Blondie or otherwise do whatever it is I have yet to decide I will do with a coat hanger to precede me.

And which it sounds like would have been rather more memorable during idle conversation this morning than it seems either it or my face were to her last night; sadly enough for both of us.

On a slightly more cerebral level, however; if such a significant portion of my blood is indeed returning to reboot my pee sized brain, the question is do I even want to use any increased thinking capacity to tackle the thorny issue of whatever it is I have yet to decide I'm going to do, or just sit here for the rest of the day?

Unless the thinking is restricted to whether I can get away with not shaving, or if I can brush my teeth both silently and without provoking my head, possibly.

And which, given this stubble, no I can't and, yes, I've got to try; unless I really do want to do nothing else but be a quasi-estate agent for the rest of my life.

Humph.

Assuming standing back up without falling over is even an option...

Hmm.

But, yes, just about.

At least my toothbrush is where it's supposed to be then.
Another thing ignored in my haste last night.

And, wow..., provoking my head it'll have to be then.

Fuck.

Toothpaste as a hangover cure is definitely over-rated.

In the absence of time for a shower and back on the subject of Blondie again for a minute though; it could at least be possible, couldn't it, that, whilst the kindest long-term option for both of us could well be a silent, if cowardly, exit, the principled option might actually be another ten-minute shag and a deceitful farewell?

Or so she might think?

Yikes, could it, might it?

As Si says, 'shag 'em once and they feel it's a sordid one-night stand, but shag 'em twice and it's a failed relationship'; and, of all people, he would know, wouldn't he?

On the other hand, having up til now not exactly had much of a reason to examine the theory, what of the details, the practicalities?

Fucking Don Juan down the hall out there accidentally neglected to explain those to me, didn't he.

Like, what if there must there be a conscionable period between the two shags – more than a few hours at least – to qualify? Or if another quickie with me is the very last thing she wants, but I find out too late to withdraw, in every sense of the word, that she's pursuing the same theory?

Humph.

Fucking relationships.

Or, make that relationships following fucking.

Blimey, waterboarding has more appeal than this.

And, notwithstanding that waterboarding is maybe what's required to fix my hair and face this morning, a quick splash-wash and dab of deodorant will have to do it.

And, no, however Si might carry on – and he's not exactly a pillar of virtue in anything else – I, for one, am going to do the right thing.

I am a supposedly responsible and considerate adult and am going to take considered responsibility for my actions.

Yes.

And let chance play its hand.

If I can make it to the front door without Blondie noticing, I'll make a run for it. If not, then I'll face the music and see what happens.

Yes, it's the fairest, most responsible thing to do.

Yep.

So, right, if that's the thorny, inner-head issue resolved, all I need do now is swat and gel my outer head back to some loose sort of normality..., mm-hmm..., and get dressed, and let fate take its course.

Yes.

Right.

The bedroom first then; calmly and quietly avoiding anything painful – yep, that's it – and into the wardrobe for my last clean and ironed shirt.

Ah.

Crap.

That isn't there.

Nope.

Another thing I was supposed to do last night.

And, whilst I somehow managed to lay the trousers of my only blue, neutral-for-interview suit over the back of the chair in the dissolute melee, the same, nope, cannot be said of yesterday's white shirt and today's only resort: which, complete with tie still clinging steadfastly to its collar, is, yep, lying discarded on the floor ever so helpfully.

Alongside what I must have trodden on: my late great Grandad's beautiful silver and pearl cufflinks.

'Yes Mum, you're right: I should and do feel ashamed.'

Luckily, the bona fide lightweight that I am, I don't seem to have bent either though.

Parking that in the embarrassment box for a minute, and as undeserving as I am, have this diehard shirt and tie combo taken similar taken pity on me?

As easy enough as they are to slip on the way they came off...

Actually...

If I flick whatever this, err..., is off and straighten it out around me a bit...

Hah!

Blimey, thank the Mirror Gods or Si's monster of a steam iron for this.

Far from great, but, yes, miraculously, still just passably presentable.

Mirror Gods or no, clean 365s and socks..., err..., yep..., and I'm almost there.

All I need to do is retrieve my suit jacket, backpack and trainers from the living room, before I can make good my escape.

Oops.

Not forgetting to grab and take my trousers, which might help. Mm-hmm.

So, right, now for the small matter of getting out of the bedroom door, across the hall, and into the living room without Blondie noticing.

And the sooner the better, in case she does indeed decide to come back to this bed.

Yep, a quick peak round the edge of the door first then.

Blondie: 'Yeah, you're right, Shirl', I know..., I know.'

Yikes, she really is here.

Undeflected and with stark clarity for the first time this morning, the real person with no name on the phone to Shirley in my kitchen at the end of my hall.

Fuck.

And factually too this time; it's like I can almost feel her against me again.

Hmm.

'Not that any renewed swell of disconcertment is going to stop you drifting silently across the wooden hall floor, though, eh John?'

Nope.

Nor, but a cursory guilt-led glance down the empty corridor later, stop me gently pushing open and easing-to behind me the living room door, and shaking open my trousers ready for my first leg.

'Wanna go for a swim, John? Yeah, let's go for a swim.'

And, nope, not one scintilla of it isn't my own doing.

Hang on: what was that?

Was that movement? Is there someone else in here?!

Yes, there, a lithe shadow set against the window blind.

And, blimey, now more than a lithe shadow.

A vision of loveliness in fact.

Still and half-dressed as I am, but in her case perfectly so, like she's been caught mid-motion, foot on couch, as she draws a hold-up stocking over a perfect leg; a veil of tousled hair and an unbuttoned white shirt framing matching bra and briefs her only defence against my gaze.

If, nope, a tousled veil she feels she doesn't need any more.

Then again, who with a face like hers would?

She's almost unnatural, ethereal.

With the possible exception of, what was that..., yep, the merest of shared grins at our – no, make that her – predicament, there the similarities between us possibly end however.

And particularly so when I'm busy making delusional jokes to myself and Ms Hold-ups is already more than a step on the couch ahead of me sending an altogether different message.

Mm-hmm.

As wholly unnecessary as it is, that's one coolly raised, straightened forefinger to her lips and glance at the door behind me that even I can't misinterpret.

As if from experience she thinks I might, on the off chance that I could.

What was I thinking about relationships following fucking again?

Only, if my rashly breaking the silence really is her sole concern, what now?

Ahh, but of course; as far as I'm concerned, absolutely nothing what now then.

The look on my face the only affirmation needed under the tacit rules of engagement in this every-woman-and-man-for-themselves-in-Pimlico world into which I have led myself this everyday morning, I am to be contained behind the tousled barrier once more while she of the perfect fingers returns simply and purposefully to the task of working the straggling hold-up up to the upper echelons of her perfect, outstretched leg.

Hmm.

And just how am I expected to react to that?

Am I supposed to feel aggrieved?

Awed?

Accepting, even?

Or just unprofessional?

At least I would happily smile if it were permitted.

And, as conscious as she's made me of my part, my tacit obligations in this unceremonious bargain, why, whichever the case, can't I look away?

What is it about this woman and her hold-ups that are so spellbinding?

Is it simply the short stretch of illusive thigh left exposed at the summit?

Or just what's implied: effortless sexiness without the need for surplus frills and overdone suspenders?

Nah, who am I kidding.

Britney, you've got a lot to answer for.

Actually, Hold-ups here is probably just as enamoured with my legs as I am with hers.

Oops.

Ahh.

Maybe not then.

Having dropped her head to hold-up level, she's directly caught my stare, my illicit thoughts, everything: openly and irrefutably.

'Oh, now you can look away Smith!'

And as well I might flush sharply with embarrassment.

Me and my cringing discomfort-cum-infantile infatuation obliged to accept in neutered shame the kind of resigned smile and directive gesture to my own legs and trousers, or absence thereof, she doubtless reserves for errant puppies – mere men like me just can't help ourselves, obviously; she and her unnerving and indomitable self-assurance completing my humiliation and her master class on counterinsurgency and the subservient male.

Like I haven't learnt enough about myself already this morning.

And the pathetic, out of my depth subject that I am, there's nothing I can do but belatedly and obediently pull on my trousers, somehow avoiding the tail between my legs.

Yep, one leg after the other.

Leaving me free to contemplate why I deserve such purgatory; and, worse, why I'm almost enjoying it.

Humph.

If absolutely not why the hell the woman is here in our living room at all, of course.

All contemplation of that being utterly forbidden until she's long gone.

And to think I had imagined such girls to be the preserve of rock stars and billionaires, rather than flatmates called Simon.

And I can only hand it to him, he did it from a standing start too.

I left him in the bar last night with only a glass for company; and this girl really is stunningly beautiful, even here and now – perhaps especially here and now – after a night before like that.

As good-looking as he is himself – and notwithstanding that he does have the sort of annoying-for-the-rest-of-us charm that only those with genuine charisma can muster, and even earns more than a few quid at a Hedge Fund – really..., what can she possibly have seen in him?

And why isn't my usual jocular jibe at him making me feel any happier about it this time?

Humph.

Him and his diamond-tipped self-confidence and sheer, indefatigable gall.

No amount of Class A could ever begin to instil the unshakeable capacity for self-admiration that he's got; nor his ability to persuade, either. And, in the sphere of sexual relations – if not everything else in this world – what value can be put on gall and the ability to charm and persuade?

Lucky for us both that I haven't had enough feelings of self-deficiency to contend with this morning.

I'm going to have to move out for the sake of my sanity.

Or if only to create room for his harem, lest anyone think I'm inconsiderate.

And yet, sitting here as I am, cowering and struggling pathetically with the laces on my trainers, should I be bitter or glad that women like this one will never have to skulk away from me in the morning without so much as a goodbye?

And should I even be bothered if I'm a disloyal hypocrite?

Humph.

How can they do this to me – Blondie, Si, this one, all of them – torment me like this?

Whilst there's every chance that Si won't be bothered in the slightest, the price of my escape from Blondie is complicity with Hold-ups. I'm willingly trading self-respect for guilt.

Surely no shag is worth this?

Then again...

Going on this one here, either in or out of that flossy skirt and fitted jacket...

Even if she does have the temerity to use that framed photo of

18

my parents – in their own youthful prime accepting – to apply that utterly superfluous dab of lipstick.

And I should obviously just be grateful for her woman-who's-worth-it generosity in granting me the honour of a close-up view of this final inverted shake of her tousled hair and a co-departure, bless her presuming cotton hold-ups.

Likewise, naturally, the visual confirmation of those, my instructions she's thrown me with her eyes.

'Your jacket, backpack and the door it will obediently be then, eh John?'

And, yep, it will.

And, whether by calculation or providence, she's now positioned herself so close behind me in the doorway that there's no going back in any sense of the phrase for either of us seemingly.

Still, as eerily and disconcertingly quiet as the hall now is, just three or four light pads to the front door, and both Blondie and Si will have had their respective opportunities.

And particularly so for Si, who, even if he is bothered, can only blame himself for neglecting in his own rush last night – and who could blame him – to turn the deadlock, hereby making it even easier for me to open the front door without breaking the silence.

Mm-hmm.

Much in the same way as a prudently de-heeled Hold-ups is able to ghost her way silently across the hard, wooden hall floor towards the front door I'm holding open for her.

And, yep, as well my blood might run cold all of a sudden.

Blimey; I can live with her making me feel subjugated, inferior even, but has she really got to make me feel cold and displaced as well? In my own home?

It's like she's obligated to Blondie under the terms of some time-honoured female pact to take every available opportunity to maximise my misery.

19

But, in my own defence, I have let chance play its hand with Blondie, haven't I? And she's highly likely to be grateful not to have to face me again in any case, isn't she?

Assuming, as I stand here watching this one here slip stealthily out through the front door and out into the common stairwell, that chance has had anything to do with any of it.

Take away my delusory, wishful thinking and I've been nothing less than intentionally evasive.

But am I not also genuinely late, in danger of missing what might be my one and only opportunity of a lifetime?

And it was a miracle I got the interview in the first place, wasn't it?

Hmm.

I'll take one, last, final, look down the hall.

'Come on Blondie, where are you? Confound me.'

But, nope, still nothing but silence and emptiness.

And no more time.

I am tied to a fate of my own making, and must accept my ability and willingness to insert a key into the outside of a front door and twist open and then closed with hitherto unrecognized deftness the latch as I close the door behind me with barely a sound, and get on with it.

Humph.

And there was me thinking I'm one of the good guys, someone who treats others with care and respect.

Today, deaf to even my own conscience, I'm just going to follow the path of the newly shoed Hold-ups down the staircase.

One, two, three, five, seven...

Yep.

Thirteen, Fifteen, Seventeen...

In a descent for me far greater than the twenty-three stairs, no matter how quickly I try to take or ignore them.

And..., oh.

And a descent which, as luck would have it, brings me out just in time to make farewell eye contact with an evermore to be one step ahead of me Hold-ups from the backseat of an opportune black cab as it pulls away from the pavement.

For whatever reason, not so much as a single word uttered between us; and, our contrasting fortunes the way they must be, there almost certainly never will.

Hmm.

Of all the experiences I ever hoped for in life, this is not among them.

To think there was a time not so long ago when I would greet and inhale this, the early morning street air of the greatest city on earth with relish and anticipation.

And just how the hell have I allowed myself to come to this?

Milking it

So, key back in the front door not so silently this time, and here goes.

Oops: Blondie.

Was she expecting me?

Nope, she looks as startled by my sudden appearance in the hall as I am.

And wearing only her sexy little Beatles vest top from last night and not much else besides...

Actually, maybe Si's right and I should just see if she's up for another quick one? It wouldn't take long, and would be as much for her benefit as mine, wouldn't it? Yes, it would be for the best all round in fact.

'Only, no, it wouldn't though, John, would it?'

And, no, sadly it wouldn't.

'Morning Blondie. Thought you might need this...'

'Yes, the carton of milk dangling on my finger, and my fabricated excuse for having left and come back.'

And which, if only to break this uneasy silence, I'll quickly drop into the kitchen for her.

Uh-oh, she's smiling hesitantly and has that unmistakeable look of regret-based worry on her face.

My first assumption was right all along then.

And why, after all, would she want to see someone like me again?

There's no need for her to worry about it though.

'Listen, don't worry about anything, okay? I had a great night last night, but things don't always turn out as we think, do they?'

And I really did, and they really don't; well, not for me at any rate.

Still.

'And I'm sorry, but I've got a really important interview this morning, so I've got to get off. But give me a call if you'd like another cocktail or two sometime. Maybe we could compare notes on, I dunno, The Beatles or, err, hangover cures or..., something.'

And, good, that wry joke's got her smiling at least.

If only as a prelude to a second departure done properly this time.

Blondie: 'Thanks, John.'

And judging by the warmth in her voice and face she might even mean it too.

At least a name like mine is easy to remember.

A farewell nod and smile before I close the door it is then.

Blondie: 'My name's Kelly by the way.'

Oops.

I'm not the only one who can make playful, magnanimous gestures then.

'Course it is Kelly. You have a great day. If you need anything before you go, just ask Simon...'

The layabout.

'I'm sure he'll be up before too long. Even good-for-nothing investment bankers have to go into work occasionally.'

The gold medallist

Right then: now for the rest of this fine summer morning.

And all hereto won't matter a jot anyway if I don't get into the office PDQ.

I need to be in Golden Square for nine; so, as long as my eyesight and watch have stopped ganging up to play tricks on me, at just gone eight twenty-three I should just about have time to get the tube into work, give a lame excuse about having to do some property inspection or other, and hotfoot it over to Soho.

In which case, if there's nothing else my conscience has forgotten to do, and having already traded, rather successfully I'd say..., yep..., my earlier world of stealth and torment for the more heartening environs of Wilton Road and a freshly made ham croissant and pressed apple juice combo from Jen's café, it's Victoria Station or bust in as quick and easy a manner as my still resolutely mutinous and acidified body will allow then.

Oops.

Perhaps trying to walk a little straighter.

Oh, and call me old-fashioned, maybe even beginning to think about what the hell I'm going to say to them in the interview if I do make it on time.

But on which subject, aside from a reassuring spiel about

proven concepts and adding value through creativity, anything really meaningful or persuasive is, yep, so far eluding me.

If indeed there is anything.

Maybe I should do simply and precisely what I want to do, and just beg?

Beg to be extricated, saved from this other person's life I'm leading.

But, when they ask why?

Not because I deserve to be saved – last night's choices are clearly contra-proof of that if any more were needed – but just because they can?

How, left to my own devices, I end up on one of the most important mornings of my life struggling to walk in a straight line and direct a croissant into my mouth?

'Harrumph.'

If nothing else, they might see what I've come to and take pity on me possibly?

Albeit, if the croissant and apple juice continue at their current rate to take the edge off my hangover and sharpen my senses, I'll be confounded on even that notion.

'You're starting to make me feel better on purpose aren't you, gut for brains?'

A second insurrectionist part of my own body that thinks it knows better than I do.

Hang on, what the...?!

No!

You've got to be kidding me!

Fuck.

Make that a second insurrectionist with the ulterior motive of allowing me to take in with blinding alacrity the telltale blue and white striped tape slowly extending out behind that police officer as she crosses the road and pavement directly ahead of us both.

Today of all days.

A fucking station closure incident.

This morning.

I don't sodding believe it.

The whole of Victoria Station.

Cordoned off under my very nose.

Actually, there are only two police officers covering this part of the road. Maybe I could slip under the tape quickly?

Oops, seen.

'Nope, okay officer, sorry.'

Fuck.

This really can't be happening; not today.

If I could get hold of the idiot who's caused this, I'd chop his gonads off.

That's if he's not bigger than me, of course.

Or braver, which wouldn't be hard.

Maybe I could outrun him after I've done the chopping?

'Fuck, John, this is not helping.'

Whatever the reason, I'm not the only one here with a look of desperation in his or her eyes.

And I must be joking if I think I'm going to find a cab.

Hold-ups had the right idea all along. Maybe looking after number one does pay. If I hadn't cracked and gone back up to see Blondie, I'd already be on the tube by now with nothing more to worry about than keeping my croissant down for a couple of wobbly minutes.

Me and my fucking goody-goody conscience.

Bollocks.

Even the buses are in gridlock.

Bollocks.

Humph.

Nope.

I have no alternative.

I can either wait here with my fellow malcontents and be late; or I can speed-walk it.

Which is just fucking great.

Fabulous even.

For two fucking miles.

In this physical state.

To Mayfair.

Arghh.

Only, short of knocking that bloke off his bike and stealing it, there really, definitely, really isn't anything else to do, is there?

If I've even got the time?

Hmm.

Even my all-time record for the walk from home to the offices of what I earnestly hope will soon be my erstwhile employers in Mayfair is twenty-one minutes and twenty-three seconds...

Although, less, say, four minutes for the distance I complacently ambled to here, meaning around sixteen or seventeen minutes?

Bollocks.

Further meaning that, yep, I can just about do it.

Possibly.

With the small matter of having to share the pavement with a hundred thousand more people than normal all pumped-up with newly acquired commuter-rage.

And unaccustomed work-walkers spoiling for some pavement argy-bargy will be all I sodding-well need.

And I don't even have my Walkman in my bag, do I?

Erm...

Nope.

It's going to seem like an hour and seventeen minutes.

But, yep, it's undeniably doable.

Hump.

Yep, it's eight twenty-five, and I've got nothing left to lose.

And no amount of self-pity or additional scrutiny of the worsening human and vehicular gridlock around me is going to change either fact.

If I stop prevaricating and get on with it.

Mm-hmm.

Lots of gesticulating and police tape, but no sign of an early resolution.

Just a multitude of pounding heads.

Like the opportunistic bastard that is mine has decided it should do again.

So, across Victoria Street and speed-walk pace through the backstreets of Westminster and St James's it is going to have to be then.

Fabulously.

And there was me thinking yesterday that I'd give myself an early night and a nice, stress-free early morning in which I could prepare myself calmly and thoroughly for the first and only interview I've genuinely ever wanted rather than needed a job from.

But, oh no, just when I thought it impossible to surpass my previous efforts at imbecility, here I am.

Scarcely half an hour beforehand and still at best a mile and a half footslog away, forced to swerve and jostle my way through London's iratest with absolutely no fucking idea if or for how long I'll be able to keep either my speed up or my breakfast down.

Ugh.

'And, no, I don't care if there are far less attractive routes on which to have to do it.'

Fuck, I really am going to be sick.

No, false alarm.

Yak.

Then again, the last time I...

Woooaaahhh, fuck me!!

Wow, that was close.

An eco-green Toyota Prius heading at an insane speed in near total silence across the shared pedestrian-cum-car path to that underground car park.

'Fuck, you nearly hit me you idiot?!'

And without so much as a backward glance or pause either.

The twat of a so-called driver has quite clearly done it deliberately, presumably believing I was jaywalking over what he considers to be car territory.

Blimey, if it isn't station-closure rage that gets me this morning it'll be road rage.

In fact, technically not even road rage but common space rage.

And what does the sign above the car park entrance denote?

Department of Transport.

Un-sodding-believable; almost killed by someone who works for the government body responsible for road safety.

Actually, I should have feigned injury from a glancing blow by his wing mirror: that would have frightened the twat. I wonder how his boss, the Secretary of State, would explain that one away on Newsnight.

JP: 'But we can see clearly from the CCTV footage that your employee deliberately veered towards Mr Smith, and it was only because of Mr Smith-here's amazing, no, superhuman, reactions that the car did no more than glance him in the bollocks.'

SofS: 'I'm sorry, Jeremy, but despite the fact that the car was entering the Department of Transport's secure underground car park, and it had a DoT sign on its bumper, there is simply no categoric evidence that it was being driven by one of the Department's employees.'

JP: 'You mean to tell me..., even though the car is registered to the Department of Transport, and notwithstanding the vast array of CCTV cameras, you can't identify the lunatic twat of a nutjob driving it at the time?'

SofS: 'No.'

Only, as usual, I'm simply not quick-witted enough.

And, with no time in the real world to indulge in now absent electric-car-driver baiting – yep, the twat of a nutjob has long since disappeared into the underground car park after all – I'll need an alternative target on which to focus my energy and expletives.

Actually, is that my sometime adversary Boney Arse up ahead? Yes, I think it is as well.

Where does she head to again? Buckingham Gate, isn't it?

In point of fact, boney-and-athletic-everything might be a fairer description.

And, hence why she walks so fast, in case I dare forget.

And why she's a worthy walk-race adversary on our part-shared route to work on the odd morning, even if she is negligently unaware of the fact.

Either that or she can walk fast because her arse is boney.

Only, if I really am going to take her on again this particular morning, Buckingham Gate isn't actually that far away now, and at my current rate of gain it'll be some chase and touch and go whether I can catch her at all in fact.

Although if I hug the building corners, I should be able to make up at least some easy ground on her.

But, ackh, yep, when needs must and all that.

And I can only die trying.

Which would be one way out of the interview.

Not that dying would be a good enough excuse for failing to get there on time as far as my goody-goody conscience is concerned.

Ditto being majorly hung over.

Even if dying isn't conducive to walking, let alone fast.

'There's no backing out now though John, you gibbering lightweight.'

Humph.

I could do with legs like she up there.

No wonder she's got such a rangy walking style with legs that long.

And all clad in her usual uniform of tight tee shirt – light pink today – over loose grey couch bottoms and white trainers, of course.

Not exactly chic, but, unless I'm missing the latest anti-chic trend, not surprising on a warm day like today, since the sole aim of a regular work-walker is to get to work, not attract the attention of passing paparazzi. But every day? When it's wet and cold enough to freeze the nuts off a polar bear? She must be bonkers.

Or into self-flagellation.

Or sadomasochism, or something.

Walk-racing even.

Christ only knows what a woman like her does for a living.

Chief of climate change prevention at Greenpeace maybe?

Head of internal design and use of the Millennium Dome?

Actually, Dome-by-committee HQ at Whitehall would vaguely be in this direction, wouldn't it?

Huh?

Or maybe it's just the obvious, and she's just a tough, no-nonsense commuter simply pursuing her own path, either oblivious to or not caring a damn about what I or any other needy and delusional work-walk racer ponders in her wake.

Nah, who's she kidding.

She's as much of a work-walk racer as I am, and is so frightened of getting beat by me again this morning that she's already enlisted one of her eco warrior mates to wipe me out in his Prius back there.

And there's obviously no way that I can allow her to use such skulduggery to get to Buckingham Gate ahead of me.

Despite the temptation to explore further what is a bizarre thought-diversion even by my ridiculous standards.

Only if I am now somehow in Boney Arse's slipstream and don't want to blow the win, I'd better plan my overtaking strategy, and sharpish.

Yep.

So.

At less than ten metres behind, and assuming I continue to gain at my current rate, I should be able to pass her a few paces before the finish line: otherwise known as the traffic lights at the top of Buckingham Gate.

Not a thrashing, but, nevertheless, a win is a win.

And even Damon doesn't have to overtake Schumacher with a hangover I shouldn't think.

Well, for his sake I certainly hope not anyway.

Only, yep, do I try to overtake her on the pavement, or take a slight detour onto the road?

On the extreme off-chance she has paid me any attention on our mutual way in these occasional mornings, I don't want her thinking I'm stalking her.

Well, no more than in the sporting sense that I am doing.

Hmm.

I've still got a little extra speed left so think I'll quicken my pace slightly and pass her on the road, just before the traffic lights.

Just to be safe.

Yes.

Okay.

Yep.

Here we go then; a few more paces, just a few more paces.

'Walk through the pain, John, just walk through the pain.'

That's it.

And now deftly out onto the road after the Rolls Royce.

Blimey they've got long cars round here.

And, now, a quick jump back up onto the pavement in front of her.

Yes.

That's it.

Just another five..., more..., metres...

Don't look back; never look back.

... and..., yes, an imperceptible dip through the line to be sure.

Yesss! Ooohh, yesss!

'Woaaarrhh, woaaarrhh,' the crowd roars.

Well, almost whispers, quietly, to myself, under my breath.

But, oh, the self-adulation.

And, if I'm crafty enough, I might even be able to take a surreptitious glance back over my shoulder under the pretence of checking the traffic at the pedestrian crossing.

Hah!

Ohh, yesss.

The lean form of my vanquished opponent continuing on her usual route, completely none the wiser about the pasting she's just taken.

'Until next time, Boney. You were quick, but just not quite quick enough I'm afraid.'

'Woaaarrhh, woaaarrhh.'

Oops.

Yikes.

Enough of that; I'm now well and truly back in work-walker traffic so had better concentrate.

And, wow, I was right: the main routes are busy today.

Good job that this throng don't know mine and Boney Arse's backstreet-insider-route.

And my usual trainer wearing, backpack carrying geek co-work-walkers these are not.

No, smartly dressed aloof types hobbling in stiff or high-heeled shoes more like; infiltrated by a fair smattering of our mutual enemy the rotund, white-collar brigade, sweating profusely and threatening to crack me on the knee with briefcases the size of the black cabs they're used to taking.

Given that the latter are probably accountants or solicitors, they deserve to suffer. I just wish that the others – still smarting as they all may be at being forced to walk to the West End by the completely unreasonable actions of the Transport Police at Victoria Station – would stop zigzagging down the pavement and walk in predictable lines; or, better still, actively get the fuck out of my way!

On the vaguely amazing and positive side, however, it's still not quite yet eight thirty, so, notwithstanding the hobbling novices like this one – arrghh!! – and barring any further mishap, I'm still on track to make the office by quarter to.

And if anyone's going to motivate me to keep up my pace around the front of the palace, that clown of a toff-type up ahead certainly is.

Blimey, I hope I don't walk as ridiculously as that.

He must have the oddest walking style I've ever seen: all knees and splay-footed heels like some jerky flamingo caricature from an old, mock-Victorian Dick van Dyke movie.

Still, for jerky flamingo caricature read ideal work-walk racer target material, with a high probability of a bit of diversionary entertainment.

And, wow, is that really a tweed suit he's wearing?

Gosh, it is as well.

Now we really are in parody territory.

And reason alone to grind him under the soles of my trainers.

'Don't you know it's central London in high summer matey?'

I should be able to nail the berk before Green Park at the latest, and that's even if he doesn't have, or cause, a proverbial..., or even real..., car crash before he gets there.

He's like some down-on-his-uppers Duke who's accidentally got lost from his shooting party – the Glorious Twelfth and all that – even if it is a month early.

Maybe the noise of the shotguns has finally sent him doolally, and he's happened upon the spontaneous and jolly marvellous idea of visiting his third cousin twice removed the Duke of Westminster?

I can almost hear him now: 'But jolly old Gerald has got to live in one of the big houses somewhere around here, hasn't he? Maybe it's this one at the end of the Mall?'

Hah.

Am I embarrassed to find myself scoffing at my scornful conjecture?

Not a bit of it Your Grace.

This line of four enormous coaches parked up along the kerb – or, more specifically, the exhaust fumes they're expunging – aren't so comedic though.

Nope.

'That engine keeping you nice and cool in there all on your own is it matey?'

Not that the lard-arse of a driver of the first one's even remotely interested in work-walker plebs like me naturally.

Crikey, I'm going to have to hold my breath.

Fuck, and there's still two more of the enormous things to go.

Where's Boney Arse and her eco warrior mates when you need them?

At least the pavement's widening, so I can move away from their exhausts a bit.

The flamingo, if equally predictably, also seems to be doing his level best to make it too easy for me.

What the...?

'Blimey, don't mind me madam.'

Hang on a minute...

'Excuse... m...'

Crikey, how can so many people get off a coach that fast?

They must have had special mass training in North Korea or somewhere.

Actually, judging by the look of them, maybe they are from North Korea.

Only, why the Kim Jong-il have they all now stopped?! Completely blocking the sodding pavement!

Fuck, it'll be easier..., and probably quicker..., to go back and take to the road.

Oh you're kidding me; not the coach behind as well!

Arrgghh.

I thought it was only olives and communist dissidents that get stuffed and jammed in jars.

I can't even blame the mad Duke either.

Every regular work-walker knows that rule 8 is 'never get caught in a jar full of tourists.'

Not only is mad Duke Flamingo up there making the most of my amateurish loss of concentration to casually extend his lead and round the corner, but even one or two of the hobbling heel and walking caravan dorks are out manoeuvring me.

And, no, being made to feel tall for once in my life is no recompense.

Humph.

The revenge of the dorks on the geek.

Actually, maybe if I try...?

'Excuse me..., please!'

That's if I'm not also a dork.

Maybe you have to be a dork to walk-work race at all? Is Boney Arse a dork? Fuck, am I actually, genuinely, a dork?

And, what's more, a dork whose excuse me is to be completely ignored, evidently.

No movement from my captors at all, in fact: just a trance-like stillness.

What the effing hell are we all waiting for for Pete's sake?

Have I just got to try to barge my way through?

Oh, no, thank God for that.

Or, more accurately, the yellow, poison-tipped umbrella god that's risen phoenix-like ahead of us, and to which, finally..., finally..., the black-haired heads at the neck of the jar are starting..., yep..., to bob forward towards in Pied Piper like pursuit.

Finally.

I daren't even look where mad Lord Flamingo has got to.

Clearly so far ahead that the loser I am can't even see him any more.

Ah, no, there he is.

Hah, looks like he's fallen for a 'can you please photograph take for us please?' tourist hazard; another basic work-walker error straight from the handbook.

Only, why on earth would you ask an obvious wally like him to take a photo for you in the first place?

They look like a nice sensible Hispanic family, but obviously they must like wonky photos.

Maybe their walls are full of them? A glorious Spanish villa adorned with photos of headless bodies and sloping panoramas.

Or more likely that they've been seduced by the palace's aristocratic charm, and mistaken tweed for competence.

Which can't be the first time that's happened – inside or outside Buckingham Palace.

Moving swiftly on though, that's also the hobbling accountant and sweaty solicitor types put back in their rightful places.

'And, no, the fact that the pedestrianised tourista in front of the palace is swamped with loitering tourists is no excuse, you amateurs.'

It's the same for everyone.

True work-walkers find a way.

In which case, it's almost unlucky for me that all I've hereon got left to navigate is the avenue of saluting poplars across Green Park then.

Assuming that I can successfully adhere to Work-walker Rule No. 7 – namely, always try to anticipate the otherwise interminable traffic lights across the four-lane superhighway work-walker hazard that is Constitution Hill in rush hour – to even get to them, that is.

Particularly, damn it, when timing is everything and the lights are going to change against me when I'm farther away from the Pelican crossing than I need to be...

And when..., nope..., bollocks, I've no choice..., I'm going to have to break the most sacrosanct work-walk rule of all and jog a few metres.

Oops.

Nope, the pedestrian signal's turned red.

But, yes, the traffic lights are still only flashing yellow, so I can go for it.

Wow, really?

'Blimey, you don't actually think you can intimidate me into not crossing by revving the engine in such a pathetic hatchback, do you mate?'

I'm definitely not stopping now.

'Alright, Small-dick, I'm semi-jogging, aren't I?'

Oops, this taxi's not happy either.

'Oh come on, really? I'm nearly out of your way already!'

Right, if he's going to thrust his grille forward like that, I'm going to stop jogging and just amble the last few paces, just to annoy him.

Woah.

'See, there, that wasn't so hard was it, Mr Taxi Driver?'

Think I'll grin at him just for good measure.

'Yes, you can go now.'

Hah!

'Yeah, fuck you too pal.'

He'll be stewing about that all day with any luck.

And, if I can't yet feel exactly smug about making the lights, perhaps I can allow myself to feel a little more buoyed.

Yes, that's it, for the first time this morning I am feeling buoyed.

Maybe I will be able to make a go of this life changing interview. They must have shortlisted me for a reason after all.

Although irrelevantly buoyed if I can't get into the office and onto Soho in the next twenty-five minutes.

And, while I'm on the general subject of buoyed, a bottle of water wouldn't go unappreciated either.

Particularly seeing this long incline and arc of the path across the park I've now got to keep my pace up on; majestic, saluting poplars or no soddingly majestic, saluting poplars.

And, in a strict literal-meaning sense, aren't I supposed to be buoyed up rather than just buoyed?

Actually, maybe she up ahead with the sexy figure and purposeful stride can up my buoyed status, whichever way it's supposed to.

I wonder if she's as spectacular from the front?

'Hang on, what's...?!'

Is this somebody actually making to overtake me?

Blimey, I think it is as well.

I may not be going flat out but I'm still going at a pretty good pace, aren't I?

It sounds like he or she's just behind me, perhaps a little to the left, so had better grab the inside line of the path to cut them off, just in case.

Yep..., here; like so.

Only, where the hell did they come from?

Crikey, they didn't actually make it over the crossing after me, did they?

Man or woman, they really must be a lunatic if they did.

I'll risk a quick glance.

Oops, we've made eye contact.

The cheeky bastard really is trying to overtake me.

'Alright, you're fucking on mate if you really want some.'

Lunatic or not, he's in cloud fucking cuckoo land if he thinks he's going to get past me today.

Notwithstanding that this is the very last thing I could be doing with doing.

But, no, I just had to look, didn't I. I had to look.

Humph.

And, now, having seen the intent in his eyes, I simply can't back out of it, whatever the cost.

Regardless of whether I've even got enough left in the tank.

Ackh.

Or that he's doubtless sensed the physical vulnerability in me this morning.

Which is my own sodding fault.

Anyhow, if the opportunistic tyro does still want to overtake me this early on the hill, he's going to have to do it the hard way by increasing his pace and taking the long way round the outside of the path.

Especially now I've lengthened my stride slightly and poked my elbows out.

Yeah, now we'll see what he's made of.

'What do we reckon John? Maybe a year or two younger than us, and, judging by his lean white-tee-shirt-under-grey-Merino-v-neck-over-subtle-dark-cheque-slim-fit-trousers look – ever so dandily accessorised with a fancy leather messenger bag and black Campers, rather than trainers – probably some kind of self-styled designer-cum-architect type?'

Only, just how committed is he going to be, that's the real question.

There's still no sign of him in my peripherals, so simply taking the inside line and upping my speed a little has been too much for the wuss so far.

That's if, true to type, he hasn't simply tucked in behind me, knife poised, to ponder his next attack of course?

Or if, rather than being driven by the need to impress his style conscious peers, the whole purpose of his attire and lame appearance isn't simply to lull potential work-walker rivals like me into a false sense of security?

Particularly if he's already sussed that many property advisers are closet wannabe creatives in the wrong profession...

Only, where is whichever-he-fucking-is in any case?

Over the course of the last minute or so he should have at least tried to draw up alongside me, but now I can't hear him behind me either.

'You haven't given up already have you, you lightweight? Your leather messenger-man-bag thing a bit too heavy for you, is it?'

Yep, I'll chance another quick glance over my shoulder.

Fuck!

No sodding wonder I can't hear him behind me!

The poncing, cheating toerag is following the informal lazy bastard walkers' route across the grass, cutting out the bend in the tarmac path in the hope of gaining a few metres.

'But at what cost to the park you lazy, lowlife twat?'

So-called people like him must drive the park keepers mad with their muddy, lazy-bastard lines across the grass and flower beds, let alone the rest of us who stick to the proper paths.

And he's got a chisel-ly, pointy nose as well, the slimy, cheating, lowlife ponce.

'Fuck, come on legs, our life is now dependent solely on burying the twat under the soles of our mass market trainers.'

Right.

Yes.

Under the soles...,

...of our...

Hang on, just what the fuck am I doing?

Would Damon or Jenson lose their heads when faced with such barefaced and underhanded trickery?

Surely, the point is to beat the deviant to the line, not burn myself out half-way up the hill?

No, losing like that would be even worse.

No, I will keep my rhythm and try to wind him in slowly and inexorably using the calm and determined skills of a professional to beat the flower-crushing and namby-pamby deviance of the creative.

Well, his over there at least.

And if the wannabe creative in me doesn't find that tragicomic, then I don't know what will.

So, right, as tragicomic and emasculating as it may be, I'll quicken my pace only as far as Messrs Hill and Button will allow, and try to: (1) save these bursts of adrenalin and frustration for the top of the hill; (2) maintain my new policy of hugging the top of the camber down the centre of the path to maximise trainer traction; and (3) ignore the fact that he has the farmers' line all to himself when I'm having to weave my way through some earlier post-pelican-crossing traffic.

Oh, and (4), try to ignore legs which, although already starting to ache at less than maximum pace, are going to have to get me within striking distance of my slippery friend when he rejoins the main footpath in around fifty or sixty metres, if I am to have any chance of catching and passing him before the park gate to claim the win.

And which, given how fast he's moving himself, is going to be tight, very tight.

Hmm.

Ackhhh.

I bet none in this bunch of teenagers is wondering this morning why they do stuff like last night.

Nope, they look like they don't have a care in the world.

'Yeah, let's amble aimlessly in a line across the full width of the path. Who cares if these sad fuckers on their way to work have to walk on the grass to get around us?'

Oh for the days of my own ignorant, carefree teens; and for the merits of the loud-cough-immediately-behind-their-heads solution.

'AHEM!'

Hah!

That worked well.

I didn't even have to break my stride.

Only, do I thank either of the two glaring indignantly at me now they've returned to the ground and re-gathered their pride, or just ignore them?

Nah, sod 'em.

I need every second for the grass-ruiner over there.

And is that deluded teenage mutterings I hear behind me?

Hah, yep, knew I could rely on them.

And even they'll catch this woman-on-the-phone here up.

Woman walker: '...anyone would think it's not *myyy* wedding the way they're going on...'

'Just ignore her John. Just focus on your rhythm and stride, and you'll be past her soon enough.'

Woman walker: '...daahhling, I can't even think about where his parents are going to stay.'

Blimey, is this slope getting steeper or is it me?

Woman walker: 'You should see them, they're an absolute nightmare. If I could think of a way of not inviting them to their own son's wedding I would, hah hah...'

'There's only one nightmare in your bloody relationship woman; and it isn't your poor bastard of a fiancé or his parents, is it?'

If only I knew her husband to be.

'FOR PETE'S SAKE WAKE UP MAN! DON'T DO IT!'

Still, given that even I've been forced to focus on getting away from her wobbling form, one day he's surely going to do likewise.

Oh, unlike my creative designer friend, who's evidently decided there's no further illicit gain to be made on the mud-line-of-shame and has doubtless tried to take advantage of my distraction with the wobbling bride-to-be-nightmare to cement his paltry two or three metre lead by rejoining me back on the path of the righteous.

'See, you cheating bastard? You gained yourself all of a few measly metres and look what you're doing to the grass?!'

Noh, was that a smirk I just saw on his face when he glanced back at me?

Fuck, I can't lose to this prick now, I just can't, whatever the cost.

No.., right..., yes.

'So..., okay..., is that pathetic increase in pace..., all you've got, pal?'

44

Hah..., yep..., it-seems-so...

Okay-then.

But..., if-I-do..., have-pace-in..., reserve..., when-to-make-my..., move..., to-get-past-him?

There's-only-about..., thirty-metres-to-the..., gate..., even-if-he-is..., overconfident.

And..., if-I-cock-it-up..., and..., let-him-back-in-again..., I'll-have-no-option..., but-to-kill-myself.

'Come on, John..., think.'

Also..., if-at-all..., possible..., I-want-him-to-think..., that-I've-beaten-him..., easily..., without-much..., effort..., but-how?

Hang-on..., that-multiple-dog-walker..., who-looked-like..., she-was..., moving-away-from-us..., on-the-path..., to-the-left..., is..., hesitating..., looking-uncertain.

Yes..., I-think-she's..., going-to-turn-back..., and-enter-our-path..., from-the-left!

'Quick..., this-is-it...; maximum-pace..., now-John..., now!'

Yes..., this-is it.

'What..., surprised-to-see-me..., are-you..., my-slippery-friend?!!'

And-now..., to-hold-his-attention..., for-just-a-couple..., of-seconds..., longer...

'Yes, that's-it..., concentrate-on-me..., in-your-peripheral-vision; concentrate..., on-me.'

And..., hah!, yes..., got him!

'Oops..., were-you-not..., expecting-this..., matey?'

And now..., to-use-my-body..., to-hold-him-to-his-line..., for-another-stride-or-so...

Hah, yes! Ms Dog-walker and her bouncing hounds and entangled leads couldn't have timed any better her emergence into my wannabe bester's immediate line of walk if I'd paid her!

...and smile, as, with nowhere to go, he is forced to jump back from the yapping mass of hair and teeth, all rhythm broken, and watch me pass the tangled mess unimpeded, and continue on my way up the path towards the winner's gate without so much as a single lost stride.

'Keep learning my friend. I am the master.'

Oh, and, given how he was such a principled opponent...

'And, yes, it was so easy that I really do have time to let my backpack and jacket fall free from my back as I walk – no, make that stroll – and swing my jacket over my shoulder by my forefinger before I claim the win over you, you complacent ponce.'

Hah!

Yes.

The tosser.

And yet again the gold medal for work-walk racing goes to Joh... Eh..., what the..., who's...?!

No!

No!!

... goes to a lanky streak of teenage backpacker.

Yep.

In my supposed moment of glory, I've been overtaken on the line by some fresh-from-the-station schoolboy, all resplendent in European sports gear and Bundesflagge.

And, yep, seeing really is believing.

Or, more accurately in this case, disbelieving.

He's reasonably athletic, right enough, but his rucksack's bigger than I am.

And he's all of twelve.

Well, eighteen, maybe.

Good enough to beat me, though; however sodding young he is.
Humph.

And likely German too.

Oh, the infuriating feeling of inevitability.

Then again, given my lamentable failure of concentration – or, worse, ponce-like complacency like the grass-ruiner back there – I should probably just be grateful he isn't a Frenchman.

Or an American even.

After all, even if being beaten by the former is ludicrously implausible – no Frenchman could possibly beat a Brit to a gate in a work-walk race: he'd be too busy philosophising on why the gate was there in the first place – the latter would already be blubbing out The Star-spangled Banner.

Which would be even more unbearable.

At least with our German friends there's always the inescapable feeling of sporting-place to fall back on.

And it was simply all in a day's walk for my Bavarian bester here, doubtless.

'How could you do that to me, you spotty sausage Münchener?'
Oops.

Fuck, has he heard me?!

But I didn't say that out loud, did I?

So why's he barrel-chesting up to me?

Backpacker: 'Can you tell me where is Piccadilly Circus, bitte?'
Blimey; up close he's bigger and older than I thought.

'I-eeek...'

Fuck.

Just when it couldn't get any worse..., no, my throat has to choke along with the rest of me and I can emit nothing more than a high-pitched, childlike squeak.

And redden at the extent of my descent into ignominy, as my compatriots mock me.

'Hold yourself together man,' from the old guy – doubtless a war hero – with the bulldog by the newsstand.

'It's one thing being beaten by him, but another losing your self-respect,' from my sexy-from-behind co-work-walker from the hill: her face still dismissively turned away from me.

Even the waif on the Les Misérables poster on the back of the bus shelter seems embarrassed for me.

Perhaps the only one without pity in his eyes is my German bester here; and in whose face – in the rare absence of a big hole in the road for me to hide in – I'm going to have to at least try to save some of my own by exaggeratedly and self-mockingly raising my fist to my mouth and clearing my throat, belatedly.

'Harrumph.'

Mm-hmm.

'It's straight down there mate.'

And, if I am going to complete my transition back to manhood, I'd better raise my arm and point manfully too I suppose.

'You can't miss it.'

Erm...

'The Circus, rather than Piccadilly, the, err..., road, err..., um, in case you were..., err..., wondering, I mean.'

Blimey, I just can't stop myself.

Backpacker: 'Thank you, vielen herzlichen dank.'

Or, judging by the way my unwitting vanquisher is already striding off down Piccadilly towards the Circus, maybe he's stopping me for me.

'You're welcome mate.'

Yes, said far more composedly and manfully.

If, again, way too late.

Fuck, on which subject, what is the time?

Very nearly eighteen to.

Hmm.

Two minutes to the office, a couple more making my excuses, then ten more to Soho.

Even now, with a bit of luck I might just make it.

Just one more thing to do.

And she who I must have already but unwittingly missed on the hill – did she stop at the kiosk possibly? – is headed in the same direction as me anyway.

Yep, there she is: under the pavement colonnade looking to cross at the lights at Arlington Street.

Still dismissive of me and my shameful defeat just now, perfectly understandably.

'Come on traffic lights, change against her for me.'

A steady flow of taxis duly blocking her way across the road?

Yesss, that'll do nicely.

If I can continue to bob in and out of these two relatively ordered lines of opposing pedestrian colonnade traffic, I should catch her in less than ten seconds.

Nope, damn it, the traffic lights are giving her a green again.

And it's like she's ambling deliberately now, just to wind me up, in a sort of work-walker Burlesque.

Oh, what?!

No!

You've got to be kidding me!

She can't go in there!

What's she gone and gone in there for?!

I was so close.

What is this place? I can't see through the door because of the glare.

Maybe with my head against the glass I can see in?

Oops.

Fuck, Iran House.

And all I've done is draw the attention of the security guard.

'Sorry mate, no, sorry, stay there behind your desk, it's okay...'

Wow, I might not like being beaten by the most casual work-walker in London, but of all the impulsive and ridiculous things for me to do...

Yes, I might well hold my hands up and slink away in embarrassment.

And quickly.

Ms Never-to-be-seen-again didn't give me so much as a consolatory nod or break her stride down the players' tunnel.

Humph.

I should have realised the finish line was Iran House not the park gate.

The second time I've peaked prematurely today.

Actually, on the subject of embarrassment, being so close to the office I hope nobody saw me impulsively crash-lay my hands and forehead against the glass door like that. It would have looked pretty odd if they did.

Uh-huh.

There's no one I know at the bank cash machines, but what about at the window counter in the coffee shop?

Hmm.

Is that the newish American temp over there? Sarah, is it?

At least hers is one girl's name I can remember this morning; even if it is the wrong one-girl's.

And, in the highly unlikely event that she does know me from Adam, she seems preoccupied with both the barista and her coffee in any case.

If not more the handsome and super-polished barista, in fact.

But, nope, no one else I recognise, luckily.

Although, if it is more relief than recognised I'm feeling all of a sudden, it's certainly not because of these increasingly over-familiar row of steps I'd rather not have to leap up.

Oof.

To another characterless glass entrance door I should never have laid my hands on.

A good night, was it?

Nope, this is one day when these oversized chrome letters forming the words Middleton Lyons Property Advisers high on the wall of the office reception are not going to crush my early morning enthusiasm.

If I can manage to make it in and out of the building without being collared by Nigel, hope is back on the agenda in the form of a potentially life changing interview with a man who might change mine in Soho.

As for the rest of this slick and polished show of marble, steel and glass..., well..., at least there's always the irrepressible Celia here to outshine it.

'Hey Celia.'

Mmm, not bad. Even I thought I sounded bright and enthusiastic.

If this morning doesn't work out maybe the stage beckons.

Celia: 'Morning John!'

Cheerful herself, as always; and giving me her usual once over.

Celia: 'You alright, darlin'? You look a bit, err...'

Blimey, I must look terrible.

And that look of genuine concern on her face is not going down at all well with the hypochondriac in me.

'Bit of trouble getting in. They closed Victoria Station.'

Well, it's half of the truth at least.

Celia: 'Uh-huh. A good night, was it?'

Whilst my brooding, enigmatic side needs more work, clearly.

'Uh-huh, a little too good.'

And if I don't keep walking that won't be the only piece of seemingly inconsequential information that her contagious grin will elicit from me.

Celia: 'Ohh...'

She'll need another gigabyte for it all soon, and that's just for the stuff she's got on me.

Celia: 'With anyone I know, was it?'

As mean as it seems to deprive her of any more titbits to trade on by not playing along with her for the usual minute or two, today's mutual efforts at cajolery will have to wait an hour or two.

Think I'll try to fend her off with a playful wink and make for the stair and lift lobby.

'Tell you later.'

Actually, I don't suppose either lift is down here, is it? My legs have got the man wobbles all of a sudden.

Celia: 'Hold you to that...'

Oh, yes, this one, luckily.

And doubtless she will as well.

Or maybe that should be unluckily. The '1' button is so far down the floor number list that it's almost embarrassing to press it.

Only, as pathetically short a journey as it is, I am in need, aren't I?

And, yikes, triply so if the pasty-complexioned triptych of the imposter in the lift mirrors is anything to go by.

Hmm.

A composition I've cunningly managed to achieve even before any pre-interview fear in the pit of my stomach.

And based on which even I wouldn't employ me.

Mm-hmm.

Yep, drastic action may be called for.

Ouch.

Crikey, not even a sharp smack on my cheeks has brought much in the way of colour or wellness to my face; my insides really must be in a sulk with me.

Just like the lift: which, unwilling to tolerate such unbecoming behaviour, has had enough of me too, evidently.

In fairness to the lift though, if Freddy's managed to make it in after his own exploits before we went our separate ways last night, only the devil knows what else it's already had to witness this morning.

And, in which case, as useful as its mirrors could be in the game of subterfuge I must now play beyond the lobby door, I'm probably not the only one happy to be leaving them and their confidence sapping truths behind me – even if that does just leave me with smoke to play with.

Still, how hard can (a) getting past Nigel and Wendy, (b) downing some water from the chiller, (c) switching and leaving on my computer, (d) making my excuses, and (e) getting the hell out again in less than two minutes, actually be?

And, no, there is no way out of it.

First up then: through the lobby door into this hybrid-cross between a bankers' boardroom and an open prison that's been our office for the last six months, and the skulkers' back way towards my desk.

Mm-hmm.

And, so far so good, Nigel's door's closed and the spaniel's away from her guard post.

Water next then.

'Don't die Johnny Boy. I'll get you water.'

I can die later.

Uh-huh.

Cor blimey, that's better.

And, so..., Freddy *has* made it in on time this morning.

Still, I need only slip into my chair for as long as it takes to switch my computer on; as ridiculously slow as it now is with this newfangled Windows 98 software on it, and which I'm sure Nigel insisted we install just to torture me this morning.

Woe betide any of us to ask him to fund new computers that'll cope with it though.

Gail: 'Morning John.'

In her softly spoken manner, and without breaking away from her own computer screen. I'm not even sure her lips moved in fact.

'Gail.'

I'll have to hope she's picked up the deference and bashfulness in me, since last in again as I am this morning there wasn't even a hint of chastisement in her voice. And that's despite the fact I'm abusing her closest-we've-got-to-a-reasoned-team-matriarch-around-here latitude, and that she's doubtless been at her desk since the crack of dawn trying to keep on top of the latest of Nigel's wholly unreasonable demands and workload for him.

Wherever he is right now.

Judging by the stress writ large across the back of her eyes again, if she isn't there already she needs to get off the tracks before she really does reach her wits' end; because if there's one person around here who won't even consider giving her any latitude – particularly when it comes to sharing fees and the building of his esteem – it's our glorious leader, Nigel.

There'll be no such namby-pamby pleasantries from these other two though.

Freddy: 'D'you win then?'

And without raising his head from a car magazine.

Fuck, come on PC. All I need is the mail screen.

'Nah, some spotty German youth caught me with a surprise thrust from behind.'

'And, no, for once my exaggerated indignation is not far from what I'm actually feeling Fred.'

Freddy: 'Typical.'

Hah!

And typical Fred, too: spitting and absurd, laced with extra mock disgust.

Freddy: 'Not that your embarrassing humiliation is going to stop me getting my new M3, though, eh?'

And this time he didn't even need to hold up and snap open his prop to exaggerate the irony.

While we're on the subject, Freddy seems very full of it himself this morning for some reason: has a glint of something or other in his eye.

If I'm right, he'll be desperate to tell me, so I'll conveniently add 'to wind him up' to 'no time anyway' as self-justification for not asking.

Andrew: 'I'd prefer a classic car myself. Something with a bit of style and character.'

'Yep, exactly Andrew...'

Freddy: 'Hah, right, says you with the fucking knackered Capri, Smith!'

Definitely a man after my own heart is Andrew, even if he is a bit posh...

Freddy: 'And you're just a graduate Horder: you can't afford a car.'

...and a bit too subtle and erudite for Freddy's complete comfort.

'I wouldn't be too sure about that, actually, Fred.'

As usual, Freddy's jibe is water off a duck's back to Andrew though.

Freddy: 'In fact, are you.., is he..., even old enough to drive?'

Actually, maybe even Andrew grinned at that one.

Ah, finally, the home page.

Mail, click.

Not even Nigel can argue I haven't already been in if he sees my mail page up and running while I'm out on unknown business for a bit.

Well, hopefully not, anyway.

Freddy: 'So, a good night, last night, was it then, eh, *Casual*?'

When needs must and all that. The energy-wasting environmentalist in me can take the morning off.

Hang on, why did Freddy dredge up that old nickname for me?

Freddy: 'Same suit, shirt and tie as yesterday is that?'

Ah.

Hmm.

And, damn it, all I can do is grin involuntarily back at him like the culpable novice in a reconstituted outfit that I am.

Andrew: 'Maybe a '71 Porsche RS..., or a DB5...'

At least Andrew can still steadfastly hold his head up.

Freddy: 'Christ, do you know how much they cost?!'

'You're not genuinely incredulous, this time, are you Freddy?'

Freddy: 'Who do you think you are: Michael bleedin' Caine?!! In The Italian Job? Hah!'

'And, yes, I had a very nice evening, thanks for asking, Frederick.'

Andrew: 'Actually, Michael Caine didn't learn to drive until he was fifty. And it was a DB4 in the Italian Job.'

'What do you need a M3 for anyway Fred? Thinking you need a bit of a status boost?'

Blimey, look at his face.

'Yes, I want to know, really.'

'No?'

'I'd have thought you'd be looking for more of a people carrier this time Fred, given how you've got your first sprog on the way.'

He-he.

'What? Don't you want that car magazine any more Fred?!'

Freddy: 'Gail, tell them how I don't need any car to boost *my* status.'

Hah, Freddy must really be struggling if he's trying to bring our impartial arbiter of last resort into it.

Gail: 'You leave me out of this, I'm busy.'

Freddy: 'See?!'

'Pah, see what?!'

Gail: 'Okay, normally I'd say not, but for you Freddy, well..., maybe it could err..., do something...'

Hah! So, Gail isn't so busy and disinterested after all it seems.

Freddy: 'Oh, great, cheers for that Gail...'

Gail: 'Now shut up, all of you, or for once I really will call the cliché police.'

Right, mail screen up, and time to get off.

'I've got to go out; meeting in Soho.'

If anybody's remotely interested..., not.

'Back in an hour or so, if anybody needs me.'

Wendy: 'And where do you think you're going?'

Oops, the spaniel: behind me. She must have been in the kitchen; I can smell her coffee.

And, yes, looking especially smarmy and arrogant without-any-good-reason-to-be she is again this morning.

'Morning, Wendy.'

And as Nigel's PA, I'd better force a broad grin I suppose.

Wendy: 'Nigel's been waiting for you to get in. He'd like a quick word?'

'But I...'

But I..., bollocks.

It was a rhetorical question. I'll have to see what he wants quickly.

Not forgetting my empty briefcase for appearances.

Actually, make that had-better-run to see what he wants quickly.

I've got about a minute, maximum, to get out of the building or definitely, without a gnat-sized shadow of a doubt, be late for my last chance at freedom from having to do precisely this.

And, moreover, from otherwise ending up in a glass bowl of an office like this one.

Just one knock and push.

'Morning Nigel. Wendy said you wanted a quick word? Only I've...'

Oh, I'm getting the hand again.

Hmm.

Another couple of clicks on the mouse to make me wait just because he can it is then.

Only, what's he now smirking at me like that for, casually leaning back in his chair with his hands clasped behind his head?

Nigel: 'So did her collars match her cuffs then?'

Because, aside from that wet grin, it was only the preamble, obviously.

However he found out, there's only one thing the salacious twat can be on about though: Blondie. And just how the hell am I going to respond to that?

'Erm...'

Erm, none of your fucking business you lecherous tosser?

Anyone would think he wasn't married with three teenagers, even though he does shag anything that comes his way; including, rumour has it, the spaniel.

Maybe, on reflection, I'll prolong my default confounded look.

'I wondered why you were late in again this morning, and Freddy told me you were last seen with a young peroxide blonde last night?'

'Cheers Fred; you could have warned me you bastard.'

Look at him, chuckling at me from his desk out there, his mouth wrapped around the top of his tea mug.

And she wasn't even peroxide.

'Sorry Nigel, I really don't know what he's on about.'

'As successful for you as our relationship may or may not be in the field of commercial property investment agency, you're in fucking la-la land if you think I'm going to extend it to include matey repartee about my sexual relations; mate.'

Or the lack thereof in the future, either.

'And, yes, that's even if you were indeed hoping for further details on the colour of Blondie's pubic hair and are looking at me disappointedly.'

Fuck, life is good.

'And yes, this is me squirming Nigel.'

Blimey, at last: he's turned his attention back to his computer.

Unless, that is, he's about to retrieve something even worse for me out of it?

Nigel: 'I need you to do a viewing for me this afternoon at Platinum House. Two-thirty. Mr Brodsky. A Russian. Couldn't make the general viewing yesterday.'

That's a relief.

'Oh, err, okay, fine, no problem...'

And if that's all he wants, I can make for the door then.

Nigel: 'Hold on..., and while you're there I want you to take a couple of check measurements of the vacant floor: the third, is it?'

'Err...'

Fuck, is it the third?

Shit.

And now he's back to his computer again.

Shit.

Nigel: 'I know it's here somewhere...'

This actually is worse than water torture.

Nigel: 'Yes, the third. Sebastian fucking Cooper-Hands is querying the floor area, the cheeky cunt.'

Hmm.

'Don't tell me: the shrewd Cooper-Hands caught you trying to justify an inflated price with your dodgy floor area measurements has he, Nigel? The ones from that magical digital measuring device of yours that somehow reads ten centimetres shorter if you're buying a building and ten centimetres longer if you're selling it?'

'I'll do my best, but isn't it now piled high with new furniture?'

Nigel: 'Oh..., yeah, it is.'

Fuck. Now I've gone and got him thinking again.

Nigel: 'You can use a measuring tape. If there's nobody else, you can take the temp..., the American girl..., to hold the other end. Okay?'

Fabulous, that's all I need.

'Right, I'll...'

Nigel: 'Oh, and while you're at it, remind her we'll need her in the marquee at Henley tomorrow. Nine o'clock.'

And the poor girl will doubtless be well chuffed at that. Hope she doesn't shoot the messenger.

But what exactly did he mean by '*we'll*'?

No, I'll worry about that later. I need to get out of here.

Nigel: 'So, where're you off to now?'

Shit.

'Think, quick.'

'Might have something for us in Soho. Mate of mine. Just a long shot at the moment, but thought it's worth a quick look.'

Not bad, sounds vaguely plausible.

Nigel: 'Well, well, against all the odds I might make an investment agent of you yet, Smith...'

Hmm.

Nigel: 'Let me know how you get on.'

Blimey, he seems genuinely surprised and pleased.

The small problem being that sooner or later I'll have to think up another lie to cover this one up.

Just not now though.

Time to run.

And literally.

First for the stairwell.

Yep.

And no need or time for the lift this time; a risky-but-don't-care three stairs at a time in near freefall is required.

Oops.

Yikes.

Woaoh ohoa....

Oww: my ankle.
Not good.

No, it's okay.

And Celia's busy with a bunch of visitors.

Just a cursory wave over my shoulder then, and..., yes..., I'm out.

And, at less than ten seconds from Nigel's office to the street, in what must be a new record.

Only, yikes, at eight fifty-four, giving me less than three hundred and sixty more to get to Soho.

And which, as quickly as I'm covering the ground, is beyond even my fastest speed-walk.

Fuck; and no fast developing state of panic is going to change the fact.

Hang on, wait a second, wait a second, is that a 38 bus?!

Yesss!

And it's an old Routemaster too.

They must've had yet another bendy-bus fire.

Suits me though.

And, wow, if I didn't know better it's like the driver's pausing just at the right moment for me to jump on board...

Which really is unbelievable.

Aaannnnddddd..., up, and, yep..., grab.

Blimey.

Yep.

I really must be dreaming, in fact.

Rather than coming to my timely rescue by ringing her mum, Blondie is actually about to nudge me awake way too late for anything other than regret and a commiserative cheerio?

Hmm?

But, amazingly, no.

This really is the wind I'm feeling as I ride the tailgate of this amazing old bus driven by an amazing driver along an amazingly traffic-free Piccadilly.

Conveying me in less than thirty seconds from hopeless of Albemarle Street to hopeful of Piccadilly Circus.

Incredible.

The only disappointing part being that I had absolutely no hand in it.

Including being given such a perfect opportunity at such a perfect spot on the Circus to jump off again!

Just like..., yep..., so.

Yikes, skilfully avoiding this lamppost.
'Oh yes, that's how it's done Johnny Boy. Twinkle toes in motion across the pavement.'
And even these twinkle toes can manage a quick one-minute speed walk from here to Golden Square, can't they?
In which case, somewhat amazingly, it looks like I'm actually going to make it!

Incredibly.

Although...
Quite what kind of person it makes me to appreciate more these shadowy, perhaps even seedy, tall-sided Soho street-canyons over the wide and decorated boulevards of Mayfair maybe only these

assorted rough sleepers here will be able tell me on my way into work in the mornings.

The media industry moguls who've chosen to locate themselves around here must also see something in its multifarious character and grittiness – even if their focus is perhaps on a different kind of appreciation.

And not even I can argue that that dazzling, road-width column of sunshine up ahead isn't my destination living up to its name; nor that, given my lamentable position at this time less than an hour ago, I shouldn't appreciate more unequivocally the reality that, at two minutes to nine, I'm stepping into it at all in fact – notwithstanding my unpreparedness for having done so.

Shame, then, that the realisation is doing nothing to reduce the tension in the pit of my stomach; the transfer of fear of lateness to that of the unknown being too seamless evidently.

Or, for that matter, that it's in no way dispelling the dangerously premature but seductive notion sparking in my head that I may never need put myself through such an ordeal again on a workday morning.

Oh, and if all that isn't enough stress transference already, maybe the minute I've got left to worry about what I don't know about the film business and how to get inside the building will be; oh so luckily and helpfully.

Mm-hmm.

'Still, nobody can tell us we can't find a so-huge-you-can't-miss-it, bronze-plated, art deco double door when we need to, eh John?'

Even if I have been here before and really would be in trouble if I couldn't.

The principal difference this time being that, rather than simply posting my hopes of a life more than sub-prime through its letter box, I've got to press the subtle entry call button marked TotalFilm Productions and try to realise them.

The life changing interview

One small buzz for a man, one giant leap for Johnny-kind.

Well, potentially, maybe.

Intercom: 'Yes?!!'

Yikes, that's shrill and direct, even from an intercom.

'Err, hi. I have an interview with..., err, Rob Smelley?'

Oops, did that sound relaxed and confident or spill over into laid-back?

Hmm.

And why's there still nothing but an unnerving hum from the intercom?

'Erm...'

Is she waiting for me to elaborate?

'I'm here for the..., err..., Production Assistant job?'

Great, and now from laid-back to hesitant.

Intercom: 'Second floor.'

She, on the other hand, sounds almost disappointed that she might have to open the door.

Oh, and, finally, the entry buzzer.

Oops.

But if not this part, which part of which door *do* I push or pull?!

Fuck.

And now I'm too late!

Fuck!

Nope, I'll have to push the call button again.
Fuck.
And Christ knows how Ms Intercom is going to react to that.
Intercom: 'Yesss?!'
'Sorry, it's me again, still..., err... here, I couldn't..., um..., wasn't...'
Ah, the entry buzzer again.
...quick enough.
'Ah, yes, this part of the door, knobhead. It's obvious.'
Gosh, it's heavy too.

And, wow, this is some huge, fancy entrance lobby.

An art deco fantasist's idea of heaven, no less: all glazed brick tiles, chrome and polished bronze sunburst motifs like the interior of some grand, 1920s ocean liner.

'Forget the street canyons; imagine coming into this every morning, Johnny Boy.'

Even the prominent chrome signboard seems original.

If not the pink logo '2 mezzanine: TotalFilm'; jarringly.

So, yep, just a quick, courteous nod to a security guard more interested in the small mountain of post on his desk, and the second floor mezzanine it is then.

And for once I don't even have to ask where the stairs are; an obligatory design afterthought hidden away behind a small, anonymous, white fire door this imperious, sweeping stone staircase is not.

Nope, a magnificent and uncompromising feature from the days before the demands for Net Internal Floor Area and cost cutting more like, rivalled only by its long-time collaborator this resplendent Lalique-esque glass window towering over us: the two of them in an eighty year battle for aesthetic supremacy if ever there was one.

So much so, in fact, that it feels almost unfair to add my own bodyweight's worth of wear and tear to the prevailing stalemate.

Hmm.

And such that, just when my own rivals will doubtless be using the pervading sense of grandeur and indomitability to reinvigorate themselves for the likely ordeals ahead of us this morning, I'm focused only on treading more lightly than the pathetic lightweight I already am, obviously.

Still, if I can't yet be sure there's no further scope for self-doubt even now I've stepped off the bloody thing, there's certainly no mistaking that I'm at the right floor and door: the latter another art deco original alright, but whose flawless design is this time marred by yet another luminous pink laminated sign marked 'TotalFilm Productions'.

Which is not a good sign by any use of the word.

Even if it is fully colour coordinated with, yep, the reception area.

Uh-huh.

So much for me expecting a quirky, retro office crammed with torn leather chairs and piles of unread scripts. This is the antithesis; the media office equivalent of bling, as if they've got too much money.

Just with nobody around to staff it.

Oh, nope, here she ambles: presumably Ms Friendly on the intercom, dressed casually in jeans and sleeveless Astroboy tee.

'Hi, I'm here to see Mr Smelley, at nine?'

At least one of us is going to look and sound keen.

And, so, no asinine pleasantries here in the flesh either then; just a well-practiced aloofness.

And an inability to operate a mouse to rival Nigel's.

Man Utd away at Newcastle, Premier League: attractive on the face of it, but a lot of fucking aggro getting there.

Astrogirl: 'You are?'

Even if, as her tone suggests, maybe I should have told her my name.

'Smith, John Smith.'

And if she doesn't already think I'm some Albert Broccoli wannabe, she will now.

As if there can't be enough of us already around here.

And, duly, that is one alarmingly long list of names she's scrolling down.

Hmm.

'Yes: shocking, positively shocking.'

At least mine's there for her to tick off I suppose.

Astrogirl: 'They're running a few minutes behind.'

And, for the first time, she's even accompanied her words with eye contact; I am privileged.

If running behind is all I need with Nigel and his watch likely to be on the prowl.

Hopefully he'll already be otherwise engaged and won't notice my prolonged absence.

Astrogirl: 'You can wait over there.'

Oh?

Wow, is that a trendy sofa or a half-deflated pink air balloon?

'Right..., thanks.'

I'm going to keep smiling at her if it kills me.

Astrogirl: 'They'll come and get you when they're ready. The toilet's there...'

Ah yes, the bright yellow door the other side of the waiting area.

'Righty...'

No, she's already strolling off again.

'...oh.'

If I ever have nothing better to do, hers would be one remarkably deluded attitude worth paying homage to.

Actually, maybe I should take the yellow door option and use its facilities while I've got the chance. It would certainly be better than looking a knob on the pink air-blancmange-balloon thing.

A prick like me might deflate it even further doesn't she know.

Oh, and the loos are unisex ♂♀.

This should be interesting.

And behind the yellow door it's...

... actually confoundingly civilised and tasteful.

Mm-hmm.

And I have it all to myself it seems.

So, a quick waz in one of the tangerine cubicles and wash of my hands it is then.

Think I'd better resist the temptation to leave the seat down, even in the vague hope of getting one back on Astrogirl out there.

She could be a colleague soon.

Well, theoretically, at least.

Okay, notwithstanding that the chance of both them giving me the job and her still being here if they do is even more remote than Red Ken becoming Prime Minister.

Oh, and this loo flushes by itself then.

No man being trusted to flush of his own free will in a unisex toilet.

Not when there are machines and technology to reliably do it for us, and without the need for any form of encouragement or mediation on the subject.

Only, whilst the central island of sinks is pretty idiot friendly, where or how the hell do I dry my hands?

There really isn't anything, is there?

Certainly nothing resembling a paper towel dispenser or hand dryer.

Mm-hmm.

The seat of my trousers it is then.

And the damp patch results of which I can't see in this full-length wall mirror in any case.

Right, where's my surnamesake and occasional adviser on all things sartorial when I need him?

'Okay Paul, what do you think? Do I look like a potential film executive?'

'Looking good, as always, John. Like the suit... oh for fuck's sake!!... and trainers combo, although I'm not sure about the tie.'

And, nope, this is no time for inner admonishment.

The only thing I really had to do in the office was remember to put my shoes on, and yet, no, I didn't.

My idiocy is now completely, fuckingly, undeniably irrefutable.

Un-fucking-believably.

'Harrumph.'

Actually, I suppose it's too much to hope they won't notice, is it?

'Oh don't be so sodding stupid; of course they'll fucking notice the trainers! You're not auditioning for The Young Ones for fuck's sake.'

Nope.

'But will they care?'

Hmm.

Ignoring the fact that pondering my own response to my own question is never a good sign of entirely stable mental health even in times of panic – the answer could, just possibly, be maybe not?

At least they're brown and gold Adidas retro classics; my mass globalisation whites would've given me no chance.

'What was that you were saying, Paul? Shame about the tie?'

I'm not sure I can bear to look.

Yep, a performer's spin jump might be in order.

'Da-dah...'

Blimey, I was right: maybe the stage does beckon if film producing doesn't work out.

Actually, tie-less me doesn't look too bad; pretty cool in fact.

'Maybe you can get away with it yet John.'

What the..?!

No! A flushing toilet!

Fuck, someone must have slipped in when I was having my waz! Can I make the door before he – or she – comes out?

No, too late, I'll have to watch via the mirror.

A late middle-aged man, emerging cautiously from the end cubicle behind me, looking uncertain whether to acknowledge my presence and, therefore, what he must have heard, or ignore me and carry on with his business.

Hmm.

He's decided on the latter it seems, at least while he washes his hands.

Ah, so that odd silver lid-less box is an air drier!

Hopefully he would have heard me wash my hands even if I did silently dry-wipe them on my trousers.

Oops, our eyes have met in the reflection of the mirror.

'Okay, you've caught me mate. And, yep, all I can do is half-grin at you.'

Oops.

Clutching at straws, he was at least smiling as he left – even if he was gently shaking his head.

'Yep; let alone the youth of today, I'm sometimes utterly baffled by me as well mate.'

Like why I was the last person here to realise that the safest option was always this pink blancmange.

Still, if he's there in the interview, so be it.

He was wearing a jacket and sneaker type shoes himself after all.

And, yikes, I need the extra grip of my trainers and a damp trouser seat just to hold myself in place on this supposedly safe-option but actually lethal oxymoron of a sofa.

Unless this relaxed, thirty-something producer type who's just magic-ed herself from behind Astrogirl has come to catch me when I fall, that is. And assuming that those high wedges don't preclude her doing anything that athletic and spontaeous, of course; which really would be a shame.

Ms High Wedges: 'John Smith?'

Despite having addressed her question to Astrogirl, she wants me too.

Astrogirl: 'Erm...'

Albeit, if we all have to wait until Astrogirl gets around to confirming or even remembering that the only person in their reception is indeed the John Smith her colleague is asking her for, then we'll be doing so for some time.

'Yep.'

'Yes, this is me trying to slide off this ridiculous sofa without breaking my neck.'

Ms High Wedges: 'Sorry, yes, of course, you *must* be, err...'

Bringing to two those of us trying not to appear foolish but failing.

Ms High Wedges: 'Jill Thompson, I'm an associate producer and office manager here.'

And if ever I need make a good first impression with a handshake – plus take her attention away from my trainers – now's the time.

'John Smith..., pleased to meet you.'

Yes, that's it: firm and keen, metro not macho.

'Thanks very much for inviting me in.'

Yep, everything about her says Liverpool in Europe in their understated 80's pomp.

Fantastic.

Liverpool Jill: 'Not at all; I'll take you through.'

And demonstrative proof that women don't even begin to peak until their mid-thirties; and hope for me yet.

Liverpool Jill: 'Sorry to keep you waiting; bit of a conveyor belt I'm afraid.'

Hmm.

'Yes, this is a rueful smile.'

Liverpool Jill: 'Sorry, what I meant was we need someone asap, and we're trying to see as many people as we can today, only we had a bit of a production issue arise first thing...'

Right, glad we got that straight then.

And, judging by the distinct lack of people in such a big floor of offices, I can't say I'm exactly surprised either.

Shame the fact doesn't make it less rather than more likely of having to renew my fledgling acquaintance with Mr Baffling-youth-of-today from the toilet anytime soon.

Oops; on which subject, that wasn't actually, really him I just glimpsed loitering with another guy in the corner office that Jill seems to be bee-lining us towards, was it?

Fuck.

Yep.

It actually, really is him.

Fuck.

Where's the way out; I might as well leave now.

Unless, this being the film business, there's no chance he has a stunt double for awkward toilet scenes, is there?

Or that I can simply hover outside the door like this without ever having to go in to face him?

Liverpool Jill: 'Come in, please.'

Hmm, maybe not on either score then.

Beckoned as I am to slaughter.

Or should that be laughter?

Liverpool Jill: 'John, this is Rob Smelley, Executive Producer and Managing Director of TotalFilm.'

To momentarily prolong my agony, the taller, younger man first then.

Rob: 'Hello John, thanks for coming in.'

And said surprisingly appreciatively too.

Maybe Mr Baffling-youth-of-today hasn't said anything and I still do have a chance. This one's certainly offering me his hand eagerly enough.

'Pleased to...'

Ackh, damn it.

'...meet you..., err..., Mr Smelley.'

How am I supposed to reciprocate a firm handshake if he overeagerly grasps too soon and tries to squeeze and shake only the feeble weakness offered by my fingers?!

Rob: 'Call me Rob, please.'

'Bang goes that first impression for us both, then, eh Rob?'

No prizes for guessing what else he probably does that's premature and disempowering.

Rob: 'And this is Joel Messenger, one of our senior producers.'

And my new friend from the toilet, where I've already left that first impression.

Joel: 'Glad to meet you, John.'

And an American, no less.

'Mr Messenger.'

At least he's still smiling; and, yes, is also even returning in kind my this-time-successfully-planted handshake.

'Nice look..., very Adrian Edmondson.'

Hah; very smart.

And delivered with a subtle grin and deadpan wryness even I can appreciate.

'Thanks, I put a lot of thought into it.'

If only to baffle these other two.

Jill: 'Joel also happens to own TotalFilm!'

Oops.

'Great: thanks, Jill. That's made me feel much happier with myself.'

Although it's probably no wonder she's taking any opportunity to gush about him if he was the unwitting funder of her reception fit-out back there.

Still, lest I want to add her indignation to owner Joel's bewilderment and MD Rob's suspicion of my feebleness – not to mention rule out completely any distant if imaginary prospect of her ever coming onto me – I'm going to have to force myself to smile sycophantically along with her, too.

Uh-huh, like so.

Eeee...

While I think about how to make a start on my second impression on Rob, who seems to be taking over the lead now we're in interview phase.

Rob: 'Please, John, take a seat.'

And which will absolutely not involve my making any comment

whatsoever on this bright orange, trendy-but-totally-impractical blobular table before I sit manfully in the chair with the target roundel on it that he's gesturing me towards.

Mm-hmm.

At least they'll all be sitting opposite me where I can see them then.

When Jill stops trying to distract me from over by the juxtaposition that is that elegant Scandi sideboard.

I can sense a legendary Smith fightback coming on.

Jill: 'Coffee, anyone?'

'No!'

Oops. As keen as I am to avoid any further opportunity to embarrass myself through incompetent handling of a coffee mug, that was a bit of an overreaction by even my standards.

Jill: 'Or tea?'

'Err, sorry, no, not for me thanks, err..., Jill.'

'Perhaps more relax and less fight Johnny Boy.'

Jill's outfit is actually quite figure-hugging, and even more now she's sitting; perfectly complimented by those super- chic glasses she's now adjusting with her super-manicured fingers around her short and effortlessly stylishly haircut.

Rob: 'Frankly, we were surprised, but very pleased, to receive your application, John.'

Crikey.

Wow.

'You were?'

Rob: 'Your CV, whilst a little unconventional for us, is very impressive.'

Eh?

'It is, Rob?'

'Well, I feel I've not done too badly for myself so far.'

That's it, nice and conversational.

'But films are where my heart and interests really are, err..., lie.'

Rob: 'Well hopefully that's something we can help you with!'

And Rob's certainly maintaining his enthusiasm, even if Joel's gone quiet. It's like they've swapped nationality or something.

'That's why I'm here Rob!'

Albeit, maybe conversational with less of the clichés and feigned laughter.

Rob: 'Films are our business!'

And, as subtly exquisit as the embroidery is on Jill's shirt – jungle theme is it? – I really must stop scrutinising it, and her.

Rob: 'And, from what I've seen and read so far, you're very good at them too!'

Oops, she nearly caught me looking that time. And would rightly suspect it wasn't at the embroidery.

'Fuck, focus and concentrate you idiot! This is possibly the most important interview of your life and, no, she almost certainly won't be into younger men.'

Besides, there's no way this dodgy table could take our combined weight anyway.

Rob: 'So which bits of your CV do you think are most relevant to us here at TotalFilm?'

Blimey, did anyone else notice that? The way she drew her hands down the sides of her shirt, or was I imagining it?

Given Rob's again looking down at my CV, and Joel's looking me straight in the eye awaiting my answer, evidently not and I was, then.

'Umm, that'll probably be the two screenplays I've written.'

Nice imagining though.

'I started working on them in my spare time, when I realised a life in investment property isn't what I want.'

'See, that's the kind of answer you give when you don't concentrate.'

And they all seem as disappointed by it as I am.

Rob: 'We were actually hoping you'd tell us about your time at Universal? I gather you worked with Tim Hudson on the Figgs' last music video?'

Huh?

Universal? Who the hell is Tim Hudson?

'Sorry, Joel. I don't know what you mean. I've never worked at Universal. I joined Middleton Lyons as a graduate, straight from university.'

Rob: 'But it says here you went to the London Film School?!'

'And you can sound as accusing as you like Rob, but I've never been there either.'

Ah...

Right.

And to think I'd hoped this would never happen to me again.

Particularly when it matters.

'That is, actually, *my* CV you've got there, is it Rob?'

At least I've stopped looking at Jill's jungle...

Joel: 'What's going on here Rob?'

... and Joel's stopped staring at me for a minute.

Rob: 'You *are* John Smith...?'

I knew it wouldn't take Rob long to play the blame game.

'Yes.'

So much for anonymised CVs.

Rob: '...of Sanderson Avenue, Camden?'

Err, nope.

'No, of Warwick Way, Pimlico.'

I never have liked that part of Camden.

Hmm.

And the way this works now, if I remember rightly, is that it's my turn to be able to assess them when they are stressed and under scrutiny.

In this case, involving lightweight Rob all too predictably and dramatically slumping back in his chair like the twat I've already taken him for, and Joel calmly placing my namesake's CV back down on the table and looking expectantly to an already lunging for the door as best she can in those wedge heels Jill.

Jill: 'Sorry Rob, Joel. I'll go and check with Karen what's happened, and get Mr Smith's correct CV.'

If for Karen read Astrogirl, I might have known that she'd have something to do with it.

Lost In Space girl more like: but one even more vacuous.

Joel: 'Sorry about this John.'

It's not even Joel's fault either; but we'd both be waiting all day for an apology from Rob, despite the uncomfortable silence.

'It's an occupational hazard when you've a name like mine, I'm afraid. I'm hoping that, by the time I've produced my first hit film with you here, the name John will have fallen out of favour. Well, among the Smiths at any rate.'

'And, yes, as cheeky as it was, that was a joke, Rob.'

Joel smiled at least; in spite of what we all already know is the inevitable.

Speaking of which, here's Jill back already and beckoning Rob to the doorway to confirm it.

Joel: 'Okay John, let's put the CV aside for a minute. Tell me why you want to be an assistant producer.'

Huh?

Is he serious or just making small talk because there's now just the two of us?

He is earnestly leaning forward in his chair towards me.

'Well, I...'

Rob: 'So we've invited the wrong guy in, yes?'

An angry Rob, on the other hand, can't even keep his voice down in the corridor. Not that I can blame him I suppose. It's a waste of his time as well as mine.

Joel: 'Don't mind them, you were saying...?'

Give Joel his due though, he's determined to give me my say, waste of time or not.

'Well, I know it's a cliché, but I've actually *always* wanted to work in films. It's been my dream job since I first started making my own dodgy efforts as an aspiring Ridley Scott and began to notice the difference between good and bad in fact. Only, when it came to a choice of career, the pragmatist in me told me it was unrealistic, that dream jobs don't exist, or were for other people. But now I know different. We only get one go at life, and I want to get up in the morning and *want* to go to work; do something I'd find fulfilling and am passionate about.'

Rob: 'And this guy's a... Chartered Surveyor?!'

'That's right Rob, Jill; I am a Chartered Surveyor.'

Joel: 'And that's it? It's a dream job for a lot of people.'

And that uninspiring collection of banalities is the final nail in my coffin as far as Joel's concerned as well then.

Still, what have I got to lose...?

'Yep, you're right Mr Messenger..., and you will find other people with more experience in the industry than I have. But believe me you won't find anyone more resourceful, enthusiastic to learn, full of ideas, and, most importantly of all, committed to being where you want me when you want me and able to get what you want done. As I think Lawrence Turman put it: I think I have taste and tenacity. And, as you've probably been able to conclude already today, I'm maybe just the right side of baffling-youth-of-today to be good at it. And, if that's not enough, well..., I might even consider lending you my Sergio Leone collection.'

'Wow John: the right side of baffling-youth-of-today, really?'

Joel: 'What, only *consider* lending...?'

Hah, yep.

I definitely like Mr Messenger here.

'Yep, *might* only consider.'

Albeit, as courteous and engaging as he's being, it's time for his less humorous MD to put us out of our collective misery in any case it seems.

Rob: 'Sorry Joel, there's been a mix-up.'

Why is it always a mix-up with people like Rob here, and never a mistake?

Joel: 'We heard.'

Rob: 'Oh.'

At least Joel's holding him to account for his lack of tact.

Rob: 'We meant to invite this other, err..., Camden, guy in.'

There is, however, a difference between showing tenacity and embarrassingly flogging the proverbial.

Until the day it's my CV being brandished with such enthusiasm, and I'm the one receiving a surprise late call-up from some other Ms Karen-I'm-too-talented-to-be-doing-this, enough of this what-might-have-been is enough. The writing is on all of their faces let alone the wall, and even if Premature Rob and Liverpool Jill do spring a surprise by being contrite or embarrassed enough to want to go through the motions of the rest of the interview – which they probably aren't, and therefore won't – my dignity and I are going to make a stand, literally, and withdraw gracefully.

Or, failing that, simply drag ourselves any which way the fuck out of the building.

'Please, I don't want to waste any more of anyone's time here. Mistakes happen. I hope the other, err, Camden John proves to be just the person you're looking for.'

Leaving this Pimlico one to say his cheerios; beginning with the kindly Mr baffling-youth-of-today here.

'Goodbye Mr Messenger. It was a pleasure to meet you. Really. If maybe not, perhaps, the bit in the.., err..., well, you know where.'

Think I'll take a different tack with Rob though.

82

'Mr Smelley.'

Hah, yes, got him!

'Yes, this is what it's like when somebody prematurely grips only your fingers in a firm and, I hope, emasculating handshake, Rob.'

It's too much to hope that someday I'll get to do the gibbering lightweight's office rent review, is it, I suppose? The one where I get to triple his rent?

As sad, blimey, as the potential implication of that thought is to contemplate on a wider level.

Jill: 'I'll show you out.'

Still, if, rather than angry indignation, I am indeed unable to muster anything more than a feeling of sad resignation, what would be even sadder – if not indulgently wasteful – would be to spurn this last chance to take in a little more of Liverpool Jill here as she leads us out.

Hmm.

And, she being embarrassed and me just embarrassing, no small talk or eye contact this time; just a slightly less casual stride trailing an awkward silence: which I very much doubt she'd break even if she did catch me surveying her curves.

After all, once a surveyor, always a surveyor, eh?

Or so they must think anyway.

They're not the ones who've got to live with the notion though.

Oh, and don't tell me, that wasn't by any chance the tail end of Karen the incompetent receptionist bolting into that adjoining office keen to avoid us..., me..., was it?

I bet she's never chosen to move so fast.

On the bright if not even luminous side, at least I won't ever have to be associated with that fashion victim of a pink sofa.

No, I can't resist.

'That pink, err, sofa, Jill?'

Jill: 'It's fuchsia, actually. Wonderful, isn't it?!'

Yes, she really is as enraptured with it as she sounds. It's certainly fuch-something, I'll give her that.

Jill: 'It's a Jason Steel. Chose it myself. Couldn't resist! Hah!'

Hah, indeed.

Probably best to just smile and nod and maintain the suitably reverential facade though. Never burn one's bridges as my Dad says.

'Bye then.'

I wonder if she is actually as supercool as she and her handshake portray? Or if that sofa and this shirt of hers belie more playful and daring inclinations?

'Perhaps this morning, all this, is for the best after all, then, eh John?'

Yeah, she almost certainly wouldn't have been able to stop herself from pestering me for adventurous sex all day every day, which would've been annoying after a while, even for me.

Especially if it was on that fuch-something sofa.

Astrogirl-Karen-the-receptionist too, in all probability.

If not simultaneously.

No, I'd never have got anything done.

Yep, I can stroll out, head high.

Well, if no longer completely deflated anyway.

'And, if you're no longer a budding film producer, Johnny boy, you might just as well take the opportunity to cast your once-a-surveyor-always-a-surveyor's eye over this beautiful art deco lift here, heh?'

Ah.

If it weren't out of order: typically.

Where's a fucking management surveyor when you need one?

Shame, though. I'll never get another chance to ride in it now.

Just another look at this ludicrously tacky but no longer funny, fuchsia 'TotalFilm' sign on the stair door, and a descent into melancholy.

Yet another what might have been to gnaw away at what was supposed to be a limitless, lifetime supply of enthusiasm.

Life is not a dress rehearsal: isn't that supposed to be the maxim? When all I've got to look forward to next in mine is playing out my lies for Nigel back in the office.

And just how do I get my head around that?

Hmm.

Perhaps in a different way to Mr Security Guard in his stellar lobby here, maybe. Unless he's just trying to outdo me in the forlorn stakes.

'Cheers then.'

Oops, I think I almost made him jump.

He also can't get much of a look-in with these media types either.

Guard: 'You have a great day, sir.'

Oh. Right.

That'll be both of us pleasantly surprised then.

'Thanks, you too buddy. Take it easy.'

And, yes, he's right as well, isn't he?

Am I not actually the one and only Johnny Smith, destined for great days and superlatives? I've told myself often enough, so it must be true, mustn't it?

Or is this great double door more than likely the closest I'll get, and closure for me in more ways than one?

So much so that I can hardly bring myself to step down from the doorstep?

Humph.

Either this is a first degree feeling sorry for myself moment or I must be the only person in this damn square that the sun isn't shining on.

Metaphorically at any rate.

'Oh, mighty Sun God I beseech you: tell me this isn't all life has in store for me.'

Eh?

Is it?

Please?

Nope, thought as much.

Then again, despite this being a degree of warmth I've so far failed to feel from any other incarnation of the Almighty, whether this one would entertain on demand the desperate beseeching of a devout atheist like me is probably a moot point in any case.

And, with the opera diva already accepting her applause for her comedic rendition of my life story, I can close my eyes and offer my face skywards like a lemon as long as I want, all the difference it'll make now.

Uh-huh.

For Sun God read spotlight of failure in fact.

Ackh, I'm going to run...

Yes, I'm going to run back to the office, or anywhere; somewhere.

Yes.

Or would if I could muster the energy.

Or the motivation.

An unnoticed implosion of frustration and autopilot mode it'll have to be then.

And, if I'm lucky, not even a spotlight of failure would dare try to follow me into the shadows of Brewer Street.

Nope: down the rest of the square maybe, but not into Brewer Street. No spotlight of any sort is safe in here, daytime or not.

Unless, that is, the spotlight is in the front window of a sex shop, obviously.

'On which subject, if you really can't stop yourself taking one last, wistful look back towards the square and all it offered career and libido satisfaction wise, it's too much to speculate that Jungle Jill's a regular visitor to Lilly's Sex Emporium here, is it, Johnny, eh?'

Yes, really, is it?

I can practically see her in that pink leopard print catsuit displayed in the front window already.

Ackh!

'No, I said Jill in the catsuit, not lightweight Rob in the black gimp gear on the hanger behind...'

Urgh.

I've now lost control of my mind entirely it seems.

Either that, or I've inhaled too much of the rank, hallucinatory staleness spewing out of the newly opened bowel doors of the Piccadilly Theatre over there and it all really has been a dress rehearsal for me this morning.

If that isn't one pun too near the mark.

Sadly, whether I am more likely accepting meekly a life mundane or just needing some fresh air, I'd better leave Jill and Rob at it in the window and move on physically at least; and certainly before my libido and credit card can step inside for a catsuit gift-wrap.

This wholly contrasting and less readily sidestepped smell of cooked breakfasts breezing out from the conflictingly named New Piccadilly Cafe – which, I suppose, like Labour must have been new at some time or other – is very definitely sending my shredded constitution an altogether less ambiguous message, however.

And, yes, I really am going to have to find something quick, stodgy and calorific to eat if I'm going to be able to fend off the impending mid-morning post-hangover shakes.

But from where is the question.

I've had enough melancholic Soho nostalgia for one day; so, with no offence meant, this place is a non-starter.

Only, given that Piccadilly Circus is now playing host to what must be the other half of tourist London still in bed for the changing of the guards at the palace earlier this morning, and that the majority of these are in the queue for the obvious target sandwich bar, that's out too.

As long as my legs don't give out in the hundred or so metres before I get there, my usual plan C and the café bar in the British Art Academy it'll have to be then.

And, in the interests of looking beyond what I've just left behind, that may be no bad thing I suppose.

Granted, this my usual stomping ground may not be as impossibly on-trend as Golden Square and its media-obsessed inhabitants, but nor is it one-dimensional and introverted either. And, when it comes to art galleries and culture and the like..., well, even Catsuit Jill would have to admit there's no comparison.

'You know what, you might very well be right, Johnny Boy; that fuchsing company probably wasn't the way to go in any case, eh?'

Yes, I think the grip of my melancholic ne claustrophobic mood is starting to loosen a little already, in fact.

And I can genuinely, almost, possibly, believe me too.

Particularly when I'm a hot, undiscovered screenwriter with two blockbuster screenplays in development. Oh yes, I can see myself on Film 1999 – no, make that 2000, to allow for production – now.

JR: 'So, Johnny Boy Smith, what a fabulous film. I really enjoyed it.'

Me: 'Thanks, Jonathan. The director obviously did a great job realising my vision.'

JR: 'I think the only thing that's obvious is that you're a really talented screenwriter.'

Me: 'Noohhh, I was just inspired by my surroundings.'

JR: 'Some surroundings.'

Me: 'Yes, London really is a fabulous city.'

JR: 'Many critics are already saying you've got the Original Screenplay Oscar in the bag?'

Me: 'It's just fabulous to be nominated with so many other great writers.'

JR: 'But you're having a fucking laugh, aren't you?'

Me: 'I beg your pardon?'

JR: 'Well, a talentless wannabe tosser like you imagining you're on my show, nominated for an Oscar?'

Mm-hmm.

I must be the only person in the world who, in the space of thirty paces, can secure and lose an Oscar nomination in his own head; under, poetically, the bemused, watchful gaze of the head office of BAFTA.

Humph.

So, from humiliation before the British Academy of Film to consolatory double chocolate muffin at the British Art Academy, melancholic mood fully restored it is then.

Or at least it would be if I didn't also find myself so laughable.

Then again, if this here in the middle of their otherwise impressive entrance courtyard really is what the curators were doing behind all the cloaking last week, being laughable can't be a state unfamiliar to them either currently.

And, nope, I don't think my eyes are deceiving me; they really have installed two giant dinosaurs made from pieces of steel plate seemingly conceived and cut to shape by a five-year-old child for assembly from flat pack by gullible adults.

Or, perhaps more accurately in this case, by brazen artists for gullible critics.

Or, maybe just as likely, by a five-year-old child with a penis for a nose for brown-nosing critics, if these artists' previous, ever so clever and provocative creations are anything to go by.

And if their intention is to provoke me into thinking even I could do better, it's working.

'But, however laughable or playful these notions may sound and the results here may look, anything for a muffin and to put off facing Nigel for another half an hour, though, eh John?'

If, from somewhere in the depths of this not so clever and increasingly provocative wallet of mine I am able to find my annual Friends membership card – yep, the one so well hidden for fear of anyone I know, and Simon in particular, using it as more evidence of my nerdism that I can't find it myself – before my hangover finally does for me.

Mm-hmm.

Ah, found it: hiding alongside its kindred spirit my Stoke City FC supporters' club card.

Oops.

'Sorry.'

The latter of which won't get me waved in by the ticket monitoring lady as effectively as the former.

And not even out of sympathy.

Anyhow, now I am through the door; to the canteen for the hugest, freshest double chocolate muffin I can find and an extra strong, takeout cup of Redbush.

Or Rooibos, to give it its proper name that I must remember to use in the rigorously culturally approropriate canteen here.

And, for once, there are only two people in the queue ahead of me too.

Moreover, and far more importantly, unless the joke characterisations really are true about pregnant women and small men, neither look ready to fight me to the death for that obviously even from here biggest of the muffins in that counter-top basket beside them, even if they are also after it.

And which, if I'm suitably stealthy, I can so snaffle, yep, by sliding my arm into the narrow gap between them, hah.

Also handily enabling me to slip ahead of them to order my tea too.

Oh yes.

You snooze you lose.

'And a regular takeaway Rooibos, please.'

Right, all I need after buying these is an empty bench in one of the galleries before the hoards from Piccadilly Circus get here.

Wow, that was quick; its like Ms Counter-Assistant's second-guessed me.

And proffered with a bashful smile and an exhibition leaflet, helpfully.

Mind you, if I had cheekbones as high as hers, I'd be smiling like that too, very probably.

'Cheers, £3, here you go, thanks.'

Either that, or she's come into work this morning via that introduction in the courtyard and knows what else is in store for me in the rest of the exhibition.

Still, if I am going to be knowingly hoodwinked by anybody...

And there are usually at least a couple of rooms in the exhibitions here that are worth taking a ten-minute pew in, even ignoring the cunningly persuasive Ms Bashful-with-a-red-bush back there.

Or the diverting thought that conjures.

Oops.

Or a Ms Bashful-now-unwittingly-nearly-making-me-spill-some-of-it, even.

And, if I am to achieve optimum satisfaction from their consumption, perhaps taking the precaution of concealing from the exhibition mess-police my tea and paper-bagged muffin under my jacket.

Yep.

Sensibly.

If deviously.

And notwithstanding that, as a Friend, I should know better.

Hmm.

Still, oh for a convenient pew in a quiet corner somewhere.

Despite my descent into deviance just now, I'll keep walking past the 'Art in architecture' room, no matter how quiet it looks in there; nor how appealing it would be to defy the poetic cries of hypocrite from my architect friends.

But, nah, fuck 'em: I'm near as damn it a successful creative myself, don't the bastards know.

Only, instead of something appealing like art in film, what does the sign plate on this next room say?

'This room is hung for people who are sensitive, intelligent and thoughtful.'

Blimey.

I can't go in there as a matter of fundamental exclusion then.

Well, maybe I would if it were stashed full of cut-price Hockneys; but only then.

And it isn't, so I'm not.

And I can't afford even a cut-price Hockney anyway.

Although conceivably I could borrow the dosh from Si and then trade it maybe?

Huh?

Now I really am in front courtyard dinosaur land.

Speaking of which, this next room looks a possibility, even if it is marked 'Conceptual'.

Specifically not 'Modern' or 'Contemporary' then, but 'Conceptual'.

Oh, and a helpful annotation too.

'Conceptual Art: where artists give the concept priority over the traditional media.'

And if that's not an advance excuse of some kind or other I've never read one.

Only, if I don't want to wander around the gallery all morning waiting for my Nobush to get cold, and because there's a space on the end bench in there next to a Miss Bamby-with-sketchpad-student-type, 'Conceptual' appeals all of a sudden.

Particularly when I can't walk much further, and the bench is looking even more inviting the closer I get to it.

Yes, ahhh.

And notwithstanding that I'm not enough of a priority in concept to merit so much as a reciprocal glance from Miss Sketchpad here; the art in here being that good.

Humph.

'Perhaps, instead, it'll have to be an inability to attract attention that, whilst bad for our ego, is good for consuming crumbly chocolate muffins in banned places then, eh Johnny Boy?'

If that's not spinning the reality more than a little too far.

With all these people milling about I should be able to get away with it if I choose the right moment to turn my back to the guard and adopt my foolproof thrust-nose-and-mouth-deep-into-bag technique, however.

Like now.

Mm-hmm.

Hah.

A large, crumbly bite plus slurp of Nobush equals instant, gooey, salvational gratification.

Finally.

And, fabulously.

And, yikes, with a sugar rush which my body needed more than I realised.
Hmm.

Back to the similarly un-realising Miss Sketchpad for a moment though, what can she possibly, really, find so much more interesting than me in here?

Certainly nothing in this video installation of a man wandering around a glass foyer in a head to paw lion costume, surely?

Even if it is by and featuring an artist who 'creates transcendent possibilities from everyday moments of life through systemising nature, the banal and the abstract.'

Presupposing that my own failure to wear a lion costume isn't where I'm going wrong; and in which case I'm having a transcendental moment of my own, if not for the reason Mr Lion Costume had in mind or would doubtless appreciate.

And as for this patchwork blanket-cum-quilt that Miss Sketchpad's so fixated on...

What are those words daubed across it?

'Andrew Kinson', 'behemoth', 'child', 'emotional execution'?
Hmm.

And with the latter also being what will happen to Miss Sketchpad here if she doesn't stop looking at it so appreciatively.

Unless, such being the young British artist zeitgeist, inspiring normally peaceable gallery-goers to turn on each other is part of the 'concept'; in which case I won't give them the satisfaction.

There must on some level, any level, be something conceptual in here to lift my mood, though, mustn't there?

No?

Hmm.

A garden shed botched together from pieces of scrap wood, and an old car painted completely pink.

Right; if not Miss Bamby Sketchpad here, the rest of my muffin's going to get a pasting.

'Arrgghhh, arrgharrrggghhh!'

'Arrgghhh, arrgharrrggghhh, arrgghhh!'

Oops.

'Yes John. If you are going to mount a savage, escapist attack on your muffin in the style of a lion at a wildebeest, then, unless you really are going to try to hide your face inside this paper bag all day, the very minimum you could have expected was a cagey retreat with a chocolate goatee.'

And without a napkin.

'Oh, so now you notice me Miss Sketchpad?!'

Aside from a lion costume all it took to attract her attention was a bit of perfectly innocent growling and wild muffin-chomping then.

Assuming, by attention, that's a face-full of panic and blind-groping-for-sketchpad-and-pencils retreat away from me.

Oops.

'Sorry..., please, don't stop or leave on my account..., it's okay, I'm going...'

Good, she's staying.

Not that I can blame her of course.

Me, the mad English lion of Piccadilly; even minus the costume.

And I quite like the sound of that actually.

Still, if I really have to stop kidding myself and simply resort to my usual fave, at least it's only hanging in the room across the corridor at the moment, on loan as it is currently from the competition in Pimlico.

Oops; only I need my Friends card again.

'Turner: the making of The Impressionists'

They got this title right.

And Ted's manning the entrance door.

'Hey Ted.'

Ted: 'Hello John. You just can't stay away, can you...'

Nope, evidently not.

Oops, he's spotted the tea and muffin bag.

'Sorry, yes, I know I shouldn't really have these in with me, but...'

No, he's gunna let me get away with it.

And the room's near empty again anyway; even when it is full of masterpieces.

Work that one out.

It would be worth coming in here just to see this one here alone.

The very beneficial upshot being that I get to stuff the whole of the rest of a muffin in my mouth..., mm-hmm..., just..., in relative solitude in front of my favourite painting in all the world, while those out there don't know what they're missing.

Woman's Voice: 'You're right, it does make one angry, doesn't it?'

Huh?

Was that directed at me?

It came from above and behind me.

It must have been from this older, silver-haired lady in bohemian garb; propping herself up on an elegant cane and staring back over my shoulder at my Turner.

And who, yep, has now looked down to catch my eye.

Oops: and the remnants of chocolate muffin around my mouth.

Maybe I've got a tissue in one of my jacket pockets?

Erm...

Nope, it appears not then.

Ah.

Ms Bohemian Garb has though, of course; kindly.

If proffered with the same errant-little-boy-smile I garnered from Hold-ups earlier.

What was it again? Mere men like me just can't help ourselves?

'Very kind. Thank you.'

Ms Bohemian Garb: 'So, go on then...'

Eh?

So..., go on then..., what?

About the, err..., this...?

'About..., this..., Snow Storm...?'

Yes?

Yes, it seems so then.

Ms Bohemian Garb: 'No, I meant about not being allowed to eat in the galleries.'

Oh.

Hmm.

No, she's pulling my leg: her mouth's twitching at the edges and her eyes have widened.

Ms Bohemian Garb: 'Unless I'm mistaken, I've seen you at this very spot in here before, haven't I?'

Blimey.

Me, really?

Okay, right.

Seems so then...

'I can't help myself – it's just beguiling isn't it.'

The great swirls of paint..., the steam boat..., and smoke, the industry...

'Its power and subtlety..., it's just amazing...'

And, yep, she thinks so too; I can see it in her eyes.

Ms Bohemian Garb: 'Unlike the work back out there then?'

Woah, what?

Has she been following me?

'Well..., err..., don't get me wrong, I love the meticulousness of..., I dunno..., a Gormley block figure say, or the precision of Hirst's winged dove in its flawless tank..., but out there it's like *conceptual* has become the go-to category for artists without the skill and application...'

Only, if that doesn't make me sound banal, nothing will.

'And those things in the main courtyard...'

Ms Bohemian Garb: 'So only superstars need apply?'

And why am I trying to impress her in any case?

Ms Bohemian Garb: 'And isn't Damien Hirst a conceptual artist?'

Hmm.

And now she's even conveying the same hint of mockery as Hold-ups, too.

I wish this one here had been my art teacher at school.

'I really couldn't say to be honest. But even Banksy's street art is executed with quality and subtlety, no?'

Particularly considering he must half expect the long arm of the law to descend on his shoulder at any moment. That's genuine application and dedication. No safety of the studio for him.

Ms Bohemian Garb: 'But many are amateurs or students, and it is an open exhibition after all...'

And from hint of mockery to dismissive, duly.

Or was it actually defensive?

Oops, that dodgy quilt out there's not hers, is it?!

Oh.

She's turned her back on me and is walking away.

Her attention now exclusively on the far inferior Monet; and the conclusion of Part II of this morning's master class on counterinsurgency and the subservient male: how to dismiss the ignorance and over-expectation of youth.

Hmm.

I'll drag myself away and finish what's left of my tea on the way out then.

Assuming she's not an academician sent down to identify the ungrateful or unworthy for stripping of our Friend memberships, and I am, therefore, even allowed out.

Notwithstanding that I was and am right.

And, nope, there are no uniformed types forcibly removing membership cards at the main exit door yet...

Nor any doing anything about the crime in the courtyard beyond it.

Andy Warhol had it right: art really is what you can get away with, and that lot in Conceptual Room 25 – and these, my new steel dinosaur friends – what he was on about.

And, if they can get away with it, why stop?

After all, when even the grand old first academician up there on his plinth seems to have succumbed to the farcicality of it all – poised as he is, brush in hand, to beckon the dinosaurs to roll over in some sort of puerile display of dinoCrufts – anything and everything is possible.

Mm-hmm.

Definitely time to get back to the office.

Before I lose entirely even my own tenuous grip on reality.

Print

Just what the hell is it about this damn Middleton Lyons sign that's so repressive?

Celia: 'You've got a bit more colour in your face. Whatever you've been doing has done you good.'

'The effects of a successful morning's humiliation, Celia my lovely.'

'Tea and double chocolate muffin.'

Celia: 'Oooh, that's just what I could do with.'

Yep, we're all in constant torment about something or other.

Definitely the stairs this time; I've seen enough dodgy sides to myself for one day.

Although perhaps at less than three steps at a time on this occasion; even if, unlike the rest of me, my ankle seems to have recovered its sense of purpose.

As much as I've missed him while I've been out this morning, I suppose it's too much to hope that Nigel's not around at the moment, is it?

Hmm?

Nigel: 'Look, Stephen, let me explain it to you this one final time. Either your client stumps up a non-refundable deposit of twenty-five grand, or I'm going to place the deal elsewhere. That clear enough for you?!'

Not only that, if I can hear him from over here by the lobby, his door must be open too, thereby putting paid to my casually slipping past unnoticed anytime now-ish.

Maybe if I walk fast enough he'll be too busy on the phone to notice me?

Or do I quickly duck into the kitchen on the way to buy another minute or two of watching and waiting time?

Yep, a quick dart through the kitchen door first then.

Ackh; SHIT!!

What or who was that the other side of the door?!

Oops.

An equally shocked Gail – into whom I've crashed open the door making her spill her coffee and drop her file and sundries all over the floor with a racket loud enough to draw attention from everybody in the office, including Nigel and the spaniel – is who and what.

'Crikey..., err, sorry Gail.'

And, yes, she does have every right to glare at me in stunned disbelief.

If even Fred doesn't know whether to laugh or sympathise, it really must have looked bad.

'I didn't hurt you, did I?'

Hmm.

Well, hopefully no more than her elbow then, anyway.

'No, let me do that...'

Picking up her pens and file from the floor is the least I should be doing.

'Okay; and, yes Gail, replenishing your substantially empty and forcibly proffered coffee mug.'

Very luckily, at least the coffee appears to have mostly missed her hand and clothes.

If not on an altogether more noticeable scale, the floor.

Oops.

And from which I suppose I'd better make an attempt to soak up the worst of it with some paper towels from the kitchenette.

All the while accepting that Gail's only censure was a raised-eyebrow message of imbecility; before – no drama, point made – she simply walked off to wash her hands.

Nigel: 'And when you think you've finished disturbing the whole office, Smith, you can join me in here...'

Unlike Nigel, who's never one to miss even the smallest opportunity to rub any of our noses in it, or assert his authority, or preferably both simultaneously, the generous soul he is.

'*Yep, yep, okay then.*'

Just nod; nod in obedience.

'*But only because you pay me Nigel.*'

Anyhow, where was I before I was so rudely interrupted?

Yes: kettle on, and one, two and three paper towels I should think.

And what the spaniel thinks she's scowling at me like that for only she knows.

'*Yes, I am actually going to tread these paper towels into the crime scene, Wendy.*'

What, does she want to see me dance while I do it or something?

'*Yeah, look away and get on with your work then, you nosy...*'

And, after deployment of these last two fresh paper towels, perhaps, yes, this is the worst of it up for now.

Yep.

The cleaners and their machines will have to do the rest.

Right, soaking towels back to the bin in the kitchenette..., while..., ah..., I rinse my hands and watch Gail complete my final task of making her another coffee.

103

Humph.

Still, right now, if that means I can follow her back to our desks and slump into the relative safety of my chair for a minute, I'll take it.

Fred: 'Nice one.'

'Thanks Fred. I tried hard to time the impact just right.'

Hmm.

If Wendy's renewed bout of scowling is designed to remind me that I still need to see Nigel, they can both wait another minute.

The very last thing I'm going to do is give Nigel another chance to notice, if he hasn't already, that I went out in my trainers, so now really must do what I should have done already and retrieve from my desk drawer these my forgotten, freshly-buffed-for-interview Oliver Sweeneys.

Edgy styling and expensive maybe, but it's not only women who are worth it.

'Andrew, are you free this afternoon by any chance? I need someone to help me measure up the third floor at Platinum.'

Gail: 'He's coming to Highgate with me.'

'Oh, right you are then Gail.'

In the aftermath of coffee-gate, and notwithstanding Andrew's apologetic shrug of his shoulders, I can't even ask her to budge on it either.

'Fred? It'll only take half an hour.'

Fred: 'Sorry mate, I've got client meet in Shoreditch.'

'Hmm, I might have to take the American temp then, the one doing all that archive scanning. What's her name? Sarah isn't it?'

Gail: 'Samantha. Samantha Palin.'

Make that another name I didn't get right this morning then.

Andrew: 'She's probably quit already. I would have if I was stuck in that back office doing that archive scanning all day every day...'

Fred: 'She's American, and should be grateful for the privilege of scanning our files.'

Gail: 'She's nice..., from New York.'

Andrew: 'With a surname like that it's almost obligatory to be nice.'

Eh?

Fred: 'What, you're suggesting she could be Michael's love child?'

Ah.

'Haven't you pair got anything better to waffle on about than Palins? I only need her to hold the end of a measuring tape.'

Fred: 'I actually think she got off lightly with Palin. She should count her lucky stars and stripes she's hasn't got one of those ridiculous made-up surnames they must have given out on Ellis Island as piss-takes...,'

Oh yeah?

Fred: '... like Palinawegger..., or Palibanaskiewicz...'

Hah.

Actually...

'Yeah, you're right... Or Paliwinzowsky...'

Hah!

Fred: 'Palinascanner junior..., the third...'

Andrew: 'Palintheyankwithballsky has an appropriate ring to it....'

Hah!

'Sounds like you've been giving it some prioe thought Andrew...'

Gail: 'Excuse me, team...'

Maybe even I would have remembered a name like that...

'Oops, sorry Gail.'

Fuck, make that double oops: the laughing has drawn Nigel to poke his head out of his office.

Fred: 'Remember: absolutely no laughing in the office.'

And Fred's sarcastic reminder is only half in the outlawed jest.

The tumbleweed's drifting across the carpet in the deadly silence in fact.

Nigel: 'It's alright! You don't have to stop enjoying yourselves on company time just because I'm here!'

Uh-huh.

Nigel: 'John, get your arse in here. I've got to go out, and there's something you're gunna have to do for me this afternoon, in Lambeth.'

And, on the basis of the looks of renewed subjugation on Freddy's, Andrew's and doubtless my face, I'm not the only one wisely keeping my defiance to myself.

They're not the ones having to take a pen and notepad into Nigel's office though.

Still...

'I thought you wanted me to go to Platinum House this afternoon?'

Nigel: 'Oh, yeah, right... You'll have to do this afterwards then...'

Right, fabulous, afterwards then.

Nigel: 'I want you to check the boundaries of the site against the title plan..., here..., make sure everything's as it should be, in the right place.'

Wow; this site's massive – for this part of town anyway.

Nigel: 'It's one I've been dealing with myself. It's an old warehouse and yard. The owner's a Mr Singh. Gone bust, forced sale.'

Humph.

And there was me hoping to get away on time today...

Nigel: 'Well you could have done it this morning if you hadn't been off in Soho!'

Oops.

Me and my traitor of a face.

Nigel: 'It shouldn't take you long, in any case.'

And, fuck, I know what he's going to ask me now.

Nigel: 'And how did you get on by the way?'

And what the hell can I tell him?

Nope, I'll have to play dumb; buy a few seconds' thinking time.

'Huhh?'

Nigel: 'Christ..., in Ssooo–hhooo?!'

And lucky for me that his delight at using slow and exaggerated sarcasm is matched only by his readiness to mistake my prevarication as obtuseness.

'Umm, not one for us I'm afraid. Wild goose chase. Just wanted a freebie valuation.'

'Don't ask me for details; don't ask me for details....'

Nigel: 'Some mate, the cheeky cunt.'

Wow.

Just how scornful would he be if one day I have to tell him the truth?

Nigel: 'Mr Singh's expecting you at four o'clock. Address is on the plan. Don't be late. You can tell me how you get on tomorrow, at Henley.'

'Okay, yep, seeing as if you asked so nicely Nigel.'

And if that is our conversation over, I am out of here.

Why the fuck do I keep putting myself in these situations? There really must be more to life than nearly getting speared by Nigel every other day, even if it does pay the bills.

As for here and now, he must have other things on his mind, because there's no way he'd have bought the freebie valuation line normally.

And, yes: for once, putting my hands, forehead and nose against the window by my desk for a minute's respite probably is the sensible thing to do.

Mm-hmm.

All those people down in the street, all seemingly with important places to go, interesting people to see and meaningful things to do.

Unlike me: whose only job is to be meaningless in some edifice in Covent Garden and some dodgy warehouse in Lambeth.

'And which, nope, is not anywhere near as comedic as it sounds, is it John, eh?'

Nope.

Lest I forget in the swell of excitement and meaningfulness, there probably is no further avoiding the back office photocopier and the task of copying this title plan to take with me.

Nor, assuming it's where she has indeed been re-stationed to do her too-awful-to-contemplate archive scanning, asking Ms Palinowski if she'll maybe do something else too awful to contemplate with me this afternoon.

If, like Andrew suggests, she's even in there and hasn't run for the Californian hills since first thing.

Now's as good a time as any to find out though.

And, nope, there don't seem to be any moving shadows behind the small etched glass panel in the door.

And, err..., yep, the room is empty.

Oh, no, hang on, who's this coming in behind me?

Ah.

Not Ms Palinowski, but Leannowski then.

Only, why's she come down to our floor?

If I don't want my already eighteen month long guilty conscience to offer her yet another empathetic after work drink, I'll need to be quick.

Leanne: 'Hi John...'

Gosh, I thought I was in the doldrums.

'Hi Leanne. How're you? I haven't seen you in ages!'

'Nor the micro-skirt and those disconcertingly long and exposed legs of yours, either.'

Leanne: 'Oh, you know, so-so...'

Yikes, this title plan's so old, stiff and well-creased it's like a concertina.

Only, if I simply crush it all down flat with the lid, I might damage it.

Leanne: 'How've *you* been?'

Actually, what might work is if I stretch it out flat with my hands and forearms, and use my chest to press it down in the middle.

Leanne: 'Saw you out last night with your mate Simon, did I?'

Ackh, bollocks; let's see how this comes out.

What did she say? How does she know Si?

'I didn't see you, where were you then?'

Damn, it's coming out A4 rather than A3.

Leanne: 'Want me to do that for you?'

'No..., err, no, it's okay, thanks Leanne. Despite my ineptitude, I think I'll manage...'

If by manage I mean wrestling the plan down on the plate and then demeaning myself by practically hugging the machine to keep it flat before trying to press the green button with my elbow: then, yes.

Leanne: 'Fun night then, was it?'

Blimey, I'd forgotten how hot it is in here.

Or does my apparent and instinctive unwillingness to become beholden to her for even the smallest help on the photocopier make me less comfortable than she is about what happened between us at the Christmas party, or just paranoid?

'No, it was a bit of a quiet one actually.'

And the latter, judging by that response.

Oh.

Nope, I am to be saved by the door.

And the entry of the famed Ms Palinascanner, no less.

Only, if she doesn't look up to see where she's going she'll...

Samantha: 'Oh! Hi..., sorry...'

Nope, she stopped just in time.

'And, yes Leanne, the three of us will be forced to continue standing uncomfortably close together unless you step back to let Samantha past, eh?'

Leanne: 'Hiya.'

'Okay, make her squeeze past you then.'

Samantha: 'Sorry, not interrupting anything am I...?'

What?! Was that mischievously?

Crikey, has everyone around here heard about mine and Leanne's Christmas snog?

It was only a fucking quick snog for Christmas sake.

Or have I just imagined her inference? She does speak American after all. And Americans don't do sarcasm, do they?

'No, no..., just taking a couple of photocopies.'

Albeit, damn it; seeing as how Leanne's just thrown her an exaggerated smart-arse smile, this American does then.

Humph.

And we haven't even met properly either, the cheeky..., I dunno..., imp.

The way she's sauntering over to her laptop and that enormous pile of files and the infamous scanning machine all anti-establishment in her black tee and wrists full of assorted bangles and skinny jeans and high-heeled, pointy-toed ankle boots – that, yes, she probably does need legs like hers to carry off – I really should have known better, I suppose.

Yep, even her shortish, dark brown bob – one side closely and rebelliously cropped around one ear is that? – and those wide, dark, almost feline eyes seem impish.

Still, just because she might actually be quite pretty in a doesn't have to try too hard kind of way and may well struggle to bend that impishness over a measuring tape, doesn't mean I'm not going to ask her, hah!

'Actually, I need to ask you a favour, err, please.'

If I can ever figure out how to refold this title plan, that is.

Ackh.

Why the prolonged, unnatural silence from Ms Palimpish though?

Oh.

She's still got her head down, and either hasn't heard me or doesn't think I'm talking to her.

Samantha: 'What..., who..., me?!'

Leanne's raised her eyebrows in surprise as well; even if she is doing her best to hide the fact by pretending to focus her attention on her own photocopying.

'Yes. I've got to do a viewing this afternoon and need someone to hold the other end of the measuring tape while I take a couple of check measurements? Nigel suggested you, if that's alright...?'

'Yes; I thought that might at first stun, and, now, duly horrify you! Just imagine having to go out on an inspection with someone like me?!'

Samantha: 'Nigel? Oh. Err..., okkaaayyy.'

And that soft American accent of hers suddenly isn't so soft after all then.

'Thanks. It's only off Leicester Square, but we'll need to leave at two, if that's okay for you?'

Samantha: 'Err..., yes, fine. Okay. Two o'cock..., I mean clock, two o'clock.'

Leanne: 'Pfffttt!'

Hmm.

And, now from impish to Smith-gaff-esque.

'And, sorry Leanne, for that reason alone, no, I'm not going to smirk along with you at Samantha's gaff.'

'Right, see you later, err, Samantha..., then.'

Oh, and given she really probably doesn't know me from Adam...

'And I'm John by the way, in Investment Sales...'

Samantha: 'Oh..., yeah, yeah...'

Hmm, maybe she does actually know of me then.

But, if I know what's good for me, nor do I want to get on Leanne's wrong side before I go.

'Nice to see you Leanne...'

'And, that's it John, give her a nice, warm smile, whatever the meaning behind her own tight-lipped effort.'

Actually, on second thoughts, given that the door hasn't quite closed fully behind me...

Maybe if I tiptoe back quietly, and avoid making a shadow through the glass, it might well be worth a quick eavesdrop?

'What do you reckon Johnny Boy? Whilst Leanne's actions towards us are almost certainly driven more by what or who Glenda and the rest of her mates upstairs think was a real low point for her that Christmas, she'll see dealing with Samantha as a matter of fundamental territorial principle. National pride and all that?'

If so, shame for me then that Brit babe versus rest of the world is being drowned out by the din of the photocopier.

Oh, no, it's stopped.

Samantha: 'No, I'm not seeing anyone at the moment, and I'm flying back to New York in a few weeks.'

Leanne: 'Shame you couldn't stay here longer.'

'Blimey Leanne, you couldn't have meant that any less if you tried.'

Leanne: 'Just a temporary visa was it...? But New York does sound amazing.'

Samantha: 'Oh, no..., I mean yeah, it is. But I'm just going back to see my Mom, then I'll be coming back to London.'

Oh, indeed. The playful Samantha is teasing her me thinks.

Samantha: 'My dad was born here so I can stay as long as I want...'

Oops.

'Sorry Leanne, but that'll be 1-0 to the interloper then.'

Leanne: 'So why are you just *temping* then?'

'Yeah, go on Leanne. You're not going to let some temping Yank tease you like that, are you?!'

Samantha: 'Well......'

Leanne: 'Suppose it must be difficult for someone like you to get anything *permanent*?'

Ouch.

Samantha: 'Well, I err...'

A speculative dig from Leanne making it 1-1 and all to play for.

Leanne: 'And, if not this time, I'm sure we'll have a girls' night out before you do, *finally*, leave...'

Yikes, I think that's the lid of the photocopier crashlanding.

Yep, time to quietly skedaddle.

Mm-hmm.

Shame; a scrappy and unsatisfying score draw between the Cosmos and the Hammers it'll have to remain then.

And, on the basis that loud and uncontrollable stomach rumblings aren't exactly conducive to covert and close-quarter surveillance even without the imminent danger of discovery, probably an opportune time to complete the recovery of my constitution with lunch.

Before George Smiley eats his heart out.

Only, while he's doing that, I'll take a modicum of solace from our part of the office becoming near deserted while I was away so busily, and maybe take advantage of the same to work on my only remaining potential ticket out of here: the hitherto undiscovered gem that is my latest draft film screenplay.

Assuming the wholly understandable heat it's generating hasn't caused it to spontaneously combust in the bottom drawer of my desk before I get to it, of course.

Ohhh, yesss.

Which would be difficult to explain away even for me, in an open-plan office in which the boss has real Smiley's people – well, on this occasion, just Wendy – checking for chronic skivers and spare time film writers looking to waste company resources.

Humph.

And even if I'm wrong and Wendy really is engrossed in her magazine and Tupperware box of salad, the very last thing I should risk is her catching me working on it on my office computer.

So, yep, the hard copy in its un-marked envelope and a takeout lunch in the park it'll have to be.

Only, did I remember to print off the last twenty-five or so pages of amendments before I put it back last time?

Nope; going on what's here, that'll be not then.

And it's those pages that I really need to look at.

Hmm.

Can I chance printing them off now?

What's the greater risk? Forty-five minutes to get caught with it up on screen as I work on it here, or a minute to print the latest pages?

Yeah, there's only Wendy, it'll be fine; I'll print it and get some sunshine in the park.

So then: memory stick from bag, yep; insert into front port of computer, yep; click on screenplay..., print menu..., pages 95 – 120, yep; communal printer next to Gail's desk still idle? Yep; still nobody around but Wendy, yep; click and send illicit endeavour to print.

Yep.

Only..., why's the printer not...?

Ah, no, there it goes.

Lights, printer and..., action!

Right; sixty or so short seconds, and Green Park here I come.

And Wendy hasn't so much as looked up once from her magazine.

Hang on, who's...?

Fuck.

Nigel.

Judging by the way he marched up to and practically barked at Wendy before he dived into his office, he's either forgotten something, or needs it; and now.

Only, needs what, exactly?

Wendy has duly dropped everything and is tapping and clicking furiously on her keyboard and mouse, so is it just information he wants?

Whatever it is she's found it.

Fuck, she's just looked at Nigel's printer. She needs to print something.

Arrggh – no, no! – what's she glanced at the communal printer for?!

'Please use Nigel's, please use Nigel's...'

There's maybe..., yes, around ten or so pages of my print to go.

Wendy: 'Is that you printing?'

Christ; how unlucky can one person be in a day?

'Err, yeah, it is. Shouldn't be long though; just another few pages.'

Yikes, her eyes have narrowed.

'Rather than get annoyed, just use Nigel's printer then, use Nigel's...'

Only, wherever that click's going, she's just sent it.

Wendy: 'This one's out of toner; I've sent something urgent, for Nigel.'

Fuck, what do I do?!

Should I cancel the rest of my print?

No, it's too late, there's no time. Nigel's will come straight out after mine. I'll have to go and guard it.

'Look and sound calm, John; look and sound calm...'

'Right you are Wendy..., I'll get it for you.'

'...forget your pounding heart and just sidle; yes, that's it, don't do anything to attract her suspicion, just sidle calmly and casually over to the printer...'

Trying, fuck, to ignore the fact that, contrary to my offer to get it for her, Wendy's doing likewise.

Fuck!

Should I take out what's already printed, or would that encourage Wendy to take what comes out next?

No, there can only be a couple of more pages to go.

I'll position myself between her and the printer, and try distraction.

'You're looking trim these days Wendy. Been going to the gym, have you?'

'Wow, what the fuck did you say that for you idiot?! You've never asked her anything like that the whole time I've been here! You might just as well have told her you're up to no good.'

Wendy: 'So you think I need to go to the gym to look this good do you Mr Smith?'

Well...

'No, John!'

'Well, I'd certainly have to.'

Blimey; this is the second office machine I've had to prostrate myself over today.

Wendy: 'Oh don't talk crap. At your age you couldn't put on weight if you tried...'

'Come on printer... How much longer do you need for fuck's sake?!'
Oops.

Time's up, she's making to reach around me.

'Sorry Wendy, but I think I'll be taking these, thanks.'
Blimey, talk about a face full of frustration.

'And, yes Wendy, I am going to keep the printed side turned away from you so you can't see what it is.'

More importantly, if that's THE END I can see through the back of the last page, the next page out will be hers then.

Yep.

'Here you go, Wendy. Allow me...'

And, whilst I probably shouldn't, I'll accompany it with a hollow smile too, I think.

Hah!

'Okay, Wendy; you can stand there with your beady eyes and hands bolted to your hips if you want, but are you really going to allow a menial annoyance like me to delay you getting what you need for Nigel? Really?'

Yikes.

Nope, thought not.

And, instead of just hanging here like a squeezed lemon, I suppose I'd better make it both of us heading back to our desks with our hard-won documents.

If, in her case, the three inadvertently life-shortening pages are already in Nigel's grasping mitts and on their way out of the office too, in fact.

Hmm.

Fuck, I was even closer to being caught up to no good than earlier, but now it's like nothing ever happened. Wendy's nose is back in her salad and magazine, and I'm back wondering how the hell I get myself into such predicaments.

Time to chill and get hot in the park for a bit.

Only this time for an authorised and genuine forty-five minutes out of the office.

Kindred spirits

Hard-earned twenty-five pages in unmarked envelope plus pencil and rubber – check; pasta carton and smoothie from M&S – check; the main gate to Green Park and evermore scene of my humiliating and effortless defeat at the hands of athletic teenage backpacker – check.

If, yep, the latter is duly an altogether different place from earlier; its ritual, mid-morning transformation from barren commuter racetrack to mock-Victorian picnic resort with multitudinous cloak of deckchairs, blankets and fellow escapees having duly taken care of that for me.

Still, if only in solidarity with these my fellow kindred spirits, a bit of escapist anonymity in the London sunshine on one of those two vacant pink and white stripped deckchairs under the extremity of this my favourite tree here will do nicely; particularly if it also affords an opportunity for a bit of surreptitious people watching.

Assuming both deckchairs aren't nabbed like that by two eager lovebirds of course.

Humph.

'Just too slow again Johnny Boy.'

Don't they know they should really be in canoodlers' copse further down?

Wow, see the mutual looks of longing in their eyes.

'Just don't let your other halves catch you, eh?'

This less fetching green deckchair is definitely mine, however.

And, yep, whose back stanchion has already been ratcheted back to the laziest of the lazy bastard notches like it knew I was coming.

Oops..., woah!

Blimey.

And which has survived intact that overeager and unceremonious throw of my backside down into its stripy depths, luckily.

But now that I'm down here and all that; I can worry about how to climb effortlessly and coolly back out of it later.

For now though, this sense of anonymity in the crowd – when, yep, nobody knows me, and nobody cares what I'm up to – is mine to do what the hell I want with.

Well, they will know and care one day, of course – when I'm a hotshot film writer-cum-producer naturally; but until then.

So..., right..., on which subject, where did I get to before I was so inconveniently interrupted by work?

Ah, yes: number 110 and twenty-fifth from last page of this my amazing, soon to be award-winning film script here.

Mm-hmm.

Except that it's not, possibly.

'Inside every head is a John Smith waiting to get out.'

Really?

Who the fuck would say that in real life?

You can type this shit George but you sure can't say it, as Harrison alledgedly put it.

And especially so when you've a forkful of honey and mustard chicken pasta in your mouth.

It might make a good logline though.

Maybe...

'Inside every head is a John Smith~trying~to get out.'?

Or is that sexist?

Perhaps then...

'Inside every head is a John~or Jane trying~Smith~to get out.'?

Hmm.

What a load of bollocks.

It was much better than this when I first wrote it, wasn't it?

Yep, a pasta overload moment is called for.

And another forkful, and another, until my cheeks are stuffed full like that squirrel's over there, no less.

'Yeah, look at me you little furry bastard...'

Fuck.

Really, is this what I've come to? Talking to and emulating squirrels? In a first-quarter-century life crisis?

That's if it's even possible to have a life crisis at only twenty-four years and ten months?

None of the other twenty-somethings here look like they're having much in the way of life crises, so how've I managed to pull it off?

Oh, hang on..., oh, but she is lovely though.

Oh, yeah.

Slimline trousers; matching jacket slung casually a-la-Smith over her shoulder; breasts bobbing gently up and down inside her flimsy white shirt with each exaggerated, audience inspired, sway of her hips up the path towards us.

The embodiment of Chelsea away at Bournemouth on a glorious day by the seaside in the fifth round of the FA Cup.

Maybe life isn't so bad.

Certainly not for her anyway.

Uh?

Speaking of glorious days, where's the sun gone?

'Hhellloo Johhnnn!'

Blimey, it's not a cloud but a voluminous, talking shadow standing over me.

And – so much for anonymity in the crowd – one that knows me too.

Only, hang on, is that the friendly rotund face of Ben Keady?

Yes, it is as well.

'Hey, Ben! How're you?!'

Was it the Research Dept he was prematurely and wholly unjustly dispatched to, to see out his last few years until retirement?

'I haven't seen you in ages. How's life in Research going?'

Why do equity partners think only they and not their staff can work productively beyond the age of sixty, when it's actually the other way around?

Ben: 'Still a wannabe writer then?'

Oops.

Yikes, good job it's only him eyeing the telltale pages on my lap.

Ben: 'May I...?'

Oh, yes; of course: the empty deckchair beside me.

'Yes, yes; of course, matey.'

'Careful how you go though, eh?!'

Oh..., right.

So that's how you ease into a deckchair without making a tit of yourself.

Just as I said: dispatched wholly prematurely.

'I was actually just admiring the view, and wondering whether I can pull-off a midlife crisis before I'm twenty-five...'

Ben: 'Oh..., that timeless conundrum.'

His usual, default jocularity aside, that sounded like a voice of experience too.

Ben: 'So you think youth alone makes you immune, do you?'

Eh?

'Well, err..., actually, yes; shouldn't it?'

Ben: 'Nice view though...'

Hmm.

Ms Al-a-Smith, and in side-profile now, too...

Ben: 'She looks lost to me... Think she needs the guiding hand of an older man?'

Hah!

'Yep, I think she just might Ben.'

Ben: 'Trust me, while it might be younger men that get women like her, only older men are equipped to deal with them!'

And, no, going on that glint in his eye, he's not entirely joking.

What's more, on this occasion it's not all mock irony he can see in my face either.

Ben: 'I've lost count of how many midlife crises I've had. At least one a decade I should think..., brought on by something or other..., hah!'

Hmm.

'I'm just struggling to accept this is it for me now: the tracks of surveyordom...'

Ben: 'Oh? So what's stopping you..., from doing this..., err..., writing..., here, or whatever else you want? What's *really* stopping you?'

Wow.

He's looking me dead in the eye and all I can do is shrug my shoulders and pull my dunno face?

And what the hell is stopping me, *really*?

'Oops, actually I'd better keep an eye on the time; I'm out early afternoon. You coming back to the office?'

Right, goodoh.

In that case, maybe I can watch and learn how he gets up and out of this thing too.

So...

Eh...?

Ackh.

Nope; not even an older man better equipped can manage to climb out of a deckchair without looking like an inept twenty-something.

Ben: 'That was more trouble than it was worth.'

'Yep.'

'But nothing that a quick straightening of one's jacket sleeves can't solve though, eh Ben?'

It's my apparent inability to get anything else in my life straight that's the problem.

Save perhaps the manner of my walk back to my dead-end of an office.

Ben: 'When you first joined you asked me if I had any regrets about becoming a surveyor, remember?'

'Yeah, just about, I suppose.'

Ben: 'Well, my answer was no, and still is.'

Uh-huh.

Ben: 'So, you want to be a writer. But aren't you a writer already?'

Well, some might s...

Ben: 'Being a surveyor hasn't stopped me doing anything I've

124

wanted to do in my life. You're not stuck in an office all day every day, you're earning good money, and at twenty-five you're living and working in the heart of one of the most life-affirming cities in the world.'

Crikey, talk about spinning it. Even No.10 would be proud of that one.

Ben: 'And where did you write this screenplay of yours? On your company laptop by any chance? In the office at lunchtimes? Did you print it off on the office printer? Did you write some of it on the afternoons you got home early from viewings?'

'Alright, alright, big man.'

Ben: 'So, rather than being the problem, hasn't being a surveyor actually *allowed* you to do what you want, to write?'

Hmm.

And, yes, I suppose his wry smile does say it all.

Ben: 'Actually, sorry John, but I think I'm going to pop down this way, to Jermyn Street...'

'Oh, rightyo mate...'

Ben: 'A small advantage of working in research: nobody wants to know where I am!'

And, yes, I suppose so...

Actually, maybe that's not a bad i...

Ben: 'But you know what, if you really want my best advice John, try to find the someone you love, and have a family. Everything else in life, as good as it all undoubtedly is, pales. It really does.'

Eh?

What?

But, yes, at that, I suppose all I *can* do is return his jovial, departing wave.

Hmm.

Love and family, eh?

Nah, who does he think he's kidding?
I'm just having a bad day.
Hollywood here I come.

The American and the Russians

Love and family indeed.

Pah.

What would Ben Keady know?

He obviously never had the wider talents or ambition that I've got.

Not.

Oh.

Nor, for that matter, a reluctant, patiently waiting, cross-armed American perched on the end of his desk to deal with.

Humph.

It is already pushing two o'cock, though, I suppose.

'Sorry Samantha, I'll be ready in a sec.'

'And, yeah, I really want to do this as much as you; believe me.'

Bleedin' Yank women.

Still, if I can just slip this masterpiece in its envelope back into its lower drawer hiding place, all I need is a set of the marketing details, my measuring tape and the door keys for Platinum, plus the hard-earned copy title plan for my oh so vital it can't possibly wait trip to Nigel's site in Lambeth afterwards.

Fred: 'You're in for a real treat of riveting conversation with John this afternoon Samantha – I envy you...'

'*Hmm, cheers Fred.*'

'I think she knows that already, thanks, Fred.'

On the plus side, if he's been hitherto trying to entice Samantha to his cause before I got here, judging by the time it's taken her to stop scoffing to herself and look up from her feigned inspection of her highly polished fingernails, he's not been having much success with it.

And, yes, as well she might view Freddy suspiciously.

Fred: 'Come on now, don't be bashful. I thought New Yorkers are supposed to be brash and in-your-face talkative..., to like a bit of acerbic banter?'

'*Blimey, Fred.*'

'Fred, I think you should leave Samantha...'

Samantha: 'Oh, in the same way that British men are.., oh I dunno..., banal and juvenile with bad dress sense you mean?'

Yikes, I needn't have bothered then.

Gail: 'Ah, but that *is* true...'

Particularly when she's also got Gail on her side.

'Juvenile maybe...'

Andrew: 'I actually do still feel eighteen...'

Samantha: 'What do you mean, *maybe*?'

Fred: 'You are still eighteen...'

'*But, no, don't give her the satisfaction of grinning back at her wry joke John, you fool!*'

Nope, too late.

Luckily, it's time to go though.

'We need to go Samantha...'

Oh, and...

'*Here, you'd better have this...*'

Blimey.

See the look of horror on her face.

'*Don't panic, it's only my business card!*'

'It's got my mobile number on it, in case..., I dunno..., my conversation really is that bad and you decide to accidentally lose me before we get there for any reason.'

Fred: 'You're right Samantha. I wouldn't want to be seen with his business card either.'

No, she's decided to keep hold of it.

Samantha: 'Don't you guys ever get tired of constantly trying to..., *out-do*..., each other..., all the time?'

Fred: 'What?!'

Gail: 'I certainly get tired listening to it...'

Oops.

Fred: 'Oh come on, you know you love it really, Gail.'

'And which is why we're going now...'

Fred: 'Just quickly, before you go, though, Samantha...'

'What, really, Fred...?'

Fred: 'You weren't seriously implying just now that I've got bad dress sense though, were you? Seriously?'

'Yes, Samantha, he is unbelievable, but lead on, please.'

Fred: 'Good, glad we finally got that sorted then. You can go now.'

Hmm.

At least she's smiling about it I suppose.

Still, if that was the first and last time my desk gets to size up her sassy presence, who's to tell me that I can't admire it for the rest of this afternoon?

Even if, for now, that jacket of hers is doing its best to obscure the most tightly curvaceous parts of it.

Oops.

Perhaps best to try not to let her see me checking her out from hereon though.

Samantha: 'Elevator or stairs?'

Eh?

Women never take the stairs, any floor, anytime, anywhere, do they?

'Err.., sorry, yes, the stairs.'

Only, yep, as tempted as she obviously must be to check out my own sassy presence beneath this ever so trendy suit and briefcase look that I'm carrying off with such aplomb, perhaps also best if I don't allow my ego any chance to test the idea by allowing her to be anywhere else but ahead of me.

In the meantime, pondering the subject of gawping...

'What, Celia? Not used to seeing Samantha and me together, are you?!'

Actually, seeing as if..., maybe pulling a mimic face at her is in order.

'Yes, Celia; this is what you look like...!'

Hah!

And, yep, immediately back to deadpan face for Ms Palin.

Oh yes.

'What, cheerio, do you mean by that mock scowl, Celia?!'

Oops.

And, yes, perhaps that is enough grinning to myself in front of my unwitting accomplice down there on the pavement.

'It's on the north side of Leicester Square. If you've a season ticket we can get the tube if you like?'

If her boots are as much for posing as they look, I wouldn't want to walk any distance in them either I shouldn't think.

Samantha: 'Sure, if you like.'

Only..., no..., blimey..., maybe those heels are made for walking then.

Jeepers.

Certainly – if jeepers isn't too much of a wholesome American word – not on-the-end..., of-her..., athletic-pins..., at-least.

'Anyone would think she's trying to lose us, eh John?'

Only..., no..., I-can, ease-down-again, I'm catching her.

Albeit, if I am nearly back with her, what now though?

Do I try to make idle conversation with her?

Would she even want me to make idle conversation with her?

Yikes..., oouueerrr...

Blimey.
That'll be not then, judging by the way she led us across that line of fast-moving traffic to get away from me again.
Still, it's only a minute or so max from here to the tube station, so how hard can that be to fill?
And I certainly can't allow Fred to prove himself right.
Just a little question to test her reaction and interest maybe? To prove that I'm not so rude or disinterested to at least try?

Or is it too much to hope that we can both just pretend to take in the scenery?

No, this is embarrassing now.

And she just smiled at me awkwardly.
'Just ask her something John.'
Yes, something.

Anything, now, in fact!

Fuck: this'll have to do.

'So what part of New York are you from then Samantha?'

Wow, inspired.

Samantha: 'Oh forget that. I wanna know what you were doing banging your head on that glass door over there this morning...'

Oops.

So the cocky, grinning so and so did see me then.

'Oh, don't go red for God's sake Johnny Boy...'

Great.

I've gone red.

Like a traffic light.

The question is, did she see the girl as well?

'Dunno what you're talking about.'

'No, you're supposed to be grinning in mock denial John, not grimacing, you berk.'

Samantha: 'Oh yes you doooo...'

'Hey...!'

Blimey, she did as well.

She jabbed me in the ribs with her finger!

Samantha: 'I saw you from the coffee shop back there.'

Hmm.

Actually...

'You know one of our client's is MI5, yeah? No? Well, that's one of their incognito offices, and I was just doing an impromptu door security check..., to make sure it's up to the task and all that.'

'What, you don't believe me? My almost indiscernible smile telling every part of you that I'm bullshitting, but don't know me well enough to be sure?'

Samantha: 'Noh, really? The head office of IranAir?'

Yikes, is it?

'Yep, and where better obviously?! But it's top secret, obviously; so if you ask me any more about it, I'll have to shoot you..., err, obviously.'

Samantha: 'Oh, obviously.'

Or, as a lesser alternative, maybe stave off any further inquisition from the finger-jabber until it's impossible above the noise of the station ticket hall.

'And, no, despite that still-expectant look on your face, that really is all you're going to get out of me on the subject of my embarrassing and all too predictable – and apparently near suicidal – behaviour at IranAir this morning...'

Samantha: 'You know I'm going to...'

'Eh?'

Samantha: 'You know I'm...'

'Sorry, I can't hear you...'

And, actually, even notwithstanding my tactical miming, we really would now struggle to hear each other above all this clanking and general din of engineering noise in the station concourse.

Particularly – if I can lay my hands on my own monthly season ticket as we navigate our way towards – *'blimey, no, don't mind me mate'* – and through its maelstrom zenith: the unyielding, ackh, briefcase-trapping ticket barriers.

Mm-hmm.

'You okay? This way and the Piccadilly Line, yeah?'

Actually, maybe if I walk down the escalator I can buy yet more time not to have to talk to her.

Oops; nope, maybe not then.

She's on a go slow and wants me to wait for her all of a sudden.

Samantha: 'And Brooklyn, since you ask...'

Eh?

'Oh..., right.'

Samantha: 'What?! You were expecting me to say Queens, or the Bronx?'

Yikes, see those eyes of hers flare again.

'No, no. I couldn't tell you which was which, I'm afraid. I've never been. Why..., is Brooklyn not that nice?'

Samantha: 'What, you've never been to New York...?! At all...? Ever?! Really?'

Well...

'I've meant to go.'

'Honest I have.'

Samantha: 'How can you never have been to New York?'

Hmm.

And, in fairness, I suppose her for the first time introspective and seemingly genuine dumbfoundedness probably is justified.

Just exactly how is it that I haven't *at all, ever, really* been to New York?

Ms Shocked-And-Lost-For-Words could at least close her mouth now though.

That woman behind her has already started to gawp at my embarrassment as it is.

'I will one day; just never got around to it.'

'And, yes, I am now feeling a bit defensive and defiant about it.'

'Lads' holidays to Corfu and Ibiza always seemed to take priority...'

Not that I can or do in any way regret them, of course.

Particularly that time when that girl with the...

'Oops, we'll need to scuttle; that's our eastbound train pulling into the platform...'

Yep, good times them.

Even if they weren't in New York.

As for here and now, if what's left of my self-esteem or inner Marco Polo are to survive the prospect of this unhelpfully empty carriage – and the reality that I am nearly twenty-five and haven't at all, ever, really travelled anywhere notable – my unsophisticated, uncultured brain really is going to have to think of something other than pretending to check my phone for emails to engage her for the next couple of minutes.

'Please..., after you Samantha.'

Especially in a place with no signal.

Rather than take the seat opposite her, I can't just stand here by the doors for the two stops, can I?

Humph.

'No, you can't John.'

Samantha: 'New York may not be on the Mediterranean..., but we do have beer and pretty girls you know.'

Oh yeah...?

Actually, if she's allowed to be playful...

'Really? That's not what I've heard.'

And her nose is really, actually quite pretty, especially when she deliberately twitches it for effect like that.

'But, that's it, maintain the deadpan Johnny, maintain the deadpan.'

Hah!

'And, yes Samantha: whilst I may no longer be able to stifle a returned grin at you, this is me trying to appear ambiguous.'

Then again, if she is daring me to elaborate...

'Yeah, got no depth or subtlety to 'em: too liable to give you a kick when you least expect it...'

Samantha: 'Oh yeah? Just goes to show how little you know about either then.'

Pah!

If very true, sadly.

And if I do want her to hold the other end of the tape measure before we go our separate ways later today and in life, I suppose I'd better quit while I'm behind.

'But, you're right; I have heard that at least the girls aren't bad.'

Boom-boom.

Samantha: 'Hmm.'

'What?! You thought even a banal man like me wouldn't make a joke that bad and predictable?'

How wrong can a girl be...

In fact, given that we're already pulling into the first station stop – and that the next and last is but a mere twenty-seconder – she should count herself lucky we're on such a short journey; otherwise there's no telling how many more I could regale her with.

Only, whether she's still smiling when, like me, she notices the expectant mob waiting for us on the platform is another matter entirely.

When, in terms of priority, even she will relegate the challenge of idle conversation with me behind the need to brace for the impending rush of travellers now staring eagerly into our near empty carriage with wolf-like, lip-licking and now nose-pressed anticipation.

Uh-huh!

'See?! Even my company is attractive in comparison, eh Yanks?'

Yikes.

Geezo!

This lard arse of a guy has sat down so hard on the airbag inside our conjoined seats that, not only have I been propelled upwards with nearly the same force and speed as a DB5 ejector seat, but much to Samantha's amusement opposite I've settled at an eye-line level several inches higher than it was previously.

Humph.

Nope.

Not cool.

At least it's so full in here now that I don't need to think of any more small talk.

And judging by my last effort, she's probably as relieved as I am.

Yep.

I fucking hate Freddy.

And, duly, no sooner have we left Piccadilly when we're pulling into Leicester Square.

Mm-hmm.

I'd better stand up off the ejector seat before my friend next to me does, lest I give Samantha another giggle; this time at an uncontrolled crash-landing.

Crikey, only just in time too.

Going on that barely concealed grin on her face, it's like she's almost disappointed at my split-second avoidance of ignominy.

Still, given that, like my weighty ejector-seat friend here, the rest of this tourist mob seem as intent as we are to get off at Leicester Square, fortunately or unfortunately she'll be afforded ample excuse in the heave to avoid small talk range until we're up and out of the station.

Crikey.

Yep.

Nope, despite the crush she's still managing to vaguely follow me.

Rather like the Les Mis waif again.

Or, make that about fifty poster waifs lined all the way up the escalator wall in fact.

Talk about wind-up saturation advertising.

I suppose there must be the odd person in greater London who hasn't already seen it, and there's nothing like a film remake to send the promoters of the theatre show into an opportunity head-spin evidently.

Unless it's all just aimed at the foreign contingent of course.

Wherever she is right now.

And ignoring the notion she's half Brit.

Oh, no, she's right behind me in fact.

'Sorry, we should've just walked.'

Samantha: 'Don't worry. In New York I'd have to pay to be carried shoulder-high up an escalator.'

Hmm.

She must be as used to this mayhem as I am, and now we've

reached the concourse it's just the ticket barrier and a short bit of slaloming through the madding throng that is Leicester Square, and Platinum House beckons.

That's if my season ticket stops taking the Mick and will leave its pouch anytime soon.

No such aggravation for the cool American though.

She's even making climbing the station exit stairs in those heels seem easy.

'Okay, yeah?'

Yep.

'It's just the other side of the Empire...'

Which rather than 'Shakespeare in Love' will soon have my masterpiece emblazoned in lights across its frontage doesn't she know.

Samantha: 'Seen it?'

'Oh..., erm..., no, I..., no not yet...'

Another thing I haven't got round to.

'I've been meaning to...'

Samantha: 'You should, it's good.'

'Yes, so I've heard.'

What has Shakespeare – or who is it..., Marc Norman and Tom Stoppard...?, yep – got on me as writers after all?

And even Shakespeare would call this design-less monstrosity here a tragicomedy.

'This is Platinum, here.'

Fuck, every time I see it I forget what an ostentatious abomination it is.

And, yep, going on the perplexed look on her face, Samantha must think so too.

It looked better with its original fifties' facade; but, no, all that had to go in the name of progress – or, more likely, fee generation – leaving us with this reclad which some committee somewhere is probably desperately proud of, and which the rest of us know to be a blot on the cityscape.

'Horrible, isn't it?'

Mm-hmm.

That'll be a yes then.

'The product of a crap architect with a large entertainment expense account selected by a French fund manager acting for the English boss of a German Institution funded by a Scottish Bank; or any combination thereof, such being the way of the modern British property market.'

Wow, I'm boring her even more now.

'And why Nigel likes it...'

And why only a bunch of Russians would want to buy it and its equally grotesque rental income, naturally.

'The Russians should be here at two-thirty, so we've got fifteen minutes to measure up...'

Samantha: 'The Russians??'

Actually, maybe I didn't tell her about the Russians.

'Just some potential buyers Nigel wants me to show around...'

'And, no, I've no idea who or what they are either...'

Just so long as they can speak English and don't bring their Kalashnikovs.

'We should be done before they get here – just two quick measurements of the third floor, with the measuring tape. As you'll see in a minute, it's piled high with furniture, so I can't use the digital..., err..., bodger thing...'

Wow, even the design of the lift and call buttons is crap.

Samantha: 'Oh, right, of course, the bodger thing...'

Still, as long as it gets us up and down the building.

'Yeah, the bodger thing...'

And at least there's no horror triptych to greet either of us inside the lift this time.

Not that it's stopping the Yank from a close-up review of her own minimal paint job.

Samantha: 'What, isn't a girl allowed to check out her eyeliner?'

And here was me thinking we aren't that well-acquainted yet.

'Crack on, don't mind me...'

And there's that cheeky-cum-sexy smile of hers again; my response, and its impudence, ignored – or is it answered? – in the way she deftly draws a smudge-removing forefinger across her lower eye lid; leaving men like me to contemplate the fastidious and constant attention that even a girl as naturally pretty as Samantha is obliged to pay in the game of public image.

Although, perhaps instead of us both checking her out in the mirror like this, I suppose I'd be better spending my time retrieving the door keys from my case here.

If I can hold it at the same time as unbuckling it, and remember which of this bunch of keys is the one to the front entrance door.

But, yep, lift doors open, and here we go regardless then.

And, wow, there's even more furniture piled up in there than I thought.

At least the key works though..., and the alarm's off.

Will there even be enough room to set up all this kit in here?

It'll be like a bloody call centre.

In Leicester Square of all over-priced places.

It doesn't look like there's even anywhere to squeeze the measuring tape through.

Actually, I might just get a clear run under and between these stacked chairs and desks here.

Yep.

And, actually, maybe if I pull her leg a little she might throw another of her scowls at me.

'Right, Samantha, you should be able to get the end of the measuring tape through to that wall over there if you crawl under these stacked tables here...'

'*Yeah?*'

Hah!

Yep.

Fabulous.

'What?! You're the one wearing the jeans..., and you don't expect me to scuff my suit crawling through there, do you?'

'*No?*'

And that'll be a bonus sigh of condescension from her too then.

However, before I do rightly get down on my hands and knees before her...

'Okay, if you really are going to make me do this, you'll need to hold the loop on the end of the tape against this wall here, like this, then..., please, Ms Palin.'

Uh-huh.

'*Wow, don't snatch.*'

He-he.

Maybe she's right and I would benefit from a stint in an asylum.

So, right then: down on the floor..., minding my head on that stanchion..., and, yep, back up to squeeze past the pillar..., and finally a few short paces to the opposite wall.

Only, if she is going to feign that much disinterest and try to use only one finger to hold the tape loop against the wall, maybe with any luck I can catch her off-balance when I snap the tape taught...

Yep!

'*What?!*'

Samantha: 'You did that on purpose...'

'What? Come on, concentrate, put your back into it.'

Hah!

'And, yes I do feel a juvenile sense of satisfaction.'

'Yes, that's better, thank you.'

Fifteen metres four fifty-five.

Oops where's my pen and pad?

She really would kill me if I didn't record and hence have to retake that measurement.

So, yep, now for the length then.

And, actually...; if I feed the tape between these desk legs, at least there's a clear run along the floor this direction, so no need to prostrate myself this time either.

'Okay, you just need to walk the end of the tape down to the end of the office now then please...'

'What, you actually think I'm joking again do you, Yank face?'

But, nope, she's actually, yep, going to do it this time kindly.

Samantha: 'Just this once...'

And, yes, I suppose all I do want to do is return her wry smile.

'And I reckon she's waving her curves at us deliberately, what do you think Johnny Boy?'

Even if it is only in goodbye-and-good-riddance.

Uh-huh.

And the fact she thinks she can now smugly use her foot to keep the end of the tape in place certainly won't stop me giving it another playful tug straight though...

Ahem!

...just to keep her on..., or in this case off..., her toes.

'What?!'

'Just making sure it's nice and taut and straight...'

I really must stop inwardly grinning like this..

And, so, that'll be thirty-nine one fifty-two then.

Let's see how Nigel manages to argue his way past these measurements with Sebastian fucking Cooper-Hands.

And whether by virtue of hangover fatigue or just general lack of practice lately, I've had enough of this tape winding malarkey.

If not yet of my nonchalant and now, very sadly, former, assistant though.

Samantha: 'So, that's it?'

'Yep, that's it. I just need to lock back up if you want to get off.'

'Yeah?'

No?

'What?'

Samantha: 'It's okay, I can wait.'

Oh, right.

Maybe she doesn't find me too repellent.

And if that's the tape wound up, just the door to lock then.

Yep, like so.

'Okay, done; down the stairs or lift?'

Oh, right, that'll be the lift she's handily already called, and which is now opening for us.

'After the Russians I've got another appointment in Lambeth, so you'll be pleased to hear that you're spared my company back to the office...'

Blimey, what is it about her when she widens those eyes of hers like that?

'Seriously, thanks for your help with this though, yeah?'

And that wry-cum-playful half smile of hers again too, for that matter.

Samantha: 'You're welcome.'

I've got to pull myself together.

Samantha: 'Beats the office, not that I really had any choice, right? With Nigel...'

Sadly, wry-cum-playful half smile or no, I don't suppose she did either.

'Oh, sorry, on which subject he said to remind you to be at Henley, tomorrow, at 9...?'

Samantha: 'Hmm, how could I forget...'

And, yep, how indeed...

Only, thus, with that, both the lift descent and our time together ends.

Oops, what the...!

Yikes, look at the size of these two lumps of men... They're filling the whole lift doorway.

And they're just as startled to see us it seems.

Oh, and stepping back for us has revealed another smaller and leaner one behind them too.

Parody or not, Nigel's Russians surely.

Only which of the three is in charge I wonder?

Not.

One of these two mountains with the square faces and long, black coats, or the maybe slightly older – maybe early forties?? – slim, balding one with the marble face and professorial specs?

Given the inquisitive, expectant look the latter's just thrown me, I must look every bit as formulaic as they do.

Mission Impossible meets Mr Bean – if the latter isn't flattering my own contibution.

And selling this monstrosity of a building to them isn't the former.

Samantha first though.

'Thanks for that Samantha. Really. See you tomorrow.'

Samantha's eyeing them and their matching black and highly polished Range Rover idling on the double yellows out front as uncertainly as I am. She did manage a slightly nervous nod though.

Still, back to the business at hand.

'Hello, Mr Brodsky?'

Yes, it seems so then.

'John Smith, Middleton Lyons...'

Petrenko: 'Yes, and..., err, well, no. I am sorry, but Mr Brodsky is not able to join us. I am his associate, Mr Petrenko...'

Duly heavily accented but near perfect English; and a gentle slender hand in a nonetheless confident handshake.

Just firm enough to show he's fully engaged, but not so firm that I'm left with the feeling he's in any way trying to impress or dominate.

'Thanks for coming. Pleased to meet you Mr Petrenko.'

There can't be an ounce of fat on him.

Maybe even I could put up a good fight with this one if push comes to shove.

'And you too my mountainous friends, eh?'

Petrenko: 'And this is Mr Chomyszak, and Mr Boyko.'

Yikes, then again, maybe not.

Petrenko: 'But unfortunately Mr Boyko does not yet speak any English.'

I get a smile from the prof here, but just respectful nods of the head from these two.

Maybe I should just be grateful they make no effort to step forward to offer their hands. For them, rather than grasping too early the risk being accidentally pulling my arm out of its socket.

Petrenko: 'Mr Plender will not be joining us?'

'Sorry, err, no; Nigel did the viewings yesterday.'

Petrenko: 'Only I wanted to discuss his, err, assistance on the price...'

146

Oh?

Petrenko: '...how Mr Brodsky might, err...'

'I see you've already got the sale details Mr Petrenko, and inside you'll see the guide price is ten million pounds Sterling, showing a true equivalent yield of seven point two five percent.'

Petrenko: 'Yes, only...'

Uh, yes only what?

Oh, he wants something from Boyko.

Petrenko: 'Hi.'

Blimey, not that envelop stuffed full of what looked like cash then.

And isn't 'no' in Russian 'niet' rather than 'hi'? Or is that just in the dodgy movies I've seen?

Petrenko: 'Pero...?'

No wonder Boyko feels the need to look so intimidating. He's a mobile fucking cash machine.

Definitely no doubting who's in charge though. As smooth as Petrenko appears, these other two seem quite scared of him – judging by the way Boyko is now urgently fumbling around inside his coat pockets.

Ah, a pen...

Petrenko: 'D'akuju.'

...so the prof here can write something on the back of one of his business cards.

For me then.

Petrenko: 'I had hoped to discuss this with Mr Plender today, but perhaps you would be generous to pass to him my cell number in London? Mr Brodksy would like very much to speak with him.'

'Okay, right, his mobile phone number, thanks.'

'Of course.'

Petrenko: 'We would like to take up his offer of assisting us in acquiring the property...'

Oh, assisting us how?

With the bidding process?

'I think we're just inviting best and final offers for it, Mr Petrenko; but I'll certainly pass on your message to Nigel in the meantime.'

Hmm.

Only, if he was inferring something else, he doesn't feel the need to elaborate here and now, plainly.

Still, I might as well get the rest of this over with.

'So, I thought you might like to start by seeing the empty floor, the third?'

'Right, come on Johnny Boy, at least try to sound enthusiastic about this monstrosity of a building.'

'There's good natural light, and a top end specification, including suspended ceiling, raised floors, full VRV comfort cooling and Category 3 cabling throughout.'

Petrenko: 'I understand that this floor is now, how do you say, rent?'

'Let, yes, it is. The new tenant takes possession next week.'

Petrenko: 'Then, thank you, no, Mr Smith, that won't be necessary. Mr Brodsky likes the building, and I have seen all I need.

'Oh, right, okay then. Great.'

I can get off to Lambeth and still meet up with Si at six.

Before then though...

Am I in denial at the control this seemingly unimposing Russian has over these other two massive men, or just unnerved by it?

The way Messrs Boyko and Chomy-whatever-his-name-is shot off to ready the car for him at the merest gesture of his eyes is certainly making me feel something or other.

Petrenko: 'Thank you, Mr Smith. I sincerely hope we meet again.'

Whereas, going on his shake of my hand there's only a sense of respectful humility.

'Mr Petrenko.'

Uh-huh.

Not that it's stopping him from climbing into the obligatory status symbol of a car.

Nor being part of what can only be a right circus for him.

Nice ride though.

The Lambeth talk

Oops, this next stop on Lambeth Road will probably be the closest so I'd better jump off here then.

Err..., yep.

And, whilst the No.3 bus may no longer be a Routemaster, never let anyone say it doesn't afford yet another multifaceted waif advertising opportunity.

Inside and out.

For what seems like the fiftieth time today.

Hmm.

Anyhow.

'Where's a warehouse in need of redevelopment when we're looking for one, eh John?'

It seemed quite close to the bus stop on the A to Z.

And Old Vauxhall Street is just down here isn't it?

Actually...

Yes, this must be it at the end then.

And, wow, it really is massive; in site area anyway.

Must be an acre or more, easy.

And only a stone's throw from the Tate Gallery and the Houses of Parliament too.

There are those four and five storey buildings between here and the river front, but above those and the views of the river would be spectacular.

Yep.

And this here must be the entrance.

'A & F Singh Imports'.

A rather ramshackle warehouse and adjoining Victorian stucco house formerly comprising Mr Singh's now evidently bankrupt import business.

There's no doubting the site and its potential are huge though.

Given these other taller buildings over the back here, you'd get planning for ten storeys minimum, wouldn't you? With a top architect and a high-quality contemporary design?

Yeah, there'd be any number of developers falling over themselves for this.

At the right price anyhow.

Given the context, it must be worth three or four million quid easy, even unconditional.

Not that Nigel's boasted he's got anybody interested in it yet.

I wonder if he's overpriced it, wants too much for it?

Can't imagine Mr Singh will want to hang onto it long, looking at the state of the place.

Oops, the roller shutter's opening.

Yep, two spindly legs are appearing inside.

And a slightly-built man in his..., what..., sixties maybe..., of South Asian descent, still busy sweeping the floor, even though the concrete warehouse is stripped bare behind him.

Hmm.

It's like he's in a trance; lost in a familiar place, his movements slow and half-hearted, as if out of habit not necessity.

And if he's not careful he'll be sweeping over my feet before he notices me.

Yep.

And even now it's more resignation in his face than surprise.

'Hello, Mr Singh?'

Nope, he's still looking blank; at even my most friendly voice too.

'I'm John Smith, from Middleton Lyons?'

Nope, still nothing. Just lost eyes.

Maybe if I show him the ownersip plan?

'I'm here to check the site boundary plan? For Nigel Plender?'

Ah, finally, a glint of recognition.

Singh: 'Oh yes, he did leave a message to say you'd be coming.'

And a half smile now too.

Singh: 'Sorry, I've been a little distracted lately.'

His hand is cold and work-weathered...

Singh: 'Albert Singh...,'

...and his reciprocal shake of my hand gentle, and yet also enquiring somehow.

Singh: '...or what's left of me.'

At least there's now a degree of warmth and sharpness in his face.

Singh: 'I thought you were another bailiff..., although there's nothing left to take, of course. Come inside, please.'

Wow, it must have been some kind of food or spice business. What is that smell?

Cumin is it? Turmeric maybe?

Singh: 'Cardamon. Really clears the nose, doesn't it?

Ah.

And, yep, it does too.

Singh: 'Sorry, what is it you need to see again? I thought you'd completed all the..., what was it Mr Plender said..., due diligence?'

Oh, have we?

Right.

'I just need to check the property boundaries against the title plan. It'll only take a few minutes if that's okay. Is that wall back there, the back of the property?'

Singh: 'Yes. The fire door opens onto the pavement, the street behind.'

And it has dual street frontage too then. Another plus on the design flexibility and density front.

Singh: 'Do you want to see the house? You can see the yard, the boundary fence, everything from the top bedroom.'

Actually, that would be handy.

'Yes, that'd be great please, Mr Singh.'

And not forgetting the eerily echoey concrete floor to complete the multi-sensory experience then.

Given the exposed joists in the north light roof, the main warehouse could be 1930s maybe?

Not that any of it will remain when the bulldozers move in.

This small internal door he's leading us to must be through the party wall to the house.

And, blimey, beaten up the door might be, but there's still a strong door-closer on it; ably assisted by this near gale of a draft too.

Singh: 'As you can see, it's mostly empty now.'

Oops, almost let the door fall back on him.

Yikes.

That was close.

Almost killing the client with his own door; not good.

'Good save Johnny Boy.'

Singh: 'My family have gone to live with my wife's brother..., Brahman help him.'

And that accompanied with a full smile now too.

Only Brahman knows why though, given what's in here, the state of this..., err..., kitchen.

From spice of life to devoid of life in thirty or so easy paces; a solitary sink, old Belling cooker and a Formica topped table and two chairs all that remains, everything else of any potential value stripped and gone.

He really has lost everything.

Still, only until the property's sold, surely.

And he seems to have recovered some spring in his legs the way he's leading us up these stairs.

Oh, and it's a little more habitable up here on the first floor.

A little more tolerable anyway, and must be where he lives.

Singh: 'I only stay here to keep an eye on the place.'

And a good view from the stair landing window.

Yep, another two or three storeys and I'm sure you'd be able to see the river, everything.

Singh: 'Some round here would doubtless tear it to shreds if they could...'

Or squat it I should think; or fly-tip it, such being the penchant of some in modern Britain these days.

Although, letting the local youths in with the graffiti cans and firelighters would be one way of saving costs on the demolition.

This second-floor bedroom window would even be the perfect vantage point to watch them do it.

Ah, so that's the adjoining yard he was on about.

And that must be the rear boundary line.

'So that fence..., the concrete posts..., and wire mesh..., is the rear boundary Mr Singh, yes?'

Singh: 'Yes. My brother and I put that in ourselves..., when we first bought the place, nearly forty years ago now, hah.'

And that's a wry smile that says it really does feel like yesterday to him; hopefully happily so.

Singh: 'You know, we were once the biggest importer of spices in the whole of south London...'

'Oh, right, wow.'

Singh: 'Back then, we were still able to use the docks in Limehouse of course..., but that's all gone now.'

And, yes, I suppose the view from up here is one you can easily lose both yourself and forty plus years of memories in.

Singh: 'Do you live round here Mr Smith?'

Oh, me, right.

'Erm, yes; not far, just across the river actually, in Pimlico.'

A client not so self-consumed to show a genuine interest in minion others.

Singh: 'Ahh, Cubitts grid, very nice.'

And a knowledgeable one too.

Singh: 'But your accent's not from London.'

'No..., Staffordshire..., originally.'

'No, not many people do know where it is Mr Singh.'

'Yeah, it is the middle of nowhere...'

Singh: 'My father brought us over here from a small town outside Bombay..., or Mumbai as they call it now..., in the fifties. Nobody knew where that was either..., hah!'

Hah indeed.

As well we might shake our heads at each other.

Two nowhere men who both thought the world was at our command, as Paul and another John would have it.

Singh: 'And to think it has all come to this. I'm glad he's not here to see it...'

Yep.

Time to head back down the stairs and leave him in peace, I think.

'Well, I'll need to take a look at the back of the property from the street, but I think I've seen all I need to inside thank you Mr Singh.'

Singh: 'Righto..., jolly good.'

It's like he doesn't know whether to feel sad or relieved at it all.

Singh: 'Will you be coming to the meeting, the day after tomorrow?'

Oh?

'I'm sorry Mr Singh, but I don't really know where Nigel is with it, I'm afraid. But I'll certainly tell him you'd like an update.'

Singh: 'I'm hoping to get at least enough to repay my creditors.'

'Crikey, and some I should think Mr Singh.'

He really would have to have huge debts if not.

'I'm sure Nigel's doing everything he can for you Mr Singh.'

Singh: 'I understand that nobody wants old warehouse sites in Lambeth anymore, the way the market is at the moment.'

Eh?

'Well, yes, they do, actually Mr Singh.'

Maybe Nigel just doesn't want to get his hopes up.

Singh: 'I want to try to repay my creditors.'

'It's a valuable site Mr Singh. I'm sure it'll all turn out well for you in the end.'

Maybe I should give him a card as a bit of additional reassurance.

'I'm sure Nigel will call you shortly, but if you don't manage to speak to him, or if there's anything I can do, here's my card, please give me a call. I'd be glad to help. Or try to.'

At least he seems a tad happier now.

In both his face and grip of the hand.

'Bye then Mr Singh. Good luck with everything.'

Blimey, why do I feel an affinity with this guy? Normally I don't give a monkey's and can usually dismiss namby-pamby feelings of sympathy for failed site owners as nothing more than occupational hazards of the business and all that.

'For God's sake shake yourself out of it, John.'

Ah yes, that's better.

I can leave him where I found him in his lost world of floor sweeping.

I've got my own problems to worry about.

Like completing Nigel's review of the site boundary.

And I'm even getting chest pains now.

It can't be just acid reflux.

I'm dying, I'm sure of it.

High off the hog

And the best way of dealing with hangover induced acid indigestion and multi-faceted heart pain is?

Another beer after work obviously.

According to the world of Mr Simon Spence anyway.

But only after his new suit fitting at some fancy tailor's shop on Mount Street, wherever the hell it is along here.

'And, no, Si – I really didn't and don't care if he is or was tailor to cool self-made British men the likes of Michael Caine..., or, even if you do say, Bobby Moore, for that matter.'

You'd think he'd move into the nineties now.

And why can't he just go to Saville Row or Jermyn Street like anyone else wanting a fancy bespoke suit?

It would certainly be a lot bloody nearer and easier to find.

But, no, not Si.

How did he describe them? As too common among hedge funders?

Blimey.

He doesn't just want bespoke, but bespoke bespoke. Edgy bespoke bespoke.

Nope: Saville Row, Jermyn Street and their like can eat their hearts out.

For, in Si's case, at nearly two grand a pop.

Really, what is the point of spending more than, what, two hundred quid on a suit?

I certainly wouldn't.

And haven't.

And does it show?

Not a bit of it.

Well, as far as I know anyway...

Hmm.

Maybe it wasn't actually my trainers that failed to make the grade with Jill and Joel this morning, but my suit?

'Harrumph.'

Oh, where the bleedin' hell is number ninety-five in any case?

What did Si say? It's close to The Audley, his when-in-west-Mayfair beer shrine?

And that's just here.

I suppose I'd first better check he's not finished early and here already, inside getting an early sharpener.

Uh-huh.

Gosh, I've thought it before and I'll think it again, it's like opening a door into a period time warp this place. Like Green Park mid-morning, save for stripes and picnic blankets read ornate brass and carved mahogany.

'Okay Si, would you be here in the bar or in the rear loungey bit?'

But, nope, as enticing as those pumps and beer headers are, he's not in the main bar.

What about the lounge then?

Oops, hang on a minute, is that Nigel over there in the corner?

Crikey, it is as well.

Lucky I came in via the main bar.

Fuck, did he see me?

No, doesn't look like it.

But who's that he's with?

Nope, don't recognise him.

What is he, Middle Eastern maybe?

Hmm.

And what's Nigel doing in here in any case? He never comes over this way. It's one of its main attractions: no chance of seeing Nigel.

There's certainly no way he's over here spending two grand on a suit, even though he probably can afford it.

Bang goes this particular watering hole for the foreseeable then.

And with, nope, no sign of Si in this part of the lounge either, I'd better beat a safe retreat back to his star-studded tailors.

Yep.

Hmm.

Yikes, that was a close call.

Suppose I should just take a quick glance back through the door to make sure Nigel hasn't followed me.

And, nope, I'm safe this time it seems.

The sooner I can find Si and make good my escape the better though.

And, fair do's to his tailors, it does certainly keep very exclusive company around here, going on this long line of luxury purveyors.

There're enough of them here to keep even the wife of an African dictator happy.

And these fancy gunmakers here would probably even appeal to her husband's inclinations too.

Failing that, she or he could buy a token tie or two from the tailor to the stars, duly here at number ninety-five.

And, yep, there Si is, the ponce.

It's not at all like him to want to be front and centre in the shop like that.

All wiry six foot three of him standing on – what's that..., some kind of plinth? – admiring himself in a full height wall mirror.

Oh, and a vintage they-don't-make-them-like-me-anymore above door brass bell to announce my arrival too.

Hmm.

Wow, no wonder he likes this place.

He really must be in heaven. It's the perfect purveyor of his two favourite things: attention and more attention.

Just to complete the vibe, I wouldn't even be surprised to find John Barry or Matt Munroe performing a selection of their sixties' classics on a grand piano in the corner over there.

'On daaaayyys like theeeesse...'

Simon: 'Alright Johnnyyy-Boyyyy...'

Hah, he's almost burst the pins of that precariously half-stitched suit he's craning to show off to me, complete with broad, self-congratulatory grin.

On days like these indeed.

'You look a right Charlie.'

Simon: 'Now, now. Don't be jealous.'

'Yeah, as if.'

He can't actually see I'm jealous, can he?

Simon: 'I'll buy you one if you like? I've had a bit of success today on Cable.'

'Yeah?'

Shit.

Walked into that one.

Bollocks.

And to make matters worse he's smirking at me like he's just nutmegged me on the school playground.

'Alright you twat.'

'You really can buy me one if you like...'

Fuck me! Look at the size of the quiff on this chap?

No wonder he's been hiding at the back of the shop before hesitantly making an appearance with his tailor's paraphernalia.

Where's my surfboard when I need it?

Gosh, it's like he's deliberately giving me a close-up of it as he drops his stuff on the countertop.

Impossible Quiff: 'Can I help you Sir?'

That really is an engineering impossibility, isn't it? Even with all the hair gel in a Premier League changing room.

Simon: 'It's alright Michael, he's with me.'

Impossibly outgunned by an impossibly dandyish young tailor in an impossibly immaculate bespoke bespoke suit.

Simon: 'Michael, John. Johnny, Michael.'

Uh-huh.

Impossible Quiff: 'Why don't you take a seat Mr Smith?'

Oh right, yeah, why not; the well-worn winged leather armchair in the corner.

Impossible Quiff: 'Should only be another ten minutes or so.'

Yep, I'm going to do what I'm told and get as far away from that increasingly emasculating quiff as possible.

Mm-hmm.

And, wow, this is some armchair.

Gosh.

Right up there as one of the most all-embracing and comfortable chairs I've ever sat in, no less.

And yet unapologetically masculine and empowering at

the same time, somehow. A throne-like and musky envelope of grandeur whose postural and restorative powers instantly elevate mind and stature to what is plainly one's true birthright.

Yep, I am indeed the lord of all I survey.

Quiff?

Pah.

What quiff.

I am the King of Mount Street.

Even the towering tidal wave seems empowered by my societal elevation – or, should that be containment – judging by the way he's now focused solely on wielding that tailor's chalk.

Hmm.

And even I'd have to admit that the way he's adjusting the pins and seams on the now outstretched arms of Simon's developing suit is quite artful.

These famous faces staring out in time-honoured fashion from their wall-mounted frames certainly seem impressed.

A who's who of cool sixties film and sports stars, plus Si standing on that odd looking plinth in the middle of it all looking like some sartorial version of Christ the Redeemer. And, no, whilst it is all surreal, unlike with Blondie this morning this is one time I'm not dreaming.

It may have seen more star-studded days, but just how the hell did two guys like us end up in a place like this on a sun-kissed late afternoon?

Playing at the effortlessly cool, self-made British man.

Well, in Simon's head at least.

No less than the King of Mount Street in mine.

It's certainly a long way from post school Nirvana sessions at Toff's house back in the day.

As the American so helpfully reminded me earlier, I may not yet have at all, ever, really strayed to the ends of the earth, but why rush to travel the world when you've got London on your doorstep? This place is the world, the London-wide net of the world, and all in the space of a short pub crawl.

Where I'm going to make cool films about quirky tailors and cool, self-made British men like me and Si.

Well, like me eventually, maybe, hopefully.

If I can get off these tracks.

Oops, Si's watching me in the mirror.

Oh, right. Might have guessed.

The quiff's now progressed to his inside leg and crotch and is on his knees in front of him.

Si's now grinning alright, but is he seeking wit and innuendo from me courtesy of the mirror, or is it more with watchful unease? Hoping I haven't noticed?

Yep, I think a bit of crass tongue bobbing in cheek is called for.

Why should I care how much homo erotica is pretend anathema to him these days, and the brutal, intolerant world of which he has become deserving?

Hah, see that all too predictable look of derision on his face.

Simon: 'Faack awff..'

And, yes, as well the attentive young Michael might shake his towering quiff at our immaturity.

And why wouldn't the average proportion of city traders be gay underneath all the bravura?

Maybe it's a case of the boy doth protest too much? All the incessant grooming has, after all, made him almost too metrosexual, almost androgynous even. And he now attracts as much attention from men, straight or gay, as from women.

But, nah.

Androgynous, maybe; gay or bisexual?

Actually, it's too much to hope that Hold-ups was scarpering this morning because he couldn't get it up for her, is it?

Hah!

His over-grooming aside, the suit does look good on him though, even half unfinished.

What an obsessively gym toned physique can do for you.

Humph.

I don't suppose that final tug on the trouser leg is it for the impossible quiff for today then, is it?

He seems to be reviewing his handiwork reasonably positively.

Impossible Quiff: 'Won't be a minute Mr Spence.'

Hmm, that'll be a no not yet then; he's off to fetch something else now.

Simon: 'Well, what do you think?'

'Fuck, it's taking long enough.'

Simon: 'Moy niame is Michuwl Kiane.'

'Ken Livingstone more like.'

Hah.

Simon: 'I'm not trying to look this good, I just can't help it.'

What was that I was saying? Too overly groomed and metrosexual?

'It bloody well should do for two grand.'

Simon: 'It's both a privilege and an obligation to wear suits this good. If guys like us..., well me...,'

'Alright, alright.'

Simon: '...don't buy them, who the fuck else will? Just ugly professional footballers and overly self-rewarded wankers at the BBC, that's who.'

Blimey, what's the quiff going to do with a pair of scissors that long? Cut the suit to size, or Si?

'I thought you're supposed to notice the man, not the suit? Look well-dressed without the looker quite knowing why, isn't that it?'

Simon: 'Yeah, but there's no need to be bashful about it is there?!'

Hmm, exactly like this, my newfound throne, indeed; which I had to sit in to notice.

Simon: 'At twenty-fucking-five we're in our absolute fucking prime. In absolute peak, fuck-off, physical and mental condition...'

As if everything in the place is here with the sole objective of subtly boosting a man's ego.

Simon: 'Women don't get there until their mid-thirties, at the earliest. If at all, hah!'

What the...?!

The wall's moving.

Or more accurately a hidden door has opened in the wooden panelling.

'*Yikes, Si?*'

Nope, he's no more the wiser than I am.

Soft Woman's Voice: 'No, I'll wear it now, thanks...'

And that definitely came from inside.

Clipped Woman's Voice: 'I'll get you a carry cover.'

Two women's voices in what must be a super-discrete changing room.

And there was me thinking this place was a last bastion of maledom.

Oops, and here they duly come.

An immaculate bob – yep, the female equivalent of the impossible quiff – in her what, early thirties maybe?

She's certainly got the same strident way of carrying her slim frame to the back of the shop as the quiff anyway.

The second woman, her evident client, has, yep, a more easy swagger to her as she emerges.

Some kind of publishing or media type possibly? Early forties? Pays for a topnotch hairstyle but is too busy to maintain it properly?

She has nothing more than a courteous glance for me though.

It's Si who's getting the power play, hah.

Blimey, is that bravura of hers for real?

It's certainly a flawless figure-hugging trouser suit she's self-surveying as she playfully grins and twists and turns alongside Si in front of his mirror.

Oh, and here's the immaculate bob back to get in on the act too.

Immaculate Bob: 'Fabulous...'

And said deliberately ambiguously, if no less playfully.

Flawless Trouser Suit: 'Oh, I agree...'

Only, are those knowing grins they're flashing for or at Si?

Don't think Si can tell either.

They're teasing him to react in some way.

Oh, the games we all play.

There's no ambiguity on Impossible Quiff's face though. Just plain and utter indignation; and not just at what must be his colleague's breach of tailors' etiquette.

Flawless Trouser Suit: 'Thank you, Judy. Oh, and please send the invoice to my office, will you? At Broadcasting House.'

Ahh, so that's it: 'self-rewarded arseholes at the BBC.'

And even Si's smiling back at that grin and wink she's just given him.

All walls really do have ears in this place.

And not for the first time for me today either, what with Soho-toilet-gate this morning.

In Si's case, that's the first and only acknowledgement of existence Fabulous Trouser Suit's going to give him, though.

She's got licence fee funded canapés and drinks to rush off to after all.

Immaculate Bob seems pretty pleased with herself too by that broad grin and look of self-satisfied mission-accomplishment across her face.

Oops; if not the towering quiff though, the way he's set off after her in such hot pursuit.

Simon: 'Was it something I said?'

Hah.

'Not for the first time, I think it might have been.'

Just where would we be without sexist banter and mock incredulity?

In a lot better world probably.

Simon: 'Fuck, I'm in love, I want to go after her...'

'The immaculate bob's not too shabby either.'

Simon: 'Don't think Michael was too happy with her though...'

'Ahh well, look on the bright side. You won't have enough money to come in places like this soon. That overpaid BBC trouser suit and her luvvy friends in new Labour will be trousering your bonuses before you can say 'but I only watch Sky'.'

Simon: 'Don't even joke about it...'

'No pun intended.'

Simon: 'Although Tony will need to watch out if he wants to keep Cherie on his dick. She probably earns more than I do...'

'Not sure you can rely on that matey. Brown would take too much pleasure in it. His fingernails would be scraping all along the Downing Street pavement as he's dragged back to the Treasury.'

Simon: 'Ahh, who cares? I've already trousered all I need to be getting on with. Pun intended.'

'So I can see.'

On which subject, here's the returning quiff again.

And a noticeably redder in the face Impossible Quiff too; cut down to size by Immaculate Bob, or vice versa.

Either way, there must be super-styled hair on the floor somewhere in the building.

Impossible Quiff: 'Sorry about that, err, interruption. I just want to adjust the back yoke and that'll be all for today, Mr Spence..., Mr Smith.'

He has impeccable manners, I'll give him that.

Simon: 'I'll tell you what, though, Johnny boy. The glory days are on their way back, I can feel it...'

Blimey, he's not actually seeking even more encouragement, is he?

'I'm sure you'll cope. You don't seem to be doing too badly already from where I'm sitting.'

Irony will have to do for him.

Simon: 'The excesses are coming back.'

That one even gets half an eyebrow raise from the quiff.

'Fuck, that's all the rest of us need. You and your City mates behaving even more excessively...'

Simon: 'Think we'll manage to keep it under control this time. My boss still has too many nightmares from Black Monday.'

Hmm.

Give it another few years for the memories to fade and God help us all.

As for today though, hopefully the quiff abruptly standing up and taking a big step back like that is a good sign.

Impossible Quiff: 'I think that's about as much as we can do today, Mr Spence.'

Yes, at last.

Even Si looks like he's had enough.

And the quiff seems happy with his handiwork, the way he's admiring it.

Impossible Quiff: 'It should be ready for a final fitting, say..., next Tuesday?'

Simon: 'Yep, sounds good, thanks Michael.'

It's impossible to tell who has now got the most swagger about him: Si as he steps down from his pedestal ne plinth in his emerging suit, or the quiff buoyed by the prophecy of abundant business.

All tied up in a mutually symbiotic relationship if ever I saw one.

Time to relinquish my own crown too, I think.

This magical chair something else to add to today's burgeoning list of remarkable things I'll almost certainly never see again.

Impossible Quiff: 'Would you care for a price list Mr Smith?'

Eh?

Me?

Is he serious, or just making polite conversation as he collects his work in progress from Simon?

'Sorry Michael, but I don't think I'd do one of your suits justice...'

Pfft.

No?

'Okay, don't contradict me then...'

And, no, going on the way he's looked me up and down and drawn down the corners of his mouth in apparent agreement, the dandy young quiff's not going to.

Ouch.

At least my wry smile at him was genuine.

My suits may cost less than two hundred quid, but I think I carry them pretty well, don't I?

No?

What does Si's mirror have to tell me?

Humph.

Maybe not then; not in here at any rate.

Simon: 'Right, where're we going then?!'

Fabulous.

'Not The Audley...'

Not with Nigel in there.

'I thought you said you wanted to go to the River Palace? And I'm only staying for one though, remember? I've got Henley tomorrow.'

'Yeah?'

Simon: 'Thanks, Michael.'

Impossible Quiff: 'Cheerio, Sir. See you next Tuesday.'

170

Nothing more than a disempowering half nod of the quiff for me then.

Wider attention strictly linked to potential custom.

And, perfectly timed, even the brass doorbell is tolling on my sartorial future.

Simon: 'Taxi!!'

Crikey, Si's not wasting any time.

And he's managed to hail it too.

Simon: 'Alright, if you insist, the River Palace it is then.'

'Yeah, you're a comedian.'

Simon: 'Southbank please driver.'

Why do I have a bad feeling about this...

Simon: 'Come on, hurry up Johnny Boy.'

Pah.

His choice being a bar on the Thames full of girls and trendy types, surprise, surprise.

Still, what's the worst that can happen?

Hmm.

Here goes nothing I suppose; not forgetting to close the door behind me naturally.

Oof.

Gosh, what does it smell of in here? Dogs is it?

'Blimey, is that your dodgy super musk body spray?'

Oops, maybe it is as well – judging by that odd smirk he's now got on his face.

'What?'

Simon: 'What?'

What's he holding back?

Simon: 'So how was your day after last night then?'

'Alright, come on, what?!'

Simon: 'It's nothing, I met Kelly this morning...'

Ahh, here we go.

171

Why is it his mood always seems to brighten when the subject of me and women, or the lack of them, arises?

His ego must love me.

Simon: 'Said you forgot her name...'

'Well..., I...'

Simon: 'Said you scarpered...'

'Shit, don't go red John, don't go red.'

'No, I just went out to get her..., and you for that matter..., a pint of milk.'

Simon: 'Left her all alone and defenceless...'

Huh?

Eh?

No...?!

'You didn't?'

Really?

Fuck, yep, he did too.

'You fucking well did, didn't you?'

Simon: 'I've told you before not to leave me alone with needy women – especially shaggable ones.'

Wow, he did, he shagged her. And he has an entirely guilt-free grin on his face, not even the least bit embarrassed or bashful.

Don't tell me, he just wandered out of his bedroom, calm as you like, little hiding his modesty, realises his own bunk-up has legged it, and simply refocuses his attention on young Kelly.

I bet he didn't give it a second's thought that she'd actually come home with me. Probably just egged him on in fact.

Simon: 'Actually, she came on to me as it happens.'

Hmm.

Simon: 'Something about you only doing half a job?'

'Yeah, right.'

Fuck, really?

Blimey, is he making that up or not?

Nah, I've just got to brazen it out and force a stiff grin back at him.

And stare out of the window at my fast-receding kingdom to buy some composure time.

Uh-huh.

So much for my gay, bisexual theory. The joke, it seems, is well and truly on me.

It must have been the booze, obviously.

Not.

Yet something else I'm no good at.

If the shaghound here is anything to go on, practice really does make perfect.

Simon: 'Don't worry mate, keep practicing and you'll get there.'

Fuck, it's like he's even reading my thoughts now.

'Pfft!'

He's only half joking too. He has that usual look of superiority in his eyes.

But what else can I do but scoff?

Blimey, that persistent grin of his is so fucking annoying.

He'll be suggesting giving me shagging lessons next.

He's probably got it all worked out in fact, the considerate soul.

A one-way mirror to his bedroom perhaps?

Or am I supposed to be in the room with him?

Aaarrgghhh!

'Enough of this John, you gibbering wimp...'

Fuck.

'You should be punching him, not prevaricating.'

At least he's no longer looking so cocksure of himself I suppose.

'Yes, perhaps this is a conflicted look of feigned amusement and embarrassment you can see on my face, mate.'

And that a conflicted and rare look of uncertainty on his now, too.

Simon: 'You're not actually bothered, are you? She said you told her it wasn't going to work out?'

He's even sounding a little humbler, if that's possible with him.

'And, he is, and she was, right, John, though, eh?'

I did say that.

What do I tell him though?

The truth?

That I didn't even mean for it to happen at all, but when it came to the moment with her back at the flat, I just didn't want to hurt her feelings by not following through?

Hmm.

Whether he considered I might have meant something different before he got his knob out is the question; his need for an excuse doubtless assuming the same level of importance as I applied the night before to sharing my own orgasm with her.

Humph.

Nope, there really is nothing for it but to take a deep, resigned breath and tell it how it is.

On days like fucking these.

'No, that's right, I did. It wouldn't have.'

And if that really is a genuine look of relief on his face, maybe we should both be glad we have an honourable way out of the situation.

'Mind you, I'm not sure you're in any position to give *me* shagging lessons, judging by the way I saw Ms Chestnut-hair flee from the flat this morning? At least Kelly was still there when *I* got up.'

Simon: 'Hah! Yeah...'

Hah indeed.

I wonder if he's as uncomfortable at our shared, forced grins as I am?

Still, looks like we're both going to be saved by the River Palace.

174

And seeing as my former best friend is already reaching for his wallet, I'll reach for the door handle.

Simon: 'Hang on, who said anything about shagging lessons?'

Oops.

'Right, it's just one drink and you're paying for all of it...'

And, ahh, bollocks. What do I know about anything, any of it? Life?

Simon: 'Thanks Driver. Keep the change.'

I need a beer.

And a waz.

A waz and a beer.

What a pisser

Quite the towering sixties edifice this place is too.

Not sure which is the more emasculating: this long and steep flight of stairs that is one too many for me today; the impossible quiff, which both I and my sartorial pride hope never to have to set eyes on again; or the twat-behind-me's sexual compulsions.

With these concrete stairs probably having the least structural integrity of all three of them.

Still, judging by the crowd, I'm not the only one thinking a brutalist concrete vibe with river view might be an appropriate venue for a consolatory beer for an hour or so this high summer evening.

Before the likely even busier bar and terrace, first things first though.

'I'm going for a waz.'

Simon: 'Right, I'll get em in. Any preference?'

'Nah, just the usual, any bottle of wuss lager, although *not* the rocket fuel, eh?'

Yeah, crafty grin or not, he would have done too.

Simon: 'I'll find us a good spot on the terrace.'

Hmm, and doubtless he will too.

Actually, where are the gents in this place again?

176

Oh yeah, that's it, at the other end of the bar.

A rather austere mix of concrete and glazed brick tiles if memory serves, with purpose-designed porcelain urinals.

All very Mies van der Rohe wannabe.

Mm-hmm, quite stylish though really.

And, blimey, yep, the urinals are just as grand and tall as I remember them.

Only, if positions one and three are already occupied, end position five it'll have to be then. All in the name of elbow room and good order naturally.

Come on then my useless mate, out you come.

Oops, hang on sphincter, my knob's caught in my boxers.

Yikes, that was close. Still, you get nothing for nearlies as my old football coach used to say.

And, ahhh, a relief in both senses.

Only, aye aye, who's this young tyro pushing his shoulders in?
'Christ, don't mind me mate!'

Fuck, my shoulder's tight against the wall as it is.

I thought the scowling-skinhead-in-nuevo-mod gear look went out with the fifties.

But what the hell is that?!

Urrghh, fuck.

Is that a high-pressure piss jet he's aiming too high up the urinal or what?!

Fuck, I'm getting treated to a fine spray of his rebounding piss.

Yep, all over my hands, arms and midriff.

'Oh, point it down will you mate for fucks sake?!'

How much has he drunk to build up that kind of urine pressure? It's only half six; he must have been drinking since sunrise.

Even the new be-suited arrival to the urinal the other side has quickly sensed or felt the invisible danger of our friend in between us and been able to take a sizable and immediate step away from him. Only, already mid-stream and pressed hard to the wall this end, what the fuck do *I* do?

Fuck, if anything, the spray's getting heavier.

Should I just confront the piss hydrant, scowling dead eyes or not?

He should by rights just say 'alright mate, sorry, I didn't realise what I was doing', but what's more likely is that he'd just turn and piss on me directly.

And, now he's closed his eyes in satisfaction, would it now be rude to interrupt him? Is there even such a thing as established etiquette on pissing in a urinal?

But urghh, this is disgusting. Should I just try to stop mid-flow and just come back when he's finished and gone?

Or, actually, yes, maybe I just could do it back to him? Yes, that's it, I'll just raise the trajectory of my knob and see how he likes it.

Yes.

Hmm.

Or maybe I could if only I could get my own pathetic arch of a stream more than a third of the way up the porcelain.

Humph.

So, if unlike some other men I'm not prepared to just punch the twat..., nope, I've got no option but to grin and bear it until either one of us finishes.

And there's a limit on how much wetter I can get anyway.

'Oh come on bladder! Come on!'

Oh, yes, that's it.

Seven, six, five, oh come on, push you bastard, four, push, three, harder, two, oh no, untapped reserves, where did they come from? I've hardly drank anything all day, push, five, deep breath, four, push, three, this time, yes, two, one, quick, right, that's it, squeeze, push, squeeze, step away, flies can wait, yes.

Done.

And thank God that's over. Just how much can one man be pissed on physically and metaphorically in one day?

I can spinelessly step back and do up my fly behind him.

Although judging by the wriggle of that boney arse and spine of his, he's done and out of here in any case.

Hmm.

And why would he need to wash his hands before returning to his drinkathon?

Not that I suppose I can overly criticise him for that, of course; he must be the only person untouched by his piss in the place.

Unlike my suit, which I will have to dry clean, and my shirt, which I'll have to wash at 2000° – although I suppose it is the second day in a row I've trashed it, but he doesn't know that – and my cuff link, which I may now never be able to wear again if I don't want to remind myself what a pathetic wuss I am.

Actually, maybe I can get the worst of it from my sleeve, jacket and upper trouser leg with a paper towel or two.

If only.

And wash my hands for a second time.

Yep.

And for a third time, just to be sure.

I'll just have to live with any lingering scent of skinhead for as long as it takes to have the one beer that'll persuade Si I haven't got the hump over Kellygate – which, if I didn't, would be even worse.

Fucking real men.

They piss on you even when they're not busy shagging your new girlfriend.

Think I'm going to go feminist.

Either that or try to grow some backbone of my own so I can stand up for myself next time and confront him.

Or tell him what he's doing at least.

Although, surely, nobody else can have been brave enough to have told him before now, otherwise he surely wouldn't be doing it any longer?

Unless, that is, he really is a nutter to be avoided and I'm lucky not to have added myself to his list of hospitalisations.

Hmm.

At least the air's comparatively fresher out here in the bar.

On which subject, where is my would-be sex guru with my appropriately inadequate lager?

Where did he say? A good spot on the terrace?

Mm-hmm.

And why I'm even trying to show that pretty bar-worker over there my good side and best swagger is beyond me.

Nor to any of the other talent in here for that matter; no one will come anywhere near me with the new musk-of-skinhead eau de toilet I must be trailing.

Maybe out here on the terrace the sunshine and breeze might evaporate it off a bit?

Ah, there Spence is, the wife shagger.

Really, how does he manage to bag these prime posing positions all the time?

Simon: 'Here you go mate...'

And duly proffering a suitably ice-cold bottle of Dos Equis too...

Simon: 'Listen, about the, err, Kelly, err, thing...'

...that, mm-hmm, hits the spot too.

'I don't know what you mean Simon..., what Kelly, err, thing...?'

So, he can be contrite occasionally then.

And, really, what else *can* I do other than just clink the bottom of my bottle against his and move on until the next time?

Simon: 'So what we gunna do for your birthday then?'

Actually, maybe, like him, I should just take the opportunity to scan the crowd.

Simon: 'Who'd have thought it, big Johnny Boy Smith, a quarter century old?'

Yeah, crikey, who would have thought it?

'You'll be there too, soon enough.'

Simon: 'So cummon, it's only a couple a months...?'

How the hell do you celebrate twenty-five years of underachievement?

As a starter, take another large swig of wuss beer is how.

'Not sure I want to.'

Simon: 'Course you fucking do. We could get Arn and Toff down, and make a weekend of it.'

Actually, maybe we could. We haven't done that in a while.

Simon: 'Ooh, this one's got something about her?'

Eh?

Oh.

Yep, she has too.

Pretty, but also dripping in the money she's used to having lavished on her.

Simon: 'Milan at Real Madrid, Champions League semi-final. Beautiful football, but they just can't help themselves being a little too defensive, even on a grand occasion.'

'She looks a bit too bashful to me. Maybe *Aston Villa* away at Real Madrid in the....'

Simon: 'Nah, doesn't look like she'd be bashful: obliging, more like.'

What was that I was thinking about wolves in sheep clothing?

181

In his case, finest Merino farmed by monks in Mongolia or somewhere or other.

Simon: 'Wouldn't complain no matter what you did to her...'

God help the female sex. I just hope one day they start to see through this devilish grin of his.

Oh, and there's the spotty river boat.

Simon: 'Particularly now we're gunna be twenty-five, eh?'

Eh?

Eh, what?

'No, really, 'twenty-five eh' what?!'

Simon: 'Come on, everybody knows that twenty-five is the turning point.'

Do they? What turning point?

Simon: 'When the tables turn?'

What fucking tables?

Simon: 'The transfer of sexual power and all that. A combination of fear of not finding anybody and desperation for a good seeing-to I reckon. Not that it really matters why, eh?'

Blimey.

Unbelievable.

Isn't it?

Simon: 'Look, you may not want to believe it mate, but it's a fact. Although it doesn't apply to *all* women, obviously.'

Oh, obviously.

Simon: 'Some women are bonkers at any age, but to most.'

Wow.

'So, is it our standards that get higher, or theirs lower then?'

Simon: 'Both, actually. It's like a vernacular railway of love. Well, sex. You've just got to know when to get off on the way up in our case, and on the way down in theirs.'

Yep, not only is he grinning but he actually believes it too.

Almost as much as my libido desperately wants to.

Simon: 'Oh, I forgot. How did you get on at your interview this morning by the way?'

Fuck, I'm not sure my ego can take much more of this.

Nope, looking at that expectant look on his face I can't even ignore him either.

Another big swig of wuss beer first though I think.

Humph.

'I was the wrong John Smith...'

Simon: 'What...?!!'

'They meant to interview another guy called John Smith, but the idiot secretary mixed it up, invited me in instead.'

Blimey, I can't believe I've just told him.

Simon: 'Shit?!!...'

Maybe if he actually had a name like mine and looked like me, he wouldn't be quite that astonished.

Simon: 'Pfffttt!'

Even if only momentarily.

Simon: 'Hah-hah!'

'Okay, laugh it up Fuzzball.'

He even looks like Chewy too.

Hah!

Nope, can't stop myself. Maybe what happened this morning is that ridiculous and funny then.

'Hahahah!'

Simon: 'Hahahahhhhhh!'

'Hahahahhhhhhhhh!'

Simon: 'You have no fucking luck, do you...'

Hmm.

'They didn't even look that regretful either; I had to get rid of myself for them...'

Simon: 'Ackh, their fucking loss, eh?'

A bit like this bunch of media luvvies round here..., taking themselves far too seriously.

'It's alright, we're only having a laugh, you can look away now.'

They're probably only paying us any attention just to make sure we're not laughing at them...

Somewhat sadly, public displays of raucous laughter not being allowed these days.

Simon: 'Hang on though, she's nice...'

Eh?

Oh, those three, strolling out from the bar.

Didn't take him long to get his talent radar re-engaged.

'Mm-hmm, not bad.'

Hang on, that one in the middle..., is that...?

Simon: 'That one in the middle, with the heavy eye-liner...'

'Yeah, that's the one.'

Oops, did I actually say that out loud?

As well as Si might look at me oddly.

Simon: 'Looks spicy.'

Fuck, it is, it's Samantha.

Simon: 'Man Utd v Leeds, FA Cup Final.'

Crikey she looks different. She's all vamped up like some rock star.

Simon: 'A great one-off fixture, lucky to escape with your life.'

My imaginings weren't so wide of the mark after all then.

She looks stunning in fact. But what's she doing here?

And has she seen me, that's the question.

Fuck, they're taking up station too close to us for her not to.

Talk about awkward.

Would she want to see me? Or would she rather we just ignore each other? Keep it work only?

Oops, Si's noticed me noticing her now too.

'What?!'

Simon: 'Well, come on, out with it.'

Crap, I'll have to come clean on this too.

'She's a temp in the office. Was out with her on an inspection this afternoon, as it happens.'

Simon: 'Wish there were girls like her in our office for inspection. She's lovely.'

'She's American. You wouldn't like her.'

Simon: 'Actually, I'm quite partial to the occasional yank...'

'And I'm probably the last person she wants to see.'

Simon: 'Fuck, Johnny Boy. You have a seriously negative attitude problem...'

Fuck, it's too late now anyway. She's clocked me.

At least she's smiling I suppose.

'I'd better go and say a quick hello...'

Simon: 'That's better. I'll come with you.'

Fuck, no, really?

Simon: 'Don't worry! I'll be on my best behaviour! Honest!'

That makes me feel so much better about it.

I suppose there are three of them though.

Can I or should I keep the banter going with her from earlier this afternoon, or play it straight?

After she meets the shaghound here, she really will never want to have anything more to do with me. Even in the office.

Nah, she can take it.

Yep.

Banter it is then.

'You're not following me, are you?'

She half-grinned at that at least.

Samantha: *'You're* the stalker, remember?'

Ah, Piccadilly. And probably the less said about that the better.

'I hardly recognised you. You look, erm...'

Samantha: 'Okay, go on, say it, a mess! I look a mess...?'

Simon: 'Hello...'

'...amazing, actually.'

'Sorry, Samantha, this is Simon. You don't want to know him.'

I suppose it's too much to hope that that wide-eyed smile she's throwing him means she's already wise to him, does it?

'Si..., Samantha.'

She seems to be playing along with his prolonged handshake happily enough though.

Simon: 'Johnny tells me he owes you a big drink for your help this afternoon?'

Samantha: 'Not just me, but all of us I think..., taking account of the Russians an'all...'

Simon: 'The Russians...? Hah! What fucking Russians...?!'

'Don't look at me mate. I haven't the faintest idea what she's on about.'

Hah, she's giving me the mock evil eye again.

'Okay, yep, yep, I give in.'

And, great, by all of us she means her friends too then.

Samantha: 'And these are my friends, Jo and Fifi.'

Nope, don't recognise either of them from the office.

And, yep, a returned smile and cursory acknowledgment is duly all I'm going to get from either of them; the appeal of their ongoing conversation greater than my attraction and or sex appeal.

'So, if it's my round for this afternoon, another of those Alcopop.., err..., things then, is it, Samantha?'

Right, yep, a Vodka Black Alcopop no less.

'Jo, Fifi? Another of the same?'

Oh, I seem a lot more appealing to them all of a sudden.

Fifi: 'Ooh, yes please!'

Jo: 'An Ice pleeaase.'

Now you've been so engaging I'll be sure to buy you the precise ones, ladies.'

'Same again Si?'

Yep.

Samantha: 'And while you're gone Simon can explain what's so spicy about Man Utd v Leeds in an FA Cup Final...'

Oops.

Simon: 'Err..., please matey.'

'Rightyo, think I'll leave you with that one Si...'

Simon: 'It's funny you should mention that Sam..., if I can call you Sam...? You see, it's a bit like the Brooklyn Dodgers taking on the New York Metz..'

Fuck, cool as you like, he has an answer for everything.

And he'll be well and truly in with her before I've even had time to return from the bar with the alcopops, given how busy it is.

Blimey, it's two or three deep.

Forget Kelly, I reckon he's engineered this deliberately in fact.

To get me out of the way for a few minutes.

Fuck, yep, I can see him trying to sidle in with her from way in here.

Talk about in close conversation.

Yep, even my gut's telling me so.

And Christ knows what he's going to tell her in the meantime. Do I really have to put up with him shagging one of my work colleagues too? Really? And one of the few girls I've met lately who I genuinely like?

Fuck, that would be too much for even my withered ego to bear.

This queue slash mob around the bar is impenetrable. Talk

about jockeying for position. Actually, that chap by the pillar looks like he's been served, so if I can just..., slide in..., erm..., here, then..., hah..., yes, wahey, it might be quicker than I thought.

I only need two bottles of girlie lager and three alcopops. I don't even have to wait for pouring. They just need to pop the lids and I'll be away.

And this bargirl here will do nicely.

Bargirl: 'Who's next?'

'Um, two...'

Oops.

Maybe this short stocky woman next to me – and who's giving me a look that could take the skin off a rhino – was here before me.

'After you, please.'

Rhino Woman: 'Two glasses of house white and a Vodka and Red Bull.'

Fuck, she didn't even say please either.

And look at her smug face now!

I shouldn't have bothered and just ignored the ignorant cow.

Oh, and fabulous; the bargirl has got to find and uncork a new bottle of wine for her.

Typically.

That shagaholic so-called mate of mine will be into phase-two schmooze-mode by now.

If not already shagging her on the terrace in fact.

Humph.

Nope, that line of pillars is blocking my line of sight, unhelpfully; or possibly helpfully.

Maybe Samantha can hold out for another minute or two?

Fuck, hang on a minute! What's happened here while my back was turned?!

Ms Rhino Woman has moved along the bar and left me in no-man's land, vulnerable to a bar position pincer-movement by these two enormous fat cat banker types; so big and focused on themselves that they're completely oblivious to me between and below them.

Didn't she fucking realise that I need to stay next to her to maintain my position as next in line in the mind of the bargirl?

Fuck, this is not good. Men like these are no respecters of queues, being more used to squashing insignificant beings like me rather than let us get between them and their fine wine.

And if I don't get served soon, not only will Si really have time to charm the pants, literally, off Samantha, but she'll also come to believe that I can't even get her a drink before closing time. And how would that make me look?

Useless and pathetic, that's what.

Even worse, like I have no bar presence.

A crap hunter-gatherer.

A fun stopper.

Still, that's the two glasses of wine added to the Vodka Red Bull, and the money's already on its way to the till.

Right, when do I call out my order? When the admittedly rather lovely bargirl turns back from the till, or when she gives Chubby-ignorant her change back at the bar?

Yep, probably the latter. I don't want to annoy her after all – in case I need another muse when Samantha succumbs to the inevitable.

Right, here she comes, yes, now.

Huuuh...

Bargirl: 'Sorry, I've run out of glasses. I'll be back in a second.'

Fuck.

'But I don't need any glasses.'

And she said it so nicely though that I really can only smile through gritted teeth.

Fat Cat No.1: 'Two bottles of Champagne please my good man?'

What the?!

Fuck, another barman, stage left.

And rather than rightly asking 'who's next?' the young chap is, like me, so intimidated by the sheer presence of these two towering over me that he can but nod and obey.

Leaving me out in the cold and out-witted again.

I could throw this one of the fat cats here a futile look of annoyance I suppose; but it would be just that: futile. I would first have had to even remotely enter his consciousness.

And in the face of such a vanguard of entitlement, even the barman didn't seem to see me.

Like I'm not even here.

The invisible man.

Am I here?

Yep, I can still see my hands on the bar, so, yes, I must be.

Fat Cat No.1: 'Can I get yours in, Simon?'

Wow, not only has he pushed in ahead of me but he's now going to get his mate's drinks in as well. And his name's Simon. Is this a wind-up?

Fat Cat No.2: 'That's very kind of you, Trevor. Two glasses of the 95 Villages Merlot please sir.'

'Trevor's a bit of a pathetic name though, isn't it, you giant ignorant excuse for a fat cat?'

Hmm.

And where is the other bargirl in any case? One minute she said. Doesn't anybody do what they say any more?

Oops, no, she's back; and is actually making a beeline for me too.

Bargirl: 'Sorry about that, what can I get you?'

'Umm, err...'

Shit what *is* my order? My mind's gone blank. Fuck, and I'm now flushing at my own sheer ineptitude.

Like I've not had long enough to think about it, obviously.

'Err, two bottles of the, err, lager, err, Dos Equis, please.'

She must be used to stammering, bumbling fools then, going on the amused yet reassuring smile she's just given me.

Oh, yes, of course.

'And two Vodka Ices and one Vodka Black, err..., please..., thanks. Please.'

Composure or no composure, I'd rather be polite; unlike Ms Rhino Skin now long gone.

And despite my ineptitude and premature doubt in her, Miss Loyal-And-Utterly-Lovely bargirl here is even giving me a tray for the bottle ensemble too, kindly.

Bargirl: 'That'll be a flat twenty please.'

Oops, money, err..., yes, I do have a twenty pound note.

'Here you go.'

'Thanks.'

Bargirl: 'You're welcome.'

She fancies me, I know she does.

And, no, I don't care if she is giving the next punter the exact same smile.

Only I could make such a palaver out of buying a round of drinks.

Still, if I can safely lift and carry this tray and hard-earned cargo outside, time to find out how Si really is getting on with Samantha out there.

Hmm.

Wow, look at the two of them, laughing, flirting with each other like that.

I suppose I really will have to prepare myself for Samantha falling effortlessly into his clutches.

Still, there are plenty of other girls to ogle at this fine evening I see, including that Natalie Portman type over there.

Mm-hmm, she is lovely. I think she's even clocked *me* as well. Mini-skirt, fabulous legs, figure-hugging vest top, no more than minimal underwear... Yes, absolutely fabu... Ackhh...!!

'Wooowaaarrgghh!!'

Oh.

Crikey.

But that was impossible, wasn't it?

I've just heavily stubbed my toe and done my best Jonathan Edwards across the terrace, and yet, yep, all five bottles are all somehow miraculously still upright, and with only minimal spillage.

Hah!
Fuck, how lucky was that?
And, also, what an amazing save!
I am Spiderman.
Gordon fucking Banks.
Incredible.

Only, oops, I'm not the only one staring at the tray, the bottles, and me, in disbelief.

Or, actually, make that swiftly moving from wide-eyed, to laughter, to slow, jocular round of applause then.

'Okay, okay...! Show's over folks.'

Including, somewhat ironically, the oblivious cause but still pert Ms Portman over there.

'Okay, you can all stop staring now, thank you, thank you...'

Going on the dumbfounded look on both their faces, Si and Samantha can't believe it either.

'What, did I miss something?'

'Shaken, not stirred...'

The sooner I offer these bottles around and get them off this fucking tray the better.

Simon: 'Fuck, I'll say...'

'Samantha...? Here you go. Yours is a Vodka Black, yeah?'

That'll be a yes then.

'Si?'

Simon: 'Great fucking save, though. Gordon Banks...'

'It's alright, you really can close your mouth now Samantha.'

Hah, yes, I suppose it does deserve a big, exaggerated swig of Vodka and, err.., Blackberry or whatever the hell it is...

'Fifi, Jo, your Vodka Ices are here when you want them...'

Rightyo, that'll be the same merest of facial acknowledgments as first time then.

'You're very welcome ladies. No, really, don't mention it. No, no, really, don't...'

And, no, they're not going to either.

Simon: 'So what took you so long?'

Well...

Samantha: 'He was admiring little miss pretty over there...'

Simon: 'No, that's why he almost fell on his face...'

'Alright, lovebirds, laugh it up some more why don't you.'

'You don't want to know.'

Simon: 'I need the gents...'

Hmm.

Do I tell him or not?

'Watch out for the skinhead...'

Simon: 'Huh?'

'Trust me, you'll know if you meet him.'

The easiest job in England

Fuck, I am seriously pissed.

Mm-hmm, and the shaghound too by the look of him.

He can't even walk straight.

Or is it me not walking straight?

What time is it in any case?

Oops, it's nearly Midnight.

So much for just one more drink.

Simon: 'She's lovely Johnnsy Boy. Think um in love...'

Get a cab at Waterloo, at this time? What was he fucking on about?!

Strange, I feel great though.

Simon: 'Think I'll have a go, if you've no object tons.'

Ten fucking feet tall, in fact. I am the King of Waterloo Bridge.

Actually, is this Waterloo Bridge?

That is a fucking brilliant view..., so yes, it must be.

Yes, the King of Waterloo Bridge.

Hang on, what was that he just said?

'What fuck you onbout?'

In fact, not just of Waterloo Bridge, of London. Forget Tony, London needs a King, and I am him. King John the second, or is it the third? Down with Tony, and up with King Johnny of London.

195

Simon: 'Shamantha...'

Ah, yes, the entirely lovely, sexy, beautiful and very shaggable Shamantha. I wonder if she really did mean what she said about modesty being sexy?

'Hasn't shtopped you fore though as it?'

Not that it matters, given what Samantha told me she thinks of him, hah!

Think I'll use the inane pleasure at this knowledge and my newfound ten foot frame to place a consoling arm across his shoulders.

Simon: 'Chus, mate.'

Blimey, he actually thinks I'm giving him the go-ahead.

The bullet-proof self-confidence of the guy.

Oh, but there is a taxi, and its orange light's on!

'TAXSHI!!'

Yes, it's stopping too.

One thing the dick-led son of a bitch *is* right about: you can indeed get a taxi at Waterloo at this time, bless him.

Only what's that on the door? Un-fucking-believable. Is there a fucking billboard, bus or taxi in London that this Les Miserables waif isn't plastered all over at the moment?!

Simon: 'Pimlico pliz mate.'

Ahh bollocks. Take me home waif; I've had enough all of a sudden, and that back seat is looking very inviting.

Mm-hmm, yep, much better than a forty-minute stagger.

Simon: 'Don't worry, I'll shag her for you too, eh? Pfft!'

Fuck, he actually does think he's making me feel better, doesn't he?

Him and his irresistible charm.

Cabby: 'Done a grand today gents? Been out celebratin?'

Eh?

Fuck, I wish.

Simon: 'More, sin ya menton it...'

Cabby: 'Eh, you look like that footballer..., Arsenal..., whatsisname?

'You might want to narrow it down a bit mate...'

Cabby: 'Cole, that's it..., Ashley Cole..., yeah?'

Simon it is then.

Cabby: 'Hah! You'll be playing for England soon, if the manager's got any sense!'

Hmm.

'Except sense maybe doesn't, always, really, come into it, though, does it, mate?'

'See, you can talk vaguely soberly when you want to John.'

Cabby: 'You are *not* wrong there, son, you are not wrong there.'

'You just have to talk slowly.'

Great footballer in his day, lovely chap, means well as a manager, but when have the powers-that-be chosen the right manager for England?

Venables is the only one since Ramsey, that's when.

Cabby: 'Now, I really, truly, desperately thought I should play centre forward for England, but that doesn't make me the right man for the job, though, eh?!'

Uh-huh.

Cabby: 'Or I did in my youth, ha-ha..., and I could play a bit too, I can tell you.'

'Yeah, so could I mate, so could I...'

Fuck, being England manager – that really would be an easy way of earning a grand a day. More even. For what actually must be the easiest job in football?

Come on! Just how difficult can it be?

That is, of course, until you factor in the decision-making element that is The Football Association. Not the English Football Association you understand, but *The* Football Association, as if they're still so important and historic that, as a beacon for astute football officialdom around the globe, they need no national distinction. And that's despite the fact that, in stark contrast to our comparable neighbours – like the multiple World Cup and European Championship winning Germans and Italians, say – they're directly responsible for the worst results at major tournaments of any so-called major footballing nation. Christ, after last year even the bloody French have won more than we have. In fact, we've actually no longer the right to consider ourselves a major footballing nation at all any more, since results prove that we're not, regardless of *The's* steadfastly lofty, self-regard. And yet none of this is *The's* fault, of course. Safe in their own closeted world of blazers, officialdom and self-recognition, this bunch of uninspiring shadows are seldom accountable, they rarely have to resign, and on it all goes. For over thirty years, in fact.

Fuck, yeah, the truth is, even I could do it.

Me: 'Okay, so serial-winner-but-forthright-so-and-so would be far better at it than me, but he isn't going to get the job because he hasn't quite got the right skill set, does he, really, *The*?'

The: 'Well, as you yourself know only too well Mr Smith, underachievement is also worth celebrating.'

Me: 'But, ahem, other than me – *if* I do agree to do it – who have you appointed as England coach who's actually won us anything lately? Eh? Oh, you did appoint El Tel I suppose. He did very well. Although wasn't he chosen by Jimmy Armfield, a football man? But, then again, you got rid of Tel; the International Committee decided not to renew his contract, didn't it?'

The: 'Ah, yes, but that would have been contrary to our established approach of only extending the contracts of coaches who won't actually win us anything...'

Me: 'Don't worry, I'll win us the World Cup on a shorter contract and at a fraction of what you paid the lot of them.'

The: 'Just how could you do that? You've not even managed a team at *any* level before.'

Me: 'Call me old-fashioned, but what is there to do, really?! All I've got to be is a good judge of a player, put the best players on the pitch, choose the best formation to suit them, the best tactics, intelligent leaders as captain and in one or two other positions, and make one or two clever-cum-inspired substitutions from time to time. Nothing much. It's easy; you lot have just made it seem difficult. Oh, and before you resort to an equally unsuccessful and massively overpaid foreigner as manager, how do you get on *The's* committee by the way?'

The: 'Oh, well, having been captain of your local golf club and semi-successful in a business entirely unrelated to football would tick a lot of boxes...'

Simon: 'Com'n Johnnsoy...'

Huh, what?!

Cabby: 'That'll be seven quid please, Guvnor.'

Oh, we're home.

Si looks like he can hardly stand up straight. Is he pissed?

Cabby: 'Dreaming of scoring the winner in the World Cup final were ya son?!'

'Hah, fucking, hah, mush for brains...'

Fuck, I got up too fast.

Yikes, the pavement!

Ackh.

Fuck.

Ouch.

Cabby: 'Aww, you alright son?!'

Simon: 'Cum'm Johnnsy Boy, ull help y'up...'

'Fuck, thanks Si.'

Oww, my knee.

And that fucking cabby has got way too big a smirk on his face.

'No, but I did score'h winna for Stafford E'gles under sexteens on us tour to Clacton...'

Cabby: 'Hah, didn't we all, son, didn't we all... Nighty-night.'

I could play a bit too he should know. Just wasn't picked up by the first division scouts. Could even have played for England, I'm sure of it.

Oops, ooofff.

Henley or bust

Near nuclear doses of Paracetamol and yet still the pounding in my head persists.

But just lucky not to have been sick so far, maybe.

Still, nearly an hour later than I should be, Henley station and all its joys beckons.

That's if Nigel hasn't already fired me, and this isn't the end of the line for me in more sense than this one.

'Actually, even you know that isn't possible John.'

Yep, the bastard would make me work the day out first of course.

On which subject, at least my late arrival should mean I've avoided most of the heavy putting-out work in the marquee with any luck.

Well, tent, more like, probably, this year, given what Nigel was telling me last week about the economy drive he's on; his gravy train of jollies at the cost of others excepting naturally.

What the fuck is it about these corporate days? Does anybody other than Nigel actually enjoy them?

Oh, and even better for me and my hangover, it also looks like it's going to be scorching out there today too.

Which is just perfect.

Statistically, aren't heart attacks more likely in the mornings?

And, specifically, if you're hungover?

I'm sure these chest pains are more than just acid indigestion. What have I consumed in the last forty-eight hours that would've brought that on?

Actually, where's my phone?

Ahh, yes, safely in the inside pocket of my suit; just where I left it last night.

At least some helpful stranger will be able to dial 999 with it, or let my Mum and Dad know which hospital I'm in.

That's if it were actually switched on obviously, hah-hah.

Urghh, did I get a waft of maturing musk of skinhead off my sleeve just then?

Fuck, so this is the source of the smell that's been following me around this morning.

Oops, did that woman opposite just sniff the air in my direction?

No, it must have been at the burger-eating troglodyte in the seat behind her.

A burger at this time in the morning for God's sake?

'Anyway, John, back to the point at issue, you spend £200 on that fancy new suit in the Paul Smith sale last month, but, no, you just couldn't bring yourself to lift it off the hanger, could you, no.'

No.

But, if I do, and perhaps should, want to hide myself away today rather than stand out like Beau Brummell, if not at a media luvvy interview or on a bright summer day at Henley, where then?

Or should that be wear then?

What a waste of sodding money.

Yep, I deserve to look and smell like a man in a suit that's been trashed three days in a row.

And if I really was too stupid to realise, even a quick going over with Fabreeze and Si's monster, ultra-steam-professional-bastard of a steam-iron-thing couldn't dent the musk-of-Skinhead.

Although, yep, I did manage to get a clean white shirt on this time, even if it is Si's.

Not too sure about this flowery pink tie, however. It looked smart hanging in Si's wardrobe before I pinched it, but it seems a bit too poncy for me now.

Not that I should be surprised, I suppose. It probably cost more than my whole suit.

'And, so, you'd better not puke or get red wine on it then, eh John?!'

Just about managed to put my watch on the right way up mind.

And, on which subject, maybe it is time to switch my phone on for the first time today and face the inevitable music.

On/off.

Hopefully it's run out of power.

Hmm.

Nope, the tenacious thing sadly hasn't then.

Oh, and speaking of tenacious bastards with limitless power, two missed calls from Nigel.

Bleep bleep, bleep bleep.

And two text messages too.

Let's see, maybe there's one from Samantha saying what a great time she had last night and how she desperately wants to get it on with me today?

Text. From Nigel: 'Where the fuck are you? You were supposed to be here at 9'

Fuck, he should just be lucky I'm on the train at all. I was very tempted to take a sicky, rather than man his fucking barbecue.

Oh, and from Si.

Text. From Si: 'R u still alive? Do u hav the lov Sams mob no?'

'Just. And no, but even if I did, I wouldn't send it to you pretty boy.'

Actually, haven't I got Blondie's mobile number? Yes, from the naughty text game we were playing at the bar. I'll send him her number instead.

Text. To Si: 'Just. 07770.....'

Send.

Hah! That should make for an interesting phone call.

At least Samantha's at Henley today, so it'll be nigh on impossible for him to get hold of her there, wouldn't it?

Won't stop him trying though.

Not that I can blame him for that.

I can't seem to get her out of my head either for that matter.

Only, did she really mean what she said last night, about Si not being her type, or was she just playing me?

She seemed to be genuine enough.

But what did I say to her after I'd had too many beers to control my mouth?

Nope, nothing that I can remember anyway.

So why do I feel there's some seemingly compelling reason I should have lots to be embarrassed about then? Hopefully it's just the raging hangover anxiety anti-endorphin bastards trifling with my brain again.

She can't feel great either I imagine – if she's there at all, which she won't be if she's got any sense.

How does a girl feel in the morning after seven or eight vodkapops the night before?

Same as me after seven or eight beers I should think.

Maybe that's the counter effect to Si's theory about the tables turning? That, after twenty-five, men are no longer able to macerate themselves with huge amounts of beer for days on end to take advantage of it?

Fuck, I'm feeling even more knackered just thinking about it.

Still, Samantha will have the opportunity to put me right on it soon enough.

The only immediate conundrum before then being whether I should text Nigel, or just surprise him with my effervescent presence?

Text. To Nigel: 'Sorry Nigel, forgot my phone, on train, will be there shortly.'

Send.

It would be good to know if Samantha's actually there though.

It's long overdue that some tech wiz invents some way of my keeping track of the girls I like. This lump of a phone Nigel insisted I buy might then have some beneficial purpose – other than allow him to keep track of *me* 24/7.

I am definitely going to have to lose the damn thing asap.

Who in their right mind actually chooses to get their work emails twenty-four hours a day?

Bleep bleep, bleep bleep.

Or allow your so-called friends to pursue you for info you don't want to give them.

Text. From Si: 'Hah, fucking hah, u bastd. K sends lov. Was right, apparent am much bette shag than u. R u going to txt me S mob or not?'

'Hah, haahhh!'

Brilliant!

Oops.

No laughing out loud allowed on GWR then.

Serves him right, the traitor.

He didn't waste any time though, did he? He must be super keen.

Text. To Si: 'Dont hav it, but wouldnt giv it 2 u even if did. Shes 2 nice.'

Send.

Ring, ring. Ring ring.

And who's this calling now?

Fuck, it's Nigel. He must've seen my text. Better let it ring out.

Why's that bloke looking at me? Does he want to ask me where I got my International Rescue ringtone from maybe, he-he?

Oops, it's a quiet carriage... I'm getting dodgy looks all round.

Still, there's no need for the miserable bastards to milk it is there?

'Alright, alright, it's finished now you miserable...., so and so's...'

Inward admonishment will have to do this morning. And I really can't bring myself to swear, even in my head, at the innocent looking little old lady sitting in front of me.

Him on the other hand...

'And particularly you, you baldy, hippy. What the hell is that shirt you're wearing anyway? It's making more noise than my phone ever could.'

Actually, the more I look at him and his horrendous bold pink and pale yellow striped shirt, the more I feel sorry for the sad fucker.

'Oh, don't take your jacket off for fuck's sake!'

Where's a train guard when you need one?

'Guard! Guard! Turn the air-conditioning up for Christ's sake. It's obviously not cold enough in here.'

Nope, not a guard in sight. He or she's obviously too busy chatting to his or her mate the steward and/or polishing his or her ticket machine to even think about saving us from that shirt. They'd be well within their rights to issue a fixed penalty notice for the crime if you ask me.

Only, why would Baldy even put it on in the first place, that's what I want to know. I'd be hiding under my jacket like a politician at a plain speaking conference if I were him.

Maybe he bought it while horrendously drunk one afternoon

– he was young, virile and had hair back then of course – only to turn away in horror when he saw it on the hanger at home the following morning?

Which is where it stayed, lingering in the wardrobe, until today, the dreaded morning when his wife, screaming baby in her arms, shouts that all of his other shirts are in the wash, and he has absolutely no alternative but to wear *that* shirt.

'Still, I'm going to Henley, and it's a sunny day, isn't it?' he convinces himself, little knowing that his wife has done it deliberately because he forgot their wedding anniversary.

Or could it be that he was so pre-occupied by something that he didn't think about what he was putting on? But that would have to have been some distraction, wouldn't it? Nuclear war maybe? Or guilty recollections of the sex he had with somebody he shouldn't have last night?

Ring ring, ring ring.

Oops, my phone again.

The office this time. What do they want?

'Hello office number.'

Celia: 'Hi John, it's Celia!'

That's a relief.

'Hey Celia...'

Celia: 'I've got an urgent message for Samantha – you're in Henley today, aren't you? I haven't got her mobile number.'

Un-fucking-believable.

'Yeah, I am. I'm on the train now.'

Celia: 'Have you got a pen? It's from a chap called Simon Spence. I'll give you his number.'

Should I tell her he's my flatmate?

That'll be not then. I no longer want to be associated in any way with the shaghound.

'It's alright Celia, I've already got his number.'

Celia: 'Oh..., okay...'

And, as curious as she sounds, this is not a time to enlighten her.

'I'll let Samantha know when I get there.'

Not.

'Oh, and if he rings again, tell him you've passed on the message to me will you please?'

Celia: 'Oh, right, yes, okay then.'

'Cheers then Celia.'

Celia: 'Bye then John. Have a good day!'

End.

Crikey, Si takes my breath away. While I stick to a forlorn and deluded hope that all the best men do have a little shyness about them, the worst men realise there's a difference between shyness and lacking initiative; and why they get the girls.

Oops, we're slowing, must be coming into the station.

'Okay legs, think you can vaguely stand now, do you, maybe?'

Yep?

Nope?

Yep, that's it.

Just one shaky step after another.

Blimey, don't mind me lady. Push out in front of me why don't you?

Actually, isn't she the one who was snoring for England earlier?

Not that you would know it from her hoity, self-regarding demeanour, of course. She really is completely oblivious.

And it's not only me who's noticed. Everybody else from our carriage also seems to be watching her, rubbernecking as she makes her way along the platform.

And looking at me too, right behind her, for that matter.

People don't think we're together, do they? I'd better back off a bit to be sure. Nigel can wait.

What's strange is it's almost as if she's used to people half staring at her as she passes; a self-regard born from years of attention, or from a Nigel-like authority perhaps.

And she does move well, I'll give her that; almost glides along the platform, her legs and backside a single mass of fluidity. And she's deceptively fast too, like a solicitor with an invoice to deliver, or a media executive late for a hair appointment.

Or more likely a voracious dignitary late for some regatta shindig or other.

More importantly, there are some lovely girls getting off the train though, absolutely lovely.

Why weren't there any like these in my carriage to gawp at mindlessly?

Brit babes taking it to the rest of the world with their relaxed, street-cred-sassy, heart-on-your-sleeve sexiness, all summer dresses flowing, all curves and lines and choicest underwear in a perfect collaboration with bright sunshine and gentle breeze.

Wow, yep, like they're living in the best decade there's ever been and they're going to relish every single moment of it.

Fucking magically.

And, aye-up, did the plum redhead just give me the eye?

Hah, I think she actually might have as well!

'Try to look cool John, try to carry it. That's it, nice long slow swaggering stride, cool as you like.'

I can't look too bad in this suit even after all we've been through together these last three days.

'Samantha, who? What do we care if she fancies my mate, eh?'

Oops, I'm practically going to sardine through the barriers with them too.

'No! Don't grin bashfully Johnny Boy! You've gone and given the game away now!'

Yep, that'll be yet another mere-men-like-me-can't-help-ourselves look notched on my ego.

It was probably worth it though.

If anyone could bottle this intoxicating combination of perfumes they're engulfed in, they'd make a bloody fortune.

Mm-hmm, I can see it now: Holy Grail in and on a bottle.

Parisian Perfumer: 'It really is a beguiling scent Mr Smith.'

Me: 'Mm-hmm, utterly intoxicating, isn't it?'

Parisian Perfumer: 'And the name Holy Grail, simple but so..., how you say..., apt...'

Me: 'Oh, so nice of you to say so Mon Amie, so nice of you to say so...'

Parisian Perfumer: 'And you really have no prior experience as a perfumer?'

Me: 'Nope, not a day. I just plucked it from the air like the natural talent I am, with a little help from my friends over there.'

Parisian Perfumer: 'But what do you mean Mr Smith? Friends over where?'

Yep, Brit women really are the best in the world if you ask me.

Parisian Perfumer: 'Ah, oui, those over there! And the way she's looking at you, I must presume you are more than just friends with the plum redhead?'

What? Okay, you can stop now my imaginary French friend.

Parisian Perfumer: 'Or you've at least got her phone number, oui?'

Hmm.

Parisian Perfumer: 'Simon would have got her number...'

'Right, you really can fuck off now, okay?'

Me: 'Even if, oui, Si would already be charming her casually but keenly as they stroll together down towards the river, I just can't direct my legs towards them, or her.'

Parisian Perfumer: 'Pah..., and you call yourself a perfumer? Pah!'

Pah?

Me: 'What? Tryin' tell me I don't have a way with women?'

Only, as always, it's too late now anyway.

No further attention paid to me and my lack of initiative, off the prime-of-life flow in search of prime time in the prime of Henley.

Without me and my steadfast inability to play anything other than the shy, disinterested type; as infuriating as it is embedded. The best in the world, the nearliest of nearly men, another opportunity gone, another chance wasted.

Although, actually...

'You do have to work today though, don't you John?'

And, actually, yes, I do. The sole point of being here in fact.

'So there was no point in talking to them in any case, was there?'

Yes, I would obviously have approached them if I hadn't been working today; but I am, so obviously there was no point.

Nope, no point at all.

`Bleep bleep, bleep bleep.`

Oops, another text.

Hmm.

`Text. From Nigel:   'You've got 5 mins or you're sacked.'`

Fuck, charming.

Good job I'm only three minutes away then.

So much for this high-spirited sense of occasion and joie de vivre when Nigel has anything to do with it.

All this rowing malarkey may not rival the absolute prime of British sporting occasions; but, yep, there's something to say for it.

It's a kind of heady blend of nostalgia and expectation and too much Pimm's; like some giant, money-no-object wedding, featuring the old with money who can't, and the young without money who could: all in ridiculous outfits.

Yep, some of these rowing club blazers would've put LIFFE traders to shame, let alone baldy on the train.

What was it?

'More than just stripy blazers, a philosophy,' as some old codger of a club member tried to put to me last year?

Oh to be able to join that bunch of university types having an early loosener in the riverside bar of the Angel over there.

Instead of having to work out which one of this identical row of green striped riverside marquees is occupied by my muse and that caricature of a boss of ours; and which one I'm most nervous about seeing.

Maybe I could just avoid them both by doing a James Bond and jumping into one of these floating V8 Chippendale side cabinets moored up along here, and make a spectacular getaway down river?

Either that or get caught, told off and thrown overboard by some snotty but muscular private schoolboy rower and his plutocrat father of an owner?

Uh-huh.

'So, a day's graft and a late afternoon hair of the dog to salve the humiliation it'll have to be then, eh John?'

And beginning sooner than I'd hope if that sign on that second marquee up ahead says what I think it does?

Yep, the dreaded two names, Middleton Lyons.

And it seems surprisingly full and noisy, even at ten fifteen and from behind the trunk of this tree back here. No wonder Nigel's been doing his nut.

Samantha: 'Morning John.'

Cripes.

Oops.

Samantha.

Grinning at having made me jump.

Over a tier of trays full of plastic glasses.

Samantha: 'Or is it afternoon?'

She must have been to the catering tent; and, wow, had jaws

212

dropping all the way there and back in that summer shirt over vest and skirt number she's donning.

Yep.

I was right, she has got fabulous legs: taut and agile, honed on a million subway steps.

No wonder Si's pursuing her.

Samantha: 'What?'

Oops, she's caught me gawping again.

Samantha: 'Yes, I can carry off a skirt when I have to you know...'

Yep, and fabulously so.

'You look..., err...'

'...err, no John.'

'Err, aren't you hungover?'

Samantha: 'Not really. I can't let myself have a hangover today...'

'Mmm, Nigel looks like he's got you busy.'

Samantha: 'Don't worry, I didn't tell him you were out on the razz last night...'

Oh, right.

That's something at least.

'Sorry about my..., err, Simon, by the way... If I'd known you were going to be there, I'd never have..., you know...'

Samantha: 'Oh..., you'd never have what...?'

'Erm.., inflicted him on you...'

Yikes, there're those piercing eyes of hers again.

Wow.

No, she's released me.

Samantha: 'Carry two of these for me and I might even pretend you've been helping me for a while...'

Really?

That's nice of her.

'That'd be great, thanks.'

And, yep, I think even I can manage to carry a couple of tiers of these.

Yep.

Actually, they're quite light.

And yet, despite the partial get out clause she's giving me, this exchange of wry smiles is all she expects in return evidently.

Like she'd do the same for anybody.

Samantha: 'Right, yeah, okay then, follow me...'

Yikes, I was right – it is busy in the marquee.

It can't be half the size of last year's, but the same number of guests I bet; doubtless because this is Nigel's turn to organise it.

Mm-hmm.

Think he must be relying on the riverside spectator area for expansion.

No sign of him yet though.

Rain would make it interesting. There wouldn't be much quarter given by this motley bunch of property mongrels in fighting for a spot undercover. Even just a few years ago there would have been enough fat, slow, arrogant white men with polished faces to slip past in the rush, but these days it's lean, mean professionals used to scrapping for turnover and fees.

Plus poor Gail over there.

And me, doubtless, eventually.

'Harrumph.'

In fact, not even being one of them but serving them.

Today anyway.

At least Samantha's managed to shield me as far as the makeshift drinks table-cum-bar though.

And, yep, it's probably simplest to just drop my trays on top of Samantha's then.

Only, where's she now going, abandoning me to my fate?

That is one enormous Grand Deluxe mobile barbecue, err, machine, err, thing, in the corner over there.

No sign of any chef though.

Fuck, that's not my job, is it?

No, thank God; this must be the chef walking back in with Samantha, all resplendent in full-on chef whites-cum-stripes, round hat and waste apron.

Only, what's she looking at her phone and me like that for?

'Thanks Samantha. So far so good.'

What? Does she want me to help her arrange the glasses out across the table?

'Think I might see if I can continue to avoid Nigel by talking to Gail for a bit.'

Wherever she is currently?

Oops, Samantha's dropped one of the plastic glasses and it's dominoed over the others.

Oh, and the fact that she's now standing bolt upright, hands on hips, glaring at me means it was my fault, then, does it?

'Oh, I see, eh, Butter Fingers?'

And she's steadfastly blanking me now.

Fine.

Si is welcome to her.

Really, where the hell is Gail anyway?

Ah yes, there she is, looking like she's in need of rescue from the attentions of Henry Gilmartin.

And, nope, still no sign of Nigel.

'Morning Gail.'

Gail: 'John.'

'Sorry to interrupt... Henry, how are you?'

Mm-hmm, he always has had a wet fish of a handshake.

Henry: 'Fine thanks, John.

Much like his negotiating technique: cold and wet, ready for gutting.

Henry: 'Gail was just telling me about some of the sites you're looking to bring to the market.'

'Yeah, there're a few...'

Yep, no surprise Gail is sporting a careworn look on her face.

'Looking for anything in particular?'

Henry: 'I'm on the hunt for hotel sites at the moment..., like everybody else..., off-prime central London... Got anything like that coming up?'

Oh, right.

'Nigel hasn't mentioned something he's got coming up off Lambeth Embankment then?'

No?

Nope, even Gail's looking blank.

Henry: 'No..., not yet..., sounds interesting though...'

That's strange.

'Oh, okay, right, I'll mention it to him then, and keep my eyes peeled for anything else...'

Henry: 'How're you getting on with that other one you put to me recently..., the one in Leicester Square, Platinum House was it?'

Yikes, who's heavy hand is that on my shoulder?

Crap, it's Nigel.

Nigel: 'Oh very well, Henry, very well. We should have a deal tied up for it by the end of next week, shouldn't we John?'

Fuck. Next week? Really?

Nigel: 'Otherwise John here may be looking for alternative employment, hah!'

Hmm.

'Hah, bleedin' hah, Nigel, you...'

Nigel: 'Are you recruiting Henry?'

I see Gail and Henry aren't too sure whether he's joking or not either.

Nigel: 'And that's only if I don't sack him now for not having an absolutely cast-iron excuse for being late again this morning, eh Gail? Hah-hah!'

I honestly think Nigel enjoys making Gail feel uncomfortable almost as much as he does me; and going on the look on her face he's succeeded.

Only Henry's smile is genuine out of all of us.

'Enjoying yourself are you, Henry?'

Nigel: 'Leaves on the line in high summer, was it?'

Shit. Think. Quick.

Nigel: 'Security alert at Paddington? Or were you just out on the piss last night with Samantha?'

Fuck.

'Hahahaaah!'

Did Samantha tell him? Or is he just guessing? It's some guess if he is.

But there's no time. I'll have to gamble that he's guessing. And even Nigel won't be able to resist smirking in agreement with this...

'I think Samantha's got higher standards than to be seen out with me, Nigel...'

'Yes, and this is my broadest, feigned grin, Nigel you bastard.'

Nigel: 'Pfftt!'

And, okay, here we go, more seriously now.

Really seriously in fact.

'Sorry, I didn't have chance to tell you, but the Russians rang me last night asking if they could take another look at Platinum..., first thing this morning. The only time he could do the rest of this week. I thought you'd agree. I'd have rung you this morning, but like an idiot I forgot my phone... Had to go back home to get it before I got the train.'

'*That's it, hold his eye, hold his eye...*'

Just a few seconds longer.

Yes, thank fuck for that, his demeanour's softened slightly, as if he's decided to give me the benefit of the doubt.

And now he seems almost gleeful even.

I really am going to have a heart attack if I have to put myself through any more of this, hangover or no hangover.

Nigel: 'Right, well, we'll both have to ask Mr Brodsky about it then. He said he might drop in later...'

Fuck.

I'm sacked.

As well I might drop the corners of my mouth and nod my head in apparent agreement.

Gail's smiling unknowingly in relief; Henry seems a little disappointed.

But, ackh, bollocks.

If Mr Brodsky comes, so be it.

For now though, thank God for the opportune arrival of our glorious leader and senior equity partner Patrick Middleton.

With some wrinkly-skinned, South American..., or is it Middle Eastern..., type in tow: a sort of walking lizard in a Prince of Wales suit.

Patrick: 'Nigel...'

And someone else who can't do without a ridiculous, if a little more discrete today, bodyguard.

Actually, haven't I seen Mr Lizard Guy somewhere before?

Patrick: 'Nigel, I wanted to introduce you to Menachem Kalin, of Orencap SA, who I think you're meeting tomorrow?'

Nigel: 'Oh..., yes, err..., that's err right, Patrick, I think we are...'

Blimey, what's come over Nigel all of a sudden?

Nigel: 'Nigel..., Nigel Plender. Pleased to meet you..., err, Mr Kalin...'

That's a first. Nigel's like a rabbit in headlights.

Kalin: 'Menachem, please...'

How odd. They're shaking hands assuredly enough, but Nigel's body language is all awry. Like he can't wait to get away.

Hang on a minute?

That's odd, very odd.

Isn't this the guy I saw sitting opposite Nigel last night in The Audley?!

Fuck, it is as well, isn't it?

What the fuck was all that acting like wary strangers about then?

Mm-hmm.

Even now, with fake introductions made and our illustrious senior partner and his valued charge off to mingle, Nigel still looks uneasy.

Hah, has Nigel been trying to muscle in on Patrick's client behind his back?

Oops.

Nigel: 'What the fuck have you got to smile about?'

'Err, nothing..., I...'

Nigel: 'I want you on the barbecue table at twelve, helping the..., err..., Samantha, and the chef, get the food out...'

'Yep, yep, fine, no problem...'

Hmm.

Yep, as back to normal as he is with me, he is rattled, definitely.

Gail: 'Sorry John...'

'Don't worry Gail. It's not your fault: it's absolutely all mine.'

Earning lunch

Blimey, where did the last two hours just go?

Chef and food-flipper-supreme Pete here is a Trojan. Think I've got repetitive strain injury just from watching him.

Talk about earning our lunch.

Even if I am the only one not to have had it yet.

Excluding the half sausage in ciabatta I had earlier of course.

And the half-burger.

Humph.

Nigel's doing it deliberately, I'm sure of it. The bastard's been watching me like a hawk, and the rest of the tent for Mr bleedin' Brodsky no doubt. Fuck, it's very nearly two o'clock and all I've managed to surreptitiously quaff is one measly glass of Bucks Fizz.

Now the racing's well and truly underway and everyone else has had their fill, perhaps Nigel will loosen the leash a little? Such that I can sneak a bit of something tasty with Samantha on the river front? She's been looking as harassed and peed off as me, not that she's anywhere obvious just now.

Nope.

I wonder if Chef Pete or Nigel will mind if I snaffle one of those last few burgers keeping warm on the edge of the barbecue as a starter for ten?

'Pete, mind if I have one of those? I think that one's got my name on it.'

'Great, thanks mate, yep, on this bun please, if you would.'

Right, a smattering of this poncy salad, a massive dollop of ketchup, and that'll do nicely.

Chef Pete: 'Actually, you couldn't do me a favour could you John? Watch over this for five minutes for me? I need the loo and am desperate for a fag.'

What, this little ol' barbecue thing?

Hell yeah, why not. I might even be able to snaffle a hot dog as well this way.

'Yeah, course. It looks like we're about finished now anyway. It'll be booze and cake only from hereon I reckon. Til they all get the late afternoon munchies at least.'

Chef Pete: 'Cheers, come and get me if you need me.'

'Yep, yep, no probs.'

I'm perfectly happy hiding back here prodding sausages for a while.

I just need to hope he comes back willingly given how well he blends in round here in those chef stripes. He wouldn't be easy to find.

And, mm-hmm, he certainly delivers a tasty burger.

Mmm.

So, what the hell is this monster of a Grand Deluxe barbecue of a thing anyway?

Everything a wannabee barbie king could possibly want, complete with back-up gas burners – if that isn't cheating? – and torture tools and built-in fridge.

Yep, just the very opportune thing on which a Chef de Garde like me – actually, no, make that my culinary mentor the Chef de Gorde – could knock up a well-tasty, romantic meal for Samantha and me on, no less.

Me: 'So, what'ya think CdeG? Can we knock up something nice on this thing to woo the gorgeous Samantha?'

CdeG: 'Sure fucking well could, Johnny mate. What would take your fucking fancy? I'll have Samantha on a fucking plate for you before even she knows it, eh? Hah, hah!'

Me: 'Oh I don't know Gorde, you're the expert at this. What would you suggest?'

CdeG: 'Oooh, yes. How about a tasty aphrodisiac of a starter of grilled fucking lobster with a fucking sexy mussel and soy sauce that you can both get your fingers right into, if you know what I mean, eh John? Fucking lovely, yes?'

Me: 'What an opener, CdeG, what an opener. And then? I need a main course that'll really start to soften her up.'

CdeG: 'You've definitely come to the right fucking place for that, John, I can fucking tell you. How about a lovely piece of rump steak, marinated for three years in a Chateau Lafitte 69 red wine sauce, and pounded to within an inch of its fucking life, eh? That's if it wasn't dead already, eh, eh? Hah, hah! So tender and juicy it'll just melt in your fucking mouths. Tell me I'm wrong, John. Go on, tell me I'm fucking wrong.'

Me: 'Can't Gorde, sounds like a winner to me. An absolute fucking winner.'

CdeG: 'Trust me, she'll melt into your fucking arms, John, into your fucking arms.'

Me: 'And for desert Gorde? I need the Don Juan of penalty shoot outs.'

CdeG: 'You won't believe it, but I've got just the fucking thing, John, my young love machine, just the fucking thing...'

Henry: 'John?'

Eh?

What?

Fuck.

And not only Henry either; the whole sodding lot of them seem to be pouring back in. It's like the crowd scene from Ben-Hur in here again all of a sudden.

Henry: 'That was some race, the last one John. Shame you didn't, err, couldn't see it...'

Shit, where's Chef Pete?

Henry: 'I'll have another of those burgers if you can manage it, though, please... All that excitement's given me a renewed appetite, hah!'

Fuck, the griddle tongues are here, and I suppose one won't hurt.

Only, where the hell is the professional?

'Okay, here you go Henry.'

Actually, that was easy enough.

Henry: 'Thanks, mate.'

Fuck, if Henry gives me just one more derogatory, smartarse smirk like that...

'Just think of Platinum, John, just think of Platinum...'

The big fee I'm getting and he's not.

Well, that Middleton Lyons are getting.

And probably not me.

Crikey, how did all these people line up so fast?

Actually, I say people, they're looking more like lions at feeding time.

Nope, I've no choice. I'll have to pop out of the marquee to see if I can find Pete.

'Sorry, I'll be thirty seconds...'

Whoever the hell that was at the front of the queue...

I'll just have to hope she's not Patrick's second most important client...

Fuck, it's dazzling out here in the sunshine.

Uh-huh.

Come on Peter...

'*Where are you, eh?*'

But, shit, nope, he's nowhere.

Well, nowhere obvious anyway.

'*Fuck, come on, Peter, Peter?*'

Eh?

Eh?

Nope, lots of blue and white stripes, but none attached to him.

Fuck.

Actually, I suppose if I peak back inside it's too much to hope he's gone back in via the main entrance, is it?

Yes?

Nope, just the crowd of lions looking like they're going to take things into their own claws any second.

And, typically, no sign of Nigel either.

He's been watching me like a hawk for hours, but not when he could be useful.

Shit, I'll have to do it.

Or should I just do a runner?

No, I promised him.

Bollocks.

Those bloody rowers. Couldn't they have slowed down a bit?

Even sodding Samantha's reappeared to grin at my predicament.

'*Well don't bother helping me then Pretty Bonce, eh?*'

Oops, my glare has made her look away.

'Okay, sorry about that everybody. I'll stand in for chef for a few minutes.'

So, how hard can this be?

Those there must be the last four of the batch of burgers keeping warm which Henry and I have had ours from, so I can dish those out; but which ones of these others are cooked?

They must all be by now, surely?

But even they won't last long looking at these piranhas.

And where's the stash of food?

Must be in the fridge.

Mm-hmm, yep, here.

CdeG: 'Calm the fuck down, Johnny Boy, it's easy. Take that tray of burgers, sausages and chicken legs out of the fridge and chuck them on the grill, splodge on some of that gloopy marinade stuff – although it looks fucking horrible – flip them over a few times and pass them out. Fucking simple.'

Right, okay, yep, okay.

Chuck them on, flip them over a few times, hand them out.

Simple.

Fuck, the grill's spitting fat all over the place.

Okay, first up, I'll just dish out this lot of burgers, sausages and chicken legs already cooked and keeping warm on the grill...

Yep.

Onto this serving dish...

...on the table.

Yep.

Like so...

'Sorry for the wait everyone; please, help yourselves. If there's not enough, chef will be along in a minute...'

And, yep, stand well back and let the pride fight over them.

Oops, crap, I've got spitting burger fat on Si's fancy tie.

Oops.

And rubbing it has made it worse.

Hmm.

Where's it from anyway?

Fuck.

Hermes.

Fuck.

I'll just have to sneak it back in his wardrobe when I get back.

With any luck he'll just think he's done it.

Um-hum.

Wow, it didn't take them long to hoover that lot up.

Ah! Flipper Pete! Thank God for that.

'Oh, it's good to see you mate, thank God you're back...'

And, yes, as well he might look concerned.

'Yeah, as you can see we had a bit of a rush on after the race at two o'clock. I've dished out everything that was on the grill, and just started to put this lot on from the fridge.'

Pete: 'You did check the ones on the grill were cooked through, yeah?'

The ones what?

Pete: 'Some of them were still a bit frozen in the middle.'

Oh fuck.

They were?

'Erm, think so...'

Fuck, I obviously look as uncertain as I sound.

CdeG: 'They looked fine to me.'

Shut the fuck up Gorde, you had your chance.

'Don't worry Peter, I think they were fine, honestly.'

Well, probably, anyway.

And, fabulous, just when I don't need him, here comes Nigel.

Oh; and, just for good measure, Samantha.

Looking even more pissed off than before, if that's possible.

Nigel: 'Everything alright?'

'Yep, all good thanks Nigel...'

Just smile at him Peter, just smile...

Nigel: 'I forgot to pick up the cake and deserts this morning. When you weren't here. I want you to go with Samantha to fetch them from the main catering marquee, by the car park.'

Christ, anyone would think I'm a skivvy rather than a property professional.

226

Nigel: 'It's aalllriiight! It should all be ready and waiting for you. All you've got to do is sign for it and bring it back.'

Oh, if that's *all* that's perfectly fine then.

Nigel: 'And when you've done that I want you to mingle, make sure our guests are happy, and maybe even some of your agent mates...'

Christ, who among this lot would I even choose to share a beer with, apart from Gail and Gemma Green possibly?

Still, at least that hopefully means Nigel will be off my back for a while. And there are obviously worse things than a stroll to the catering tent with Samantha.

Assuming she decides to start talking to me again.

Hmm.

Although, judging by her demeanour now, there's not much hope of that anytime soon.

And Flipper Pete seems happy enough flipping those fresh burgers and sausages on the Grand Deluxe back there, now he's put the potential for mass salmonella poisoning behind him. Either that or the thought of the litigious consequences is so horrendous that he's just trying not to contemplate it.

I suppose I should have told him I'm a crap cook.

Anyhow: next, Samantha.

'Right, the catering tent it is then, yeah?'

At least she actually acknowledged me this time.

And I suppose I should really tell her in a minute about Si wanting to get hold of her – literally as well as metaphorically – much as it pains me.

'Go on then, you lead on Misery Guts.'

'Do you know where it is then?'

Samantha: 'What?!'

Wow.

'The catering tent...'

Samantha: 'I fucking well should do, I've been there about five fucking times already today...'

Ahh, so, is that it? She's pissed off at me being late and not here to help her?

It's not my sodding fault Nigel's a cheapskate slave driver.

But, yep, it's back to the silent treatment again nevertheless then.

As usual, she's not hanging about either, like she just wants to put distance between us again too.

This must be some secret skivvy-only back-tent thoroughfare between these webs of guy ropes and pegs to the caterers' marquee.

Right, I suppose if she's already cross with me I might as well get it over with.

'Simon wants your number by the way. I told him I didn't have it, which I don't of course, but that I'd pass on the message and his number...'

Yikes, that certainly got her attention. Talk about an abrupt about turn and unnerving stare.

'What...?! That's it...'

Samantha: 'I know, Celia already texted me. Apparently she spoke to you on the train? Like hours ago...'

'Well, I didn't think..., you'd..., err...'

'Blimey, if you're going to be shredded by her you could at least show a little backbone, John.'

Although it has only been an hour or two for fuck's sake. Well, five at the most. Surely she can wait that long if she fancies him that much.

Samantha: 'Even fucking Leanne texted me!'

Yikes, she seems really angry.

And Leanne as well? Is there anyone in the office the Shaghound hasn't left a message with? The guy's unstoppable.

'I can give you his number now if you like?'

Samantha: 'I've already... Aggghhhrrr... I don't even want it! Particularly...'

Christ, what the hell does that mean?

And did she say that like she knows I fancy her? Am I that transparent?

Or is it just that every man fancies her: me, Simon, everyone. There's just something about Samantha and all that?

Samantha: 'Oh fuck it, I give up, let's just get those fucking deserts...'

Give up on what?!

Hmm.

Namely, give up on ever talking to or even walking with or being seen in even the same approximate vicinity as me again, then.

'And it worked for him, the shaghound, didn't it John?'

Yep, and it always does of course.

And maybe he actually is her type after all.

Humph.

Albeit was that last glance back towards me at least slightly less stern in its intent?

Now we've managed to weave our way into this general melee that is the service area and makeshift car park – on these, what are they normally, sports fields...? – she's probably just thinking how she can accidentally lose me.

If only so she doesn't have to feel sorry for me and my unrequited lust probably.

There may not have been any knowing errant puppy dog smile this time, but I just can't help myself doesn't she know.

Samantha: 'This is it.'

Eh?

Oh, right.

Gosh, it's more like a hanger than a catering tent.

And, given the way she's marching towards it, that side door must be the way in then.

Yep.

'And still don't wait for me then Yanks.'

Right, and a long counter and hive of activity too; Samantha and I being not the only lackeys sent to take possession of its lunchtime delights.

Blimey, that didn't take her or them long. It's like this impossibly youthful student type with his apron, hat and clipboard was expecting us.

And, so, this'll be four large, cellophane wrapped trays of what, fruit trifles?

Yep, fruit trifles in individual plastic bowls, and a large box with clear plastic top window, containing..., yep, of course..., an ultra large cream-covered cake.

Mm-hmm.

About the same size as a dustbin lid because that's where a large part of it will end up later no doubt.

Only, why has this twat of a budding youth-authoritarian stickler felt the need to do that? Haughtily mark a cross next to where a momentarily uncertain Samantha's got to moniker it?

She should have just signed his forehead.

Christ this guy's going to be a nightmare when he finishes school and gets a real job.

Samantha: 'Okay?'

'Yep, how about you take these top two tiers, here? I can manage the rest.'

Yeah?

No?

'What?'

Samantha: 'Are you sure one of us shouldn't just come back for the cake?'

'*What, don't be silly, it's nothing.*'

'Nah, it'll be fine, I'll just put the cake on top. They're not even that heavy, see?'

Samantha: 'I don't mind coming back, really...'

'Nah, it'll be fine, trust me. Just got to watch out for the tent pegs and guy ropes!'

Samantha: 'Hmm, that wasn't the cause with the tray of bottles last night, though, was it?'

Pah, the sheer cheek of her.

Despite our exchange of funny faces, she wants to trust me really..., doesn't she?

'*No?*'

'*Yep?*'

Yep. Finally.

'*Here you go, see?*'

Yep, she seems happy enough now.

Right, next my turn then.

Cake box gently on top of these my two trays of trifles, and, gently does it, lift.

Yep, this'll be no problem.

Guy ropes and tent pegs.

Blimey, what's she of the shaking head and little faith waiting for now then?

'*So, go on then, there's the door...*'

Right then.

Five mins back to the tent, and we can both take it easy.

Or easier.

Well, me, anyway.

Doubtless Nigel's got no such intention for Samantha sadly.

Only, what's she slowing up again for now?

Samantha: 'So what do you think I should tell him then?'

Eh?

'Who..., Nigel?'

Samantha: 'No, Simon. You know, your persistent friend?'

Oh, him.

'He's no longer any fucking friend of mine.'

'Nothing, just ignore him.'

Uh oh; she seems hesitant. And probably rightly.

'Actually, you're right, that wouldn't work. He is way too persistent.'

Samantha: 'Mm-hmm, I can guess.'

'And if you tell him you just don't fancy him, he'd just take that as a challenge, and pursue you even more.'

Samantha: 'I didn't say I don't fancy him, just that he's not my type...'

Humph.

Nope, she's giving me a sly grin.

Bloody women, don't they know when a joke's no longer funny?

Hang on?

Wow, look at that gorgeous boat that's just been trailered into the car park. Is it one of those classic Riva Aquaramas?

Wow I think it is as well.

Samantha: 'Maybe I could tell him I'm already seeing somebody?'

Fuck how beautiful is that?

The fabulously flowing lines, the detailing in it.

It's like a DB4 Zagato for the water; another Italian designer masterclass from an era full of them.

'But didn't you tell him last night you were single?'

Gosh, it must be worth a small fortune.

And the two women who've just jumped out of the car towing it aren't too shabby either.

Ooh, yep, not bad at all...

Samantha: 'Okay, if not that, what then?'

Their lithe, tanned legs are practically the same colour as the boat.

Fan-tan-tastic.

And, yes, despite the lingering doubt in Samantha's eyes, I am still in total control of these trifles.

'Not sure there is anything you *can* say to put him off to be honest...'

Only, what would be even better is if Madames Tanned-legs own that Aquarama and not some spoilt and undeserving man who isn't me. They certainly look the old money chic type in their cut-off jeans, and the beat-up Landy they're using to tow it would fit the mould.

Samantha: 'Maybe I could just tell him I'm *about* to start seeing someone?'

It seems like they're trying to find the slipway to launch it too.

And it must look even better in the water.

Particularly with me and them sitting in it.

Samantha: 'You're not even listening to me, are you?'

I wonder if two women like those might appreciate a free driver for the afternoon?

To help them apply suncream and serve the sparkling as they settle back into that exquisite marine upholstery while we cruise the river looking for a quiet place to moor up and appreciate the merits and opportunities of that sublime, elongated engine bay with its counterintuitive convex sides...

Samantha: 'Watch that tent peg and guy rope...'

What?!

Shit! Tent peg!

'Wooaarhh!'

233

Fuck, that was close.

I half caught my foot under it too, but still my supreme skill and balance are such that the cake box hardly moved.

Hah, is that look on Samantha's face one of relief or annoyance?

'It's alright, calm down, it's all under control...'

Maybe I am, actually, Gordon Banks's love child?

Hey, on which subject, look at that, a football!

A wild shot from one of those boys having a game over there, and it's curling towards me a treat.

I'll just knock it back to them quickly.

Crap, white van man over there's also spotted it, and the kid goalie's now chasing after it like a whippet now too.

Samantha: 'No, John...'

Wow, white van man's not holding back, but I should still just get there before him, and I need only open my body slightly to be able to give it a nice curl with my right peg.

Samantha: 'So you are going to...'

Hah, yeesss, Johnny fucking Smi...

Oh fuck, woooaaahhh..., aarrgghh..., ooff.

Ouch.

Hmm.

Oops.

That must be why I never played football in leather-soled shoes on slick grass then.

Still, given the sudden impact of arse with ground, I should probably just be pleased the trifle trays now looking back up at me from my thighs look vaguely intact.

If not so the cake.

Which, fuck, I suppose is what happens when it crash-lands and somersaults across hard-baked playing field.

Oops.

And, if not for the first time in our short acquaintance, as well might Samantha stare back at me with a mixture of incredulity and disbelief.

'*Yeah, go on, laugh, I dare you.*'

White van man over there isn't even trying to contain his hysterical laughter.

'*I could play though mate, I could play. See the way it cleared the kid and curled towards the goal? Even Becks would have been proud of that one.*'

Becks: 'You're right, John. Sweet. You're a natural. Can't understand why you weren't picked up by one of the scouts.'

Mmm.

Becks: 'I might have tried to cling onto the cake though.'

The only one of the main protagonists not finding my actions hilarious appears to be the kid goalie I thwarted.

And who's now scowling at me like I've just broken his Nintendo DS.

Yet another, like me, for whom football is just far too important to laugh about.

'*You'll get over it matey. I did. It's a rite of passage thing.*'

As for the two Riva girls and all the other bystanders now watching me and my every potentially ridiculous movement, I suppose I'm just going to have to try to ignore them and recover a semblance of my dignity.

And maybe take a rain check on my Aquarama away day.

As for her, the transfixed Yank here, I think a bit of mock bravura may be called for.

'You alright with that?'

'*Heh?!*'

Samantha: 'Yep, course.'

And, yes, I suppose there is a limit on how long you can contain a straight face at such inane stupidity.

Samantha: 'You're the one who's gunna have to explain it to Nigel...'

Hmm.

And she's right too.

Oh, and while a combination of my incredible skill, but mostly the cellophane, seems to have saved both trays of trifles, it looks like, yes, I've finally killed Si's flash tie.

Um-hum.

And, no, not even carefully removing the cream splodges with my finger makes any difference.

Even if, yep, it does taste nice.

As to what's left of the cream and cake in the principal wreckage...

Samantha seems to think it's worth taking a closer look at.

Oh, fuck.

Or should that be halle-fucking-lujah?

Wow, given the extent of cleavage she really can't be wearing anything below that vest top and shirt then.

The latter two all too willingly abandoning their charges as their gorgeous owner bends forward.

But, fuck, I should really look away, shouldn't I?

Should I, will I?

Can I?

Yes.

But the view from just half a step closer would likely be too fantastic for that, wouldn't it?

Her breast or breasts in all its or their fabulous glory?

And what if they're as perfect as the rest of her?

Fuck, I'd have thrown the cake on the ground as soon as we'd stepped out of the catering tent if I'd known this could happen.

Oops, she's making to look up at me.

'Quick John, the cake.'

Samantha: 'It's a gonner...'

That was close, she almost caught me.

Well, almost caught me only thinking about looking; not that she'd have known the difference.

Samantha: 'Although, we might be able to use some of it..., for small pieces or something...'

Oh, no, she's doing it again.

And, oh, wow, this time she's even dipping a finger in the gooey mess to taste it!

Fuck, this is moral torture.

Do I try to get an even better glimpse of cleavage and maybe more, or just glory in her smiling ruby red lips and the finger she's licking clean of cream, or none of them?

Or all three if I could get my angle of vision just right?

Samantha: 'Mmm, not bad...'

I'll fucking say.

And I really am going to have palpitations if she mischievously licks her lips and grins up at me like that again.

Oops, she's going to notice the stirrings of interest down here on me too in a minute.

'Quick, think of the football, John, think of the football...'

Nope, no good, I'll have to turn away from her.

Actually, that gives me an idea.

'Can you wait here a minute? I've got an idea.'

Samantha: 'What? Where are you going now?!'

'I'm going back to see our young friend with the clipboard in the catering tent...'

And try to preserve my modesty in the process.

'We've had more than enough excitement for one day, haven't we matey?'

237

Then again, I don't want to be rash. Maybe there's always time for a bit more.

Just not between here and the catering tent ideally.

Maybe.

And particularly when it's only my resolve that needs stiffening.

If this doesn't work, Nigel's going to give me a right bollocking.

As a minimum.

And the door's now wedged open – which must be a good sign, mustn't it?

They must have a spare cake or two left or something stored in this hangar, surely?

Only, firstly, I just need to catch the eye of Master Clipboard Obsessive.

No, he's seen me first.

Master Clipboard: 'Everything okay with the order Sir?'

'Umm, apparently there should have been two cakes in our order, not just the one?'

Master Clipboard: 'Err, I don't think so Sir...'

There he goes with that annoying clipboard again.

Master Clipboard: 'Who's it for again?'

I get the impression his world would end if he lost it.

'Middleton Lyons, Nigel Plender?'

Master Clipboard: 'Ah yes, here we go. No, no, look, see, just the one.'

Oh, and I get a helpful circle round the '1' next to the letters LCC on his order sheet this time too.

'Ahh, well, that's a mistake then I'm afraid; we actually need two please?'

Hmm?

Wow, indignant isn't the word.

Even admitting guilt and begging might have gone down better with him.

238

Doesn't young Master Super Efficient here understand that accepting mistakes – even when they're manifestly not of his own making – is part of his and everybody else's job description in Britain?

Or has he not been alive long enough to know yet?

Fuck it, let's have another look at this clipboard of his.

'Do you have another of these..., err, LCC's that we can have please?'

Master Clipboard: 'I don't know, the large creams are very popular..., and you did only order the *one*.'

Fuck, he's now looking suspiciously at my cream splodged tie; and suit for that matter.

Master Clipboard: 'I'll need to ask the manager.'

'Fuck, I may have thrown the other one across Henley Park but do you want to sell us another one or not?!'

'I'd be grateful, thanks.'

Wow, I may be bullshitting, but all this obsessive, organisational efficiency is really getting on my tits. This is modern Britain where we still don't do anything efficiently. He's the sort of smartarse from whom in ten years' time we'll all end up having to try to buy the right to use our own names for some new vital internet-based technological innovation or other.

And me especially.

'I'm sorry, but johnsmith101872 is no longer available for this new essential cyberspace network, Sir.'

Maybe I should just strangle the bastard now to save us all the grief?

Manager: 'Sir! What are you doing?!'

Me: 'I'm strangling the spotty bastard, of course.'

Manager: 'But Sir!! You're really hurting him.'

Me: 'I know.'

Manager: 'Leave him alone, you can have your LCC.'

Me: 'You don't understand. If you knew, you'd be helping me.'

Manager: 'But he's just on a summer job.'

Me: 'The grief and aggravation he's going to cause us, you, me everybody....'

Manager: 'But Sir!!!'

He should just stick to sex, football and imbecility like the rest of us males.

Mm-hmm.

'Yep, shouldn't you mate?'

Although he is carrying a large cake box by the looks of it?

Master Clipboard: 'I'm sorry, Sir, the manager says there are no spare LCC's. But you can have this LCHC instead?'

Ahh, yes, of course, CHocolate.

'Yep, this'll be great, thanks.'

And, even better, if I'm in a hurry and it's here, why wait?

Master Clipboard: 'Sir, you'll have to sign for it?!'

'Don't worry, please just add it onto the invoice...'

Hah, I can hear the ruffle of his clipboard from here...

Master Clipboard: 'But Sir...!!'

With any luck the lack of a signature will torment him for weeks. If Nigel pays them for it at all.

It's a cruel world, but someone's got to maintain it.

Head candy

If this mirror and pathetic mini sink were bigger in these ridiculously small mobile event toilets, maybe I could actually see what I'm doing.

But, nope, even practically soaking Si's tie in water isn't making any difference at all to the Jackson Pollock art piece it's become.

Humph.

No wonder Master Clipboard was so suspicious. I look like a vagrant in a suit and tie he's found in a refuse bin with the smashed remnants of an LCC in it, only grubbier. If ever there was an outfit in need of an executive re-build and premium dry clean, this is it.

Mind you, even I look better than this chap who's just emerged from that cubicle back there.

Fuck, is that remnants of some Class A he's finishing sniffing up his nose?

Surely not off a toilet cistern in this fucking place?

Really?

Wow.

And, yikes, was that Dave Poole from Maxwell Brown who I just saw dive-bomb into the first cubicle?

I think it was as well.

It sounds like he's heaving his guts up in there.

Actually, did I see him in our tent earlier?

Oops, I hope it's not one of my frozen in the middle offerings from the Grand Deluxe he's evacuating in there...

The sooner I get out of Henley on Thames the better for all concerned then.

Yep.

If we three in here are anything to go on, so much for having a relaxed, enjoyable sporting day out.

I should probably not even bother going back to the marquee and just head straight for the train station.

I can't even take this tie off either, because of the dress code police.

You can sniff as much Class A as you like, but whatever you do just dress the part; such being the perceived pressures of working in investment property these days: to seem self-assured and successful when you're anything but, the bravado hiding a weakness of character unable to sustain ambitions without a crutch, the sense of entitlement leading down the road to oblivion.

Just don't take your fucking tie off.

'And, yes, extra evidence, if any were needed, on why you're right to not give a fuck about any of it, Johnny Boy.'

Notwithstanding that, yep, it would be nice to be able to afford a fancy pair of shades like this here dandy dude's on a day like today.

Hmm.

Not that I'd likely need them when back on station inside this marquee again.

Actually, maybe if I slip back in through the chef's back flap, so to speak, I'd be able to avoid Nigel and skip straight out onto the river front?

And maybe even snaffle a surviving trifle or a piece of LCfuckingHC on the way?

Yep, it's got to be worth a try at least.

I'll just have to hope Nigel hasn't yet found the remnants of the LCC Samantha made me bring back.

How did she put it again? 'Just to remind me of my stupidity'?

Good job I hid it well under the main table then.

'There was no need to draw Nigel's attention to it was there Johnny Boy?'

Nope.

So, phase one of operation trifle: a quick peek through the gap in the canvas flap.

And, nope, can't see Nigel by the food table anyway.

Right, yep, let's do this.

Nigel: 'Ah, John, there you are.'

Eh?!

Fuck, Nigel.

With Pete and Samantha behind the bar table, hiding on purpose where I couldn't see them.

Nigel: 'Thanks for fetching the deserts for me earlier, with Samantha...'

Hmm.

Why the thanks though? He never says thanks. For anything. He must want me to do something else for him.

Nigel: 'I thought I'd ordered a cream cake, but this chocolate one seems to be going down alright.'

Fuck, Samantha's stifling a grin. Why's she doing that? Has she told him?

'Just smile John, just smile.'

Nigel: 'I forgot to ask you earlier, how did you get on with the client in Lambeth yesterday? The site boundary all okay, is it?'

Ah, so that's it.

'Err, yes, Mr Singh, fine. All as on the OS. It's a great site...'

Nigel: 'Hmm, maybe.'

Blimey, that was half-hearted. It's a belter, surely?

Nigel: 'I'll get the plan off you in the morning. You can now go and, err..., mingle..., for a bit...'

Okay, right, good; that's a relief.

Only, given his demeanour, he has no such luxuries planned for Samantha and Pete though.

Can I catch Samantha's eye before I go?

Does she even want to catch my eye?

No.

Sadly, she's too busy taking Nigel's fresh orders for that.

I'll just have to take my own pathetic attempt at defiance out on one of these lucky trifles and make my first foray out onto the riverside instead.

Going on the Mexican wave of polite applause and cheers of encouragement making its way up the riverbank towards us, there's certainly still no lull in the racing.

Nope.

Hopefully the accompanying rhythmic pounding of the protagonists' oars getting nearer and nearer and louder and louder isn't a foretaste of what I can expect if a certain Mr Brodsky and his crew decide to make an appearance.

But is this trifle worth all the effort, that's the next most immediate question?

Mmm, actually it's not bad.

If I throw in a bit of closed-eyed sun-worshipping, it's a bona fide multi-sensory experience in fact.

Gemma: 'Things can't be that bad can they John?'

Ah, a smiling Gemma Green.

'Oh, hey, Gemma...'

Nigel did actually invite one or two nice guests then.

She's all glammed up and looking fabulous too.

'Not now Nigel's off my back, for a while at least...'

Gemma: 'Yeah, I saw him giving you a hard time earlier...'

'I'm still feeling a little hungover from last night to tell the truth..., but don't tell him though, eh?'

Gemma: 'Hmm, that guy really is a prize wanker..., but don't tell him that either, eh?'

Hah.

'No, as much as I'd like to, I think I won't Gemma.'

'So, how're things with you then Gemma? Enjoying the racing?'

Gemma: 'Oh yeah, what's not to like about all this?'

Hah, yes; and she's one that deserves all this too.

Particularly given how hard she must have found it to get where she is in this business in just her early 30s, as both a woman and black.

And with a focus on both environmentally sustainable and ethical investment too.

'Who's in this race then?'

Oh, and she can even juggle her glass of sparkling to rustle up an event Programme.

Gemma: 'Erm, The Thames Tradesmen and the Tideway Scullers, I think...'

'Looks like a close race.'

Gosh, and they look near exhausted accordingly.

'Go on Tradesmen!'

Gemma: 'Go on Tideway!'

Hah!

As well we might both grin and shrug our shoulders.

'Go on Tradesmen!'

Gemma: 'Come on Tideway!'

Gosh, the agony etched on both crews' faces as they approach the line.

Maybe there *are* worse things to be doing here today.

Gemma: 'Who the hell are the Tradesmen?'

'No idea at all. Who the hell are the Tideway?'

Hah!

'No, and I suppose it doesn't really matter, does it?!'

What a bit of mindless shouting at some young athletes can do for a person's enthusiasm.

Gemma: 'Erm..., it looks like the 'Sons of the Thames' versus 'Dynamo Club Moscow' will be along next...'

Yikes, no, Dynamo Club Moscow?!

'Oh, crap, really...?'

Gemma: 'Yeah..., why?'

'There's a Russian prospective purchaser of Nigel's I'd rather didn't make an appearance...'

Gemma: 'Well, he'd need to be here by now if he wants to watch the finish from here...'

'Trouble is, I don't even know what he looks like, just his sidekick!'

Gemma: 'Ahh...'

'Hah, yeah, ahh...'

Not that there's much I could do to keep them away from Nigel in any case.

And, if that distant crack a couple of minutes ago was the starting gun, as Gemma says the likelihood is they're already watching this race somewhere else, aren't they?

And, yep, there's still no sign of Mr Vlad The Smooth Petrenko for now.

'Did I see Dave Poole earlier, he's from your place isn't he Gemma? He didn't look too well.'

Gemma: 'Yeah, I heard he was sick on the train over.'

'Oh, right, poor Dave.'

'He didn't look so well in the toilets earlier either...'

At least it wasn't one of my dodgy sausages then.

I can almost hear Flipper Pete's sigh of relief from over here.

And, yes, on which connected subject, I suppose, like Gem, I really should really finish my own trifle. After what I put it through, it's the least I owe it.

'So, you got much on the go at the moment?'

Gemma: 'No, not much. The summer slowdown... It's why I've been able to come really. Although I did think I might have been able to talk Davenport into bidding for that office in Leicester Square you sent me...'

'Platinum House.'

Gemma: 'Yeah, but no joy I'm afraid. I do have a client looking to buy development sites, planning gain opportunities though. Don't suppose you've got anything like that have you? Somewhere in town maybe?

'Nigel has an acre close to the river..., in Lambeth...?'

Nigel, or Wendy more like, must have forgotten to send the marketing details to her.

And, oops, that seems to have encouraged the two guys closest to us to sidle over.

Gemma: 'No, what's that then?'

They must be bored with each other's company, not that I can blame them. I would be, looking at the two of them.

'An old warehouse on Old vauxhall Street, behind Albert Embankment, but it sounds like it's gone if he hasn't mentioned it to you already... I don't know for sure whether you'd get resi or hotel use through the planners, but I reckon you'd get ten or more storeys on it in some use or other.'

Dougie: 'I've got a couple of guys who'd be interested in that too...'

'Yeah, you and everybody else in London mate.'

Gemma: 'John, do you know Dougie and Michael?'

'Nope, don't think so, do I?'

Gemma: 'Dougie's at RealProp, and Michael's at Appletons?'

Ah, so this must be the mythical Dougie Ardern then.

Even Nigel kowtows before this guy and his connections.

Gemma: 'Dougie, Michael, this is John... He works in Nigel's team.'

'Hey both...'

Michael: 'So, come on John, tell us more about Old Vauxhall Street then...'

Actually, if none of these three know about it, Nigel must really be keeping it QT.

'It's more than my job's worth I'm afraid gentlemen, but I will mention your interest to Nigel though...'

Hmm.

'And you can fucking glare at me all you want Dougie, but that's gunna make me even more certain to keep my mouth shut.'

Gemma: 'Yeah, we can talk business tomorrow. You going to the HedKandi after party tonight, John?'

Oh, and Nigel's let Samantha make an appearance out on the riverside now too. If only with a bin bag.

Umm?

'Probably not, sadly, Gemma...'

Unless Samantha wants to take me that is. Fat chance of that though.

'Are you going along then?'

'Christ, Dougie, you really don't like taking no for an answer, do you?'

Michael: 'Who or what the hell is Head Candy?'

Blimey, even Samantha's eying me suspiciously now too. What have I gone and done now?

Gemma: 'I don't think it might be quite what you're hoping it is Michael...'

Hah.

Michael: 'Oh, that's a shame...!'

'Yeah, you're right Gem, what a plonker.'

Both of them are fucking dildos in fact.

More senior, better connected and a lot richer than me they may be, but at least I wasn't born with a penis growing out of my forehead.

Oh no.

I had to earn mine.

Tiger Brodsky

What a bleedin' bombsite that was.

I must remind Nigel to add 'help Samantha and the rest of the catering staff clean up after the company's annual jolly' to my job description.

It was good of Gail to muck in too mind.

She and Samantha look as knackered as I feel – even if they are managing to console themselves in their chairs here with a bit of the LCC remains.

Still, eight hours of torture almost over, and a no-show from Mr Brodsky too, which was a bit of luck.

'So, was today good for you both, too, then?'

Not.

Samantha: 'What, the remnants of this cake, or running around for Nigel all day?'

'See, if I hadn't tactically dropped it, we wouldn't have been able to eat it now, would we?'

Gail: 'Tactically?! That's not what I heard...'

What?!

'I don't know what you can possibly mean Gail.'

But, on that note, definitely time to finish the cake and go then.

'Nice cake though eh?'

Hah.

Oops, Nigel. I thought he'd gone.

Nigel: 'What's that you're eating then?'

Fuck.

I'd better play for time by using my hand to exaggerate that I've got my mouth full.

Bollocks, this'll do.

'Think it must be the cream cake you thought you'd ordered earlier, although it's a bit bashed up for some reason. Found it under the table.'

Crap, he's noticed what's left of the LCC in its crumpled box.

I can see the coin spinning behind his eyes.

'Why, would you like some?'

Great, he's broken his gaze.

Nigel: 'We all done then?'

Blimey.

'What do you mean 'we' Nigel?'

Samantha's eyes are screaming the exact same thing.

Samantha: 'Yeah, think so...'

Even she knows when to contain her combative side.

And, yep, even here and now, after all that today, still beguilingly so.

Nigel: 'Well, I suppose you can all get off home then! Unless any of you'd prefer to join me and the senior partners in the Bull?!'

Yeah, right.

Good job Gail was behind him when she pulled that horror-filled face.

Nigel: 'Right, see you all nice and early tomorrow morning then...'

Yep, right indeed; let's get the hell out of here.

Oh, actually...

'Oh Nigel, I need to have a word with you tomorrow about the site in Lambeth. Only, I mentioned it to a couple of people this afternoon, and they want details. One of them's got a hotel client that might be interested, and another after a planning gain opp...'

Oops.

Yikes, maybe I really shouldn't have done that after all.

Nigel: 'Oh you did, did you? I thought I told you I'm dealing with it?'

'Right, err..., yes, but..., well, none of them seem to have got the usual mail out? I thought there might have been a problem with the mailing list? Maybe Wendy...'

No, I've made it even worse. His eyes have narrowed and his brain is whirring again.

No, he's taking a breath and restraining himself.

Nigel: 'Yes, it's probably just a glitch in the mail out. Thanks for telling me, John.'

He's probably had a hard day too, in fairness.

Nigel: 'Go home. Leave it with me. I'll sort it in the morning.'

And now he's happily smiling again.

Fuck, he's like Jekyll and Hyde, and all in just a few paces.

Think I really will let him go this time. Even Samantha looks a little spooked.

Samantha: 'You know what, I'm not even going to ask...'

And, nope, she's really not wrong to, either.

And, yep, these are definitely one set of tent flaps I really don't want to see again.

Gail: 'Right, I'm off too... My husband's picking me up, if either of you wants a lift?'

'Thanks Gail, but I'll just walk to the station.'

Samantha: 'I'm getting the train too, Gail, but thanks. I'll just walk with John.'

Oh, right.

'Err, yep, fine..., great, Samantha.'

Gail: 'Okay, well I'm off this way, so see you tomorrow then...'

'Okay, yep, see you tomorrow Gail, have a good evening...'

Samantha: 'Yeah, thanks again for your help Gail, really...'

And, mm-hmm, going on the warmth in the smiles they've just exchanged, at least Gail's been succeeding where I've been failing.

A bit of mutual woman to woman appreciation in a world where neither expects any.

Actually, I don't suppose the two of them might be...

Nah.

Not a bad thought though.

'Right, let's get the hell out of here then, shall we?'

Only, who's this now?

Fuck, I don't believe it! It's Master Clipboard Obsessive from the Catering Tent!

He must have come over here to try to find me..., or Nigel..., presumably.

Wow, is it lucky or unlucky he's only just missed Nigel by seconds?

Whichever, you really do get nothing for nearlies.

Master Clipboard: 'Mr Plender?'

Erm?

As surprised as you're looking, what do you reckon Samantha, yes..., or no?'

'Err, yep, I can deal with this...'

Master Clipboard: 'I brought a copy of your revised invoice Mr Plender, and you forgot to sign the receipt for the second cake you hadn't ordered...?'

Fuck, the annoying prick's still on about his sodding order book. I really am going to strangle him in a minute.

'Oh, sorry about that, where do you want me to...?'

Ah, of course, as if there wasn't already going to be a cross marking the spot...

253

'Oh, yes, of course..., N. Plender..., here you go.'

Master Clipboard: 'Thank you. Good night, err, Sir.'

'Yeah, what are you smiling and shaking your head at Yanks?'

Samantha: 'You know what, I'm not even going to ask about that either... I just want to go...'

Hopefully Nigel will deny ever approving it.

Either that, or, if I just fold and hide the invoice in my inside jacket pocket, maybe the dry cleaners will accidentally frazzle it for me.

'What did you do with the rest of the bloody cake anyway?'

Eh?

'What? No? The bin?!'

Samantha: 'What, you wanted to take it with you?'

'Well.., err, no..., but we've been through a lot that cake and me...'

That made her half smile anyway.

And she's not even trying to leave me behind as we walk any more.

Samantha: 'You know what, I don't think Nigel could've made it any harder for me today if he'd tried...'

Um-hum.

'Nope.'

Samantha: 'And *you* owe me big time...'

Yep, and that I do.

'Yep, thanks.'

Only, does my imbecility rule out my trying to make it up to her with a pre-sex bite of pizza or a bit of head candy together, that's the question.

'Well, does it?'

Yes?

No?

Samantha: 'I could've actually hit him when he asked me to try to clean ketchup off one of his smarmy client's ties.'

'And you could always ask, though, couldn't you Johnny Boy? Not for the sex, maybe, sadly, but a pizza, possibly? Show a bit of Spence-like initiative?'

Samantha: 'D'you see him? The one who looked like he'd a dead groundhog on his head?'

'Hah, yeah, that rug was a bit obvious wasn't it...'

'Welcome to my world Samantha...'

Hell, yeah.

But, eh, why's she now looking at me so quizzically?

Oh.

'The tie, err, part, I mean, rather than the, err, dead groundhog....'

Hmm.

Wow.

Even I think that sounded ridiculous.

And, yes, justifiably, here comes another of those super-cool-women smiles again.

Blimey, I'm an idiot.

Samantha: 'It wasn't even a good tie...'

Actually, maybe I could pull her leg a little.

'Actually, given how you did such a good job, I don't suppose there's anything you can do with Si's tie, here, is there?'

Oops.

Hah!

Yikes.

'Yep, I was only joking, you don't have to try and hit me.'

Samantha: 'So that's Simon's, is it?'

'Mm-hmm.'

Samantha: 'Hmm. The ketchup actually improved the groundhog's tie...'

Hmm, indeed.

'Anyhow, getting back to the point at hand, and putting aside that I can be a daft imbecile and everything...'

How about...

'Hey look, I know I shouldn't really ask and everything, what with us working...'

Uh?

Whose is this car stopping next to us?

Fuck, I know this Range Rover with its blacked-out windows don't I?

And, yep, a blacked-out window lowered to duly reveal the smiling face of Vladimir Petrenko indeed.

Yikes, he hasn't just bumped into Nigel, has he?!

Petrenko: 'Mr Smith, good evening..., I was hoping to see you here...'

What, really?

Petrenko: 'Ms Palin...'

'Mr Petrenko...'

Samantha's looking decidedly nonplussed to see him too.

Petrenko: 'I'm sorry to impose, but my employer, Mr Brodsky, would very much like to meet with you. Can you spare him a few minutes please? He'd very much like to talk to you about our meeting yesterday.'

'Well, I err...'

Samantha: 'What, *now*...?!'

Petrenko: 'We can take you to him... It is not far...'

Oh, and given at how, at the merest of nods from Mr Smooth here, the driver has so very helpfully jumped out to pre-emptively open the door for me, that'll be a rhetorical request too then...

Petrenko: 'Ms Palin too, if you would prefer?'

Fuck, what a pain in the proverbial.

But I've got no choice, have I?

Samantha's looking at me with a mixture of exhaustion and annoyance.

Actually, no, make that more with frustration, or anger even.

But, nope, I don't think I do have any choice.

'No, that's alright, thanks, Mr Petrenko. Sorry Samantha. You go on ahead. There's no need for you to come. I'll try to catch up with you at the station...'

'*Yep?*'

Going on that decidedly unimpressed raise of her head, that'll be no, don't bother then.

'*Sorry, Samantha, but I really don't have a choice sorry...*'

Hmm.

Assuming I can actually climb up into this thing...

'*And I'm probably too much of a wimp to get around to asking you for a pizza anyway.*'

Ah, a foot plate.

'*Okay Mr Petrenko, let's get this over with...*'

And the quicker the better please.

I can't even make eye contact with Samantha or wave through these blacked out windows either.

Not that she's even trying to look back at me as she stomps off.

Humph.

The mysterious Mr Brodsky had better be worth all this.

Or at least buy Platinum House for me.

Petrenko: 'Mr Brodsky asked me to offer his apologies for not having been able to join you at your, err, event today..., only he had commitments elsewhere.'

'*Don't worry mate, it suited me just fine as it happens.*'

So, we're heading back over the bridge and back along the other side of the river.

To one of the other hospitality areas in Fawley Meadows possibly?

Erm, nope.

Given that was the Fawley entrance we've just rocketed past, evidently not then.

Only, isn't it just open countryside out from here?

And we're accelerating even harder now.

Mr Sodding Brodsky does actually know I'm just a nobody, yes?

Or does that just make me extra expendable?

The type you can kill just to send a message to the important people?

If I went missing, even the police missing person headline would scarcely garner any attention:

Wholly unimportant junior surveyor in mystery disappearance

'We didn't even notice he was missing at first, although he never really was very noticeable anywhere in the firm to be honest,' says Mr Nigel Fucking Plender.

Or maybe it should actually just read:

Junior surveyor gladly buried alive by the Russian mafia to save himself from a life of mundanity

Even if, right now, this is anything but mundane.

'So..., err..., where did you say we're going Mr Petrenko?'

Petrenko: 'Oh..., erm...'

'Crikey, what do you fucking mean 'oh..., erm'?'

And what's he looking at the driver for? To agree on the burial spot for me?

Petrenko: 'Vin khoche znaty, kudy my ydemo...'

Driver: 'Haw haw haw...'

'Oh, what, you both think this is funny do you?

Petrenko: 'Err, Mr Brodsky has, err... Ahh, we are there nearly... You will see Mr Smith, you will see...'

Blimey.

'*Do you expect me to talk Mr Vladimir? No Mr Smith, we expect you to...*'

Oops, no, we're turning off onto this narrow lane.

Crap, missed it; what did that road sign say?

Nope, it's gone.

Wherever or whatever it is is certainly brightly lit up ahead though.

Hang on, wow, I know what this long, low timber clad structure enclosed in high mesh netting is...

'*A secret KGB torture camp in the heart of middle England, Mr Smith?*'

No, just a golf fucking driving range.

After all that.

Hah!

Do I laugh myself to death, or piss myself to death?

The choice is almost a disappointment.

Luckily for me they chose a lawful place where criminal acts are committed with clubs.

And, yep, there's another sister Range Rover and a Merc duly already here of course.

And we've barely stopped moving before the watchful driver of the Merc is already opening my door for me.

Funny; not.

Given the way Petrenko and his driver are still covertly grinning, maybe I'm not the first to have felt a little uneasy on the backseat with them on narrow lanes in dark forests.

'*Hah fucking hah, you too gentlemen...*'

Yeah, I could put big guy here in hospital easily if I wanted to.

Even if I would probably need an elephant gun to deliver on my threat.

At least Petrenko has put his serious head back on.

Well, as much as he can when he's gesturing for me to follow him through a doorway emblazoned 'Hooky John's Golf Centre'.

Typically.

And despite the sight we must make in this otherwise Spartan reception, we deserve barely more than a glance from the teenage girl receptionist sitting watching TV behind the counter over there.

The complete opposite of her clipboard obsessed peer of earlier, in fact.

And we aren't even carrying any golf clubs.

Then again, there can't be much here to steal I'd imagine. Just a few plastic buckets, thousands of chipped rubber golf balls and a few hundred quid in coins. Probably not enough to even get out of bed for in this neighbourhood.

Nope, the only thing of any value in this place is the much prized and sought after 'thwack' of ball connecting sweetly with steel.

Or, cavity backed steel, either forged or cast, with Urethane Elastomer, to be exact.

Or, occasionally, frying-pan-sized titanium head and Urethane Elastomer, such being the myriad golf equipment made these days for the true fanatic.

Like my Dad.

And I used to be.

And, evidently, Mr Brodsky; wherever he is?

Hmm.

If I could in any way see past the vast bulk of the driver as we follow this narrow walkway, I might actually be able to spot anyone fitting the description of a rich Russian oligarch.

Oh.

Crikey.

As ridiculously obvious as it may be, that must be him.

A bear of a man in, what, maybe his late forties...?, hmm, but, whatever, making very bad attempts at hitting golf balls in the second last bay from the end; watched by two more burly men in more of the same archetypal black leather jackets – including Mr Chomyszak was it, from yesterday? – both standing, very wisely, well behind their club wielding boss.

No wonder Ms Teenage Lass back there didn't even bat an eyelid at mere mortals like Mr Smooth and me. If it were possible to take divots out of plywood and artificial grass, this man would be doing it. He doesn't need bodyguards, he needs a keeper, and one used to dealing with Siberian born varieties.

Ouch, yep, if he actually connected properly with one of those balls it'd go for miles.

Brodsky: 'Ahh Vladimir...'

Like a true obsessive, even Vlad's arrival doesn't stop him going at another defenceless golf ball on the mat before him.

Da-bang.

Yikes, that one didn't even clear the bay, did it?

Nope, the loud bang must have come from the ricochet off the wooden board dividing – or actually protecting in this case – other range users.

The three bodyguards duly jumped with surprise; if not, perhaps predictably, the ever cool Prof here.

Still, yep, going on the way Mr Brodsky inspected it before he roughly discarded it against the handrail as he stepped down from the mat towards us, it's duly the club that's at fault.

Petrenko: 'Mr Smith.'

Announced as if mission accomplished; me obviously being the mission.

Petrenko: 'Mr Smith, this is my employer, Mr Brodsky...'

Brodsky: 'Aaahh! Mr Smith, very pleased to meet you! Thank you much for coming...'

Hmm, heavily accented and not as fluent as Mr Smooth here, but otherwise perfectly understandable English learnt somewhere or other.

'Mr Brodsky...'

And, yes, as intimidating as he is physically, I suppose I should shake his hand.

Or bucket might be a better description, and another hand I couldn't even begin to get my fingers around.

Yikes, yep, I'll just have to grasp it as firmly as I can and hang on until his warmth and enthusiasm abates.

Bizarrely, he has a kind face though: which must be quite the occupational hazard in his profession.

Brodsky: 'Do you mind?'

Not that he lets it stop him from doing what he wants to do then; in this case killing golf balls.

Brodsky: 'An obsessive, how you say, hobby? But, ackh, I do not get much the opportunity...'

No, crack on mate. And literally...

'No, no, not at all Mr Brodsky. Please...'

'And you certainly need the practice, mate. But I think I'll take a step or two back here, if you don't mind.'

For once, even his over-familiarity is disarming; genuine, and not making any sort of point. Just a frustrated golf addict who simply can't help himself. A hobby that's got him by the dangly bits: hair, scrotum and testes.

And, yep, a less faulty and more obedient club is called for this time.

Uh-huh, maybe an easier seven iron.

Brodsky: 'Do you play this terrible game Mr Smith?'

And he seems to have a deft touch the way he used the club head to gently press the ball delivery button on the automatic ball feeder machine.

'Not as much these days as I perhaps need to Mr Brodsky...'

You don't even have to lift a ball out of the bucket in these well-to-do parts then.

Brodsky: 'So, Mr Smith, how is business?'

Oh, erm...

Twodd.

He's hit that one low and sharply duck hook left.

Brodsky: 'Hi, hi...'

And as much as he's almost protesting at and chastising himself, he actually has the makings of a decent golfer.

'Well, it can always be better Mr Brodsky, but pretty good, I think. What's the market like for you back home in Russia at the moment?'

Eh?

Uh, oh.

Yikes.

Why's he now looking at me like that?

Brodsky: 'So, you think we Russian, Mr Smith?'

Fuck, he's now gesturing with mock surprise to Vladimir and the men around us too...

Brodsky: 'Hah! Vin dumaye, shcho my Rosiyany...'

And, given the way they're all scoffing nervously, that's precisely where they're *not* from then.

But if not Russia, where *are* they from?

Fuck, if they're from one of those former Eastern Bloc countries *oppressed* by the Russians, I really am dead.

Brodsky: 'Russia is not only former Soviet country with..., how you English say?..., *oligarchs*...?, yes...?, who supposed pillage their country natural resources... Hah!'

Lucky for me, then, that he's more interested in addressing and swinging at the next ball rather than me.

Brodsky: 'We in the Ukraine have more than enough of our own of those...'

Oh, right. Ukraine.

Thwoot.

Yikes, another brutal and ill-timed swing, and this time he's topped it barely two feet off the ground.

Brodsky: 'Ackkhh!'

Do Ukrainians and Russians hate each other? They're close neighbours so I don't think they do, do they? I hope not, anyway.

'Sorry about that Mr Brodsky, Mr Petrenko...'

'And, no, we British don't think you're all the same, I promise.'

There's dangerous humour, and then there's fucking dangerous humour; circumstances considering.

'I'm sure you know we British are still coming to terms with the new world order. And who supplies our gas, of course...'

Brodsky: 'Ah, very good, Mr Smith. I am happy to hear the memory of empire is alive and well in Great Britain these days. But we do not in reality supply your gas. We are but a pipeline for our Russian comrades. Only minerals, and some of your grain...'

Oh, right.

Actually, he's not scary, really, just intimidating in a sort of all-consuming, larger-than-life kind of way. Just a pretend gangster desperately trying his best to conceal a kind side; which, given the world he inhabits, can't exactly be his most useful attribute.

Probably best not to test that particular theory here and now though.

But what he *is*, is a fanatic golfer with a swing fault.

Fuck, there we go again...

Twook.

This one's banana sliced right so much that it almost hit that guy in the bay at the other end of the building! No more than head height too. It would have killed him.

Brodsky: 'Tebe sobaka!'

Whatever the fuck that self-chastisement means, it can't be good.

But the most annoying thing – and especially for him, no doubt – is that he doesn't actually have a bad swing. He's just swaying as he swings, not keeping his head still.

Brodsky: 'Tell me Platinum House...'

'Ignore the next ball, John, ignore the next innocent ball...'

'Well, as a pure investment, it has a lot going for it. Strong tenant covenants, good income, and at ten million pounds it shows a pretty good true equivalent yield I'd say...'

Actually, that sounded quite convincing, didn't it?

Brodksy: 'Mmm...'

Nope, back to the next innocent victim of a ball then.

Oh God, not like that. Not again.

Thwod.

High and straight right this time, almost clearing the fence in fact. A better connection, though.

He's just swaying as he swings.

'No, John, no. Just keep your gob shut. You can't help him. He needs a professional...'

The poor bloke is sighing with frustration.

'No, John. No! Don't do it!!'

Nope, I can't stop myself.

Cooking and cake football I'm crap at. Golf I can play.

'Excuse me Mr Brodsky..., but I play a bit of golf myself and....'

Actually, if I really am going to show him, I suppose I'd better take my jacket off.

Oops, I'd better stop right here, actually.

These two immediate minders have jumped forward like I've triggered an international incident...

Brodsky: 'Idiots, he is my guest! Vin nash hist!'

Maybe he's not too kind-sided then.

'There's no backing out now though John.'

He's now looking at me with a mixture of amusement and anticipation.

Golf obsessives will consider suggestions from little old ladies in bus queues if they thought it could improve their game. Or from Chartered Surveyors at the Henley Royal Regatta too it seems.

Think I'd better lay my jacket over the handrail.

'If I can take the club for a second Mr Brodsky?'

'May I?'

'Yep, that's it, if you'll just let me have the bay for a second or two...'

Only, fuck, I don't think there's one of them not looking at me expectantly.

What the hell have I done?

'So you think you can play golf, do you John?'

'Erm, I'm no professional, obviously, but I couldn't help noticing that you're swaying as you swing, Mr Brodsky...'

Nope, he's looking at me blankly. I'm going to have to show him myself then.

Just, yep, exaggerate the sway of my head from at first over my right foot to over my left, yep, like this..., or that..., I think.

'Do you see?'

Fuck, nope, he still hasn't a clue what I'm on about.

Fuck. I'll try again.

'Just watch my head?'

'Yep, gently does it, same again John.'

Yep, that should have done it this time, surely?

Fuck.

That'll be another no then.

In fact, all of their faces are not only still blank but also borderline suspicious, and especially Mr Brodsky's.

I'm actually going to have to hit a ball. And after just two creaky practice swings too.

'I'll show you...'

'Or fucking try to anyway...'

Blimey, even the ball feeder is whirring for longer than normal to prolong and heighten the tension.

Ah well, here goes nothing. It won't be the first time today I've made a complete twat of myself.

'Nice and smooth John, don't snatch at the top, and for fuck's sake keep your head still.'

Mm-hmm...

Thwack.

Well, the ball contact felt okay. Where's it gone though?

Hah, yesss! Straight as a die down the middle of the range, without even a hint of draw or fade.

Womanising and pretty much everything else I'm crap at, golf I can play. And thank the devil for that.

Or my Dad.

'Right, no need to look relieved when you turn around, Johnny Boy. It's exactly what you expected after all.'

Wow, Mr Brodsky's face is not only a mixture of excitement and enthusiasm, but he's obviously chomping at the bit to test my theory.

Just as I thought, even little old ladies in bus queues.

'Yep, okay, over to you Mr Brodsky.'

But, yikes, if he could address the ball when I've stepped back a bit...

'Right, Mr Brodsky, just keep your damn head down, and don't sway...'

Thwook..

'*Oh for fuck's sake. I said* don't *sway.*'

The ball has shot high right, straight into the fence again...

Worse, he's looking at me as if I've just broken his favourite train set.

'You're not....'

Fuck, he's already...

Thwoh.

And that swing was even more vigorous.

Crap, he's barely made any contact with the ball at all this time, and it's just bobbled along the ground and stopped no more than five metres in front of us.

Fuck. The look on the not so kind Mr Brodsky's face is no longer one of frustration, but of anger.

And it's now all *my* fault.

He's way past blaming the club.

If I'd just kept my sodding gob shut I would simply have finished telling him about Platinum sodding House and now be on the train back to London, ogling at the lovely Samantha.

But no, I had to try telling him how not to hit a golf ball.

Although there is one more thing I could try, to redeem myself, if he'll let me?

'I'm so sorry Mr Brodsky, but I'm obviously not explaining myself properly...'

And, yes, I might be taken aback by my persistence too I suppose.

Vladimir must now be watching events from back there through metaphorical fingers.

Either that or he likes having to find places to bury clubbed corpses on a weekday evening in Buckinghamshire.

There really, really, is no going back now though.

'If you could address the ball for me?'

And, yes, after only the briefest hesitation, in fairness to Mr Brodsky he's game for trying.

Only, now for the tricky bit. If I can manage it?

I need to place my feet as close to the other side of the ball from him as I can..., yep, like so..., and now raise myself up onto my toes and reach out my right arm towards his head.

Fuck; God in heaven, or you stars up there, help me survive this.

'Right Mr Brodsky, just try to keep your head under my hand as you swing.'

'And, nope, you're right Mr Brodsky: I don't know either which one of us is the more incredulous!'

Or how on earth our respective golf obsessions have brought us to such an absurd moment of desperation and mutual reliance.

Me about to place my hand on the bald patch of an obviously very rich, probable gangster, Ukranian oligarch-cum-mafia boss – with every chance of having my toes cleaved off with his wayward seven iron or, worse, waking up in a box on my way to eastern Crimea – and he risking the ridicule of his subservients by allowing a property agent and near total stranger to do it.

On the very outside chance I can help him to hit a golf ball.

Luckily for us both, what unites and binds us utterly and unbreakably is our mutual and absolute desperation for him to hit the ball clean and straight down the driving range.

So, yep, hand as lightly as I can on the top of his head and here we go...

And, actually, he did keep his head vaguely still this time.

Twack.

Sounded like a slightly thin contact, but I can still feel my toes..., and..., YESSS!.., the ball's rising gradually straight down the middle of the range.

Fuck, is that me or the mat I can hear crying out in relief?

Or just Vlad at not having to get his shovel out?

Not perfect by any means, but his best shot of the day by a country mile.

The fucking beauty.

Oops, Mr Brodsky's not satisfied though.

Brodsky: 'Again...'

Blimey, he's already addressing the next ball...

'Quick John: tiptoes, arm, hand...'

Thwack.

Fuck, that was close.

He kept his head pretty still again and the contact sounded even better this time.

And, yep, the perfect trajectory and shape of a well-hit seven iron!

Tiger bleeding Brodsky...

Wow.

Amazing.

Even Vladimir the Prof is quietly chuckling and shaking his head.

And thank fuck for that.

Uh, oh.

Not only is he now grinning broadly, but my erstwhile pupil is making to put his arm around my shoulders...

Yikes.

No, he's just playfully walking me off the mat.

And, yep, that is definitely enough of that for one day.

Un-fucking-believable.

Brodsky: 'Thank you, Mr Smith, or may I now call you John?! Hah!'

'Yep, you can call me whatever you like Mr Brodsky... You too for that matter Vladimir.'

'Of course...'

Brodsky: 'Thank you, John. We must have round some time...,

so you can give me your advice as we play. My putting is also not so good...'

'I'd like that, Mr Brodsky, but I'm not sure Nigel would let me get away with it, I'm afraid... He doesn't like golf...'

Brodsky: 'Ah..., yes..., Mr Plender...'

Blimey, that was contemplatively.

Brodsky: 'I have submit offers on number properties to your Mr Plender in past one or so years, but sadly none them accepted. Did you know that, John?'

Oh, right, really?

'Sorry Mr Brodsky, I didn't.., but I wouldn't, necessarily. Nigel tends to deal with a lot of the offers himself, I'm afraid. Up to now I've only gotten to deal personally with the smaller properties.'

Brodsky: 'Hmm, I thought that might be so. Only, I ask Vladimir here to make some enquiries of the, err, Land..., how you say...?, Registry? Is amazing what can learn there. Is not that way in Ukraine... Only it seems that two of properties were sold for less..., *much* less, than I offered...'

Oh, what, really? Okay then.

Brodsky: 'Do you know why that might have been John?'

Hmm, what's he implying here?

That Nigel won't take him seriously? That he's corrupt, on the take, even?

Or have I lost it in translation?

'I'm sorry Mr Brodsky, I don't, but I'm sure Nigel must have had his reasons.'

Christ, is Nigel corrupt?

Brodsky: 'Very well, John, if you say. Only, I would like submit offer for Platinum House... I am not sure yet what price... Vladimir is dealing on with my advisers..., but when I do, I would like you to deal with for me, John...'

Nigel's a lazy twat, yes, but corrupt?

Brodsky: 'Can you do that for me?'

'Well, I...'

Brodsky: 'Vladimir thinks you honest, John, and I agree.'

Oh, right.

Brodsky: 'And I wish only for fair opportunity. No special favours..., only fair opportunity. I have enough of the, err..., other..., in Ukraine.'

Okay, if that's all then.

'Yes, of course, Mr Brodsky. Send your offer to me when you're ready, and I'll make sure our client, the owner, is aware of it, I promise you.

Brodsky: 'Good, thank you John.'

Right, good, that'll be that then.

Brodsky: 'Oh, and I also looking for site in London..., build hotel..., somewhere near tourists. Big Ben, Buckingham Palace, you know? But cheap. Not much expensive. I do not suppose you have site like that?'

Blimey, not these guys too.

'Would you consider a site without planning permission?'

Brodsky: 'Certainly, as long as hotel is possible. Vladimir?'

Petrenko: 'Yes, in principle..., although, naturally, that would need to be reflected in the price...'

And, nope, I can't argue with that.

'Of course...'

They won't be able to discount it too much though.

'It's an old warehouse on an acre in Lambeth, behind Albert Embankment... Just over the river from the Houses of Parliament, close to Lambeth Palace.'

Brodsky: 'Lambeth Palace?'

Petrenko: 'The London home of the Archbishop of Canterbury...'

'Ahh, very good Vladimir.'

'It's at 1 to 9 Old Vauxhall Street if you'd like to do a drive by?'

272

'Yep?'

It must at least be a possibility if Vladimir has felt the need to whisper something in his boss's ear, no?

Brodsky: 'Ah, yes. Vladimir reminds me we have meeting in West End tomorrow, so we will look on way, in morning...'

Oh, right, great.

'So, if that really is it now then gentlemen?'

Yep; looks like it.

'Well, thank you Mr Brodsky. It's been a..., pleasure.'

Brodsky: 'Yes, thank you again for coming see me this evening, John, and for your assistance with my little, err, hobby. An infuriating game...'

'Yep, and that it certainly is Mr B. That it certainly is.'

And, yes, we can indeed shake hands like we're golfing soul mates now.

Petrenko: 'Come Mr Smith, we will take you to the station...'

And I'm even still alive and in one piece too.

Amazing.

Thwack.

Eh?

Brodsky: 'Tak..., tak!'

Hah!

That one sounded and must have been good too then.

I just hope he doesn't reach for his one iron.

Even God can't hit a one iron.

Whether in amusement or relief, Vladimir's also still smiling.

Oh, and even opening the door for me himself this time.

Petrenko: 'After what I have just seen..., please, allow me...'

'Thank you, Vlad, my new mate, you're very welcome.'

Yep, I could just about get used to this being chauffeured about malarkey.

On the other hand, what it's cost me with the fair Samantha, only she knows.

Actually, or my phone possibly.

Hmm.

That'll again be not then.

Petrenko: 'From Ms Palin?'

If I wasn't already, I really must now be in her bad books.

Eh?

Oh, right, Vladimir.

'Err, no...'

Blimey, talk about an inquisitive grin.

'I think she must have got the train already...'

Petrenko: 'Shame...'

Fuck, he's jokingly smirking again.

Blimey, are my inclinations towards her really that obvious then?

Yep, seems so.

Even to the driver.

'And you can just keep your eyes on the road, square face.'

Petrenko: 'If there is anything I can do to make amends, please be sure to let me know...'

'Actually, maybe..., now you say that Vlad...'

'Actually, there is one thing you could do for me, Mr Petrenko?'

Petrenko: 'Vladimir...'

'Vladimir...'

'*Yes?*'

'What were you doing at nine o'clock this morning?'

Bluffing

I'm going to get another swipe of Sandalwood out of this deodorant stick if it kills me.

Or should I just have done with it and start one of the three new ones I've got ready and waiting in the bathroom cabinet?

'Nope, think of the environment Johnny Boy, think of the environment.'

My recycled plastic bottle lampshade out there will get the hump and stop working otherwise.

Actually, what if I over-screw the deo-stick's head off its housing..., err..., yep..., and then maybe use the surplus deo-goo on the underside?

Hah, yep, it worked; brilliant!

There really are no ends to my talents.

And when I finally do up the rest of the buttons of this crisply cleaned and ironed shirt..., yep..., I'll even look the part too!

Oh, yes.

Samantha and the rest of the girls in the office – or the bus and the tube even – won't know how to hold themselves back from ravishing me.

Or..., well..., at least make myself a tad more noticeable to them than normal possibly.

Maybe.

I wonder if they'll appreciate the courage it's taking for me to actually wear this hitherto virgin Paul Smith summer suit?

Oops, fuck, what time is it?

Nope, five to seven, still good.

Just one last half slice of toast and jam to devour, and I can get off.

There's no guarantee I won't beat Nigel in otherwise.

And what would be the point of all this early-morning-riser palaver if I didn't at least achieve that?

So, right, plate and mug back to the kitchen and out.

And Si's door's still closed this morning.

He did eventually make it in last night then, whatever he got up to.

But not before I managed to slip his tie back into his wardrobe though, he-he!

'Too late, mate, too fucking late.'

He must have a mother complex; he can't seem to face a night alone.

'And it definitely feels good not to have a hangover today, eh John?'

Only, did I really try to give a possible gangster, Ukrainian oligarch a golf lesson yesterday?

Fuck, I've just imagined the whole thing, haven't I, surely?

It was odd what Mr Brodsky said about Nigel though.

Maybe he just misunderstood the offers process, lost it in translation?

Hmm.

Not Vladimir, though, no way.

Or, I wonder if Nigel has suspicions about where his money's coming from, what with the new anti-money-laundering hoops we're going to have to jump through?

Yeah, that could well be it.

Not all rich people in Ukraine have got their money through corruption, though, have they?

Christ, what's this half-arsed chalk message Si's not written on the kitchen blackboard?

Josh 07710 391something something something is that?

Blimey.

Oops...

Simon: 'Morning Matey...'

Ahh, Mr Spence. Duly looking a little dishevelled, but otherwise resplendent in his Union Jack 365s.

Lovely.

'What's this message here?'

'Yes, this gobbledegook on the blackboard...'

Nope?

'Right, well, that'll be neither of us who knows then.'

And nonchalantly so in his case.

Simon: 'How'd you get on at Henley?'

Blimey, yeah, just take a swig of orange juice direct from the bottle then.

And fuck knows where that mouth has been earlier this morning; pun intended.

'Yeah, it was alright as it happens. I assume you finally managed to get hold of Samantha in the end?'

Simon: 'Mm-hmm.'

Oh, right.

'Yeah? What did she say?'

Eh, what's he got that look in his eyes for?

'What?!'

No...

Fuck, did he really just grin and gesture smugly towards his bedroom?

Simon: 'She was well up for it as it happens... Although we were both completely hammered to be fair.'

Fuck, is he pretending..., just joking..., I can't tell.

He must be bluffing, surely?

'Yeah, right...'

Simon: 'Go and take a look for yourself if you don't believe me. You know what these girls are like; playing hard to get when actually they're gagging for it. Particularly the Americans...'

What, so Samantha's really, just down the hall..., in there..., his bedroom?

No, he's bluffing, I can tell.

Only do I give him the satisfaction of looking?

No, I'm not going to look.

I've finished in here, and I'm just going to grab my bag and get off.

If I can swallow this last mouthful of toast down that is. It seems very dry suddenly.

Blimey he's left his bedroom door wide open though.

Wow, no...

Fucking no.

Or fucking yes evidently.

Samantha.

Just a head on a pillow, but her head, even from out here in the hall.

Her..., head.

278

But...
How...?
Hmm.

Only, if she did just throw me a startled look of her own through her hair for a moment, what does it matter...?

Yep, out.

Anywhere but here.

Yes, just close the door on them both, all of it.

Laters

Yep, even Celia's eyes are telling me I'm late in again.

Or, going on that dated reception clock, make that 9.33am precisely and a near comatose two hour No. 38 joyride to Dalston and back later than I thought I was going to be.

'Afternoon Celia...'

'Morning...'

I may have caught her a little by surprise, but I'm not even a name today.

'Thanks for your message yesterday. I told Samantha.'

'Yes?'

But, nope, still nothing more than a glance and courteous smile.

Making a phone call is far more important that engaging with Mr Invisible today then.

But rather Mr Invisible than a terrifying triptych in the lift I suppose.

Yep, it'll be up the stairs two at a time if only to release this strange combination of adrenalin and inertia I can't shake out of my legs.

And I wonder if Nigel's actually in yet anyway?

Surely after a late one in The Bull he'll be in late himself too, won't he?

Actually, no, his door's closed, so that must be him in his office. So that's another excuse I'll have to think up.

And Gail's at her desk.

Fred too.

Maybe if I just dump my bag and get straight on with my work, no one will pay me any further attention today, and I can just mope my way through til five.

Assuming I can avoid the muse, if or when she gets here.

I suppose I'd better give Gail at least some sort of apologetic explanation.

'Sorry, domestic incident...'

Only...

Huh?

Gosh, Freddy and Gail are both looking back at me like a bomb's about to go off.

'Hey both, what's up?'

And, blimey, what are they now looking at each other so uncertainly for?

'Well? Yes, one of you has to tell me?'

Oops, Wendy.

Wendy: 'Nigel wants to see you John, right away please.'

Oh, right, okay then.

'Wow, Fred? Gail?'

And, yes, for now I suppose Wendy's stern beckoning does trump anything Fred and Gail won't or can't tell me.

Hang on, is that what Celia was doing? Ringing Wendy the moment I arrived?

281

After all the empty threats, is Nigel actually going to sack me?

Wow.

If so, I certainly won't miss a boss who merely glances up at me with annoyance every time I enter his office – actually, make that with barely contained aggression while he finishes doing something unimportant on his PC – a disgruntled sigh being the sign he's ready to address me.

Nigel: 'I think we both know we've come to the end of the line John. I want to say I'm sorry, but I can't. If you agree to resign, voluntarily, this morning, you can have two month's salary. I need to make cuts to the department and, well, I don't feel your heart's in it. And then there's this...'

Oh, and-then-there's-this-what in this envelope he's tossed towards me?

Ah.

Right.

And then there's this, some pages from my screenplay.

Fuck.

And, nope, not even a good part of it either.

Nigel: 'Wendy found it..., a book or whatever it is, on the printer. I take it it is yours, isn't it?'

Hmm.

Wendy.

Humph.

How delightful of her.

She is one not very nice person.

Even now, knowing what's happening in here, she's glaring at me through the glass with her unique blend of smugness and bitterness.

'For what it's worth, it really was only in my own time, lunchtimes...'

Nigel: 'What own time?!!'

Hmm.

Of course: what own time.

'Okay, if this is what you want Nigel.'

'Okay, draft what you want me to say and I'll sign it Nigel...'

'And the sooner the better please. I've really had enough for one day.'

At least I'll never have to step in or out of this, his tasteless, anaemic office again.

Nigel: 'I fucking told you, but you just couldn't fucking leave it alone, could you?!!'

Eh?

What?

Told me to leave what alone?

Nope, he's just dismissively showing me the hand and waiving me out again.

Blimey.

That guy really needs some serious man and anger management training.

Oh, and, perfectly timed at her guard desk, here's the lovely Wendy with a cardboard box for me.

Mm-hmm.

Yep, duly loaded with my personal items – isn't that the phrase? And obviously the reason why Gail and Freddy looked so spooked earlier, given how joyfully Wendy must have cleared my desk under their noses.

'Think I'll just empty the contents into my backpack if it's okay with you Wendy?'

Nope?

'Like I care that you don't want me to go back to my desk.'
Wendy: 'Harrumph, I'll also need to take your phone.'
Hah.
Really...

'Sorry, Wendy, but the phone's mine. Nigel demanded I get a phone, but refused to pay for it, remember?'
Hah.
Christ if her face was to tauten any more her head will implode.
Wendy: 'I'll just see you out then.'
Blimey.
Okay, but not before I say cheerio to Fred, Gail and Andrew though.

'Laters yaw'l...'
After today, all of them could well be following me out of the door soon enough.
If more by choice in their cases.

'Take it easy and don't work too hard, eh? Really...'
And maybe the reason why even the normally undemonstrative Gail is openly shaking her head at the perceived wrong of it.
Andrew: 'It's a joke.'
Only, scoff as Andrew might, he hasn't been here long enough to know.

'Thanks, Gail, Andrew. But don't worry about it, seriously. You lot are the only thing I'll miss. Well, except you Fred, obviously.'
Yes?

Wow.

Fred's mouth hasn't even twitched, and for once no hint of any riposte either.

Things really must be serious.

'It'll all be alright Fred.., really, I'll call you...'

Fred: 'No..., no it won't, John...'

And for once maybe he's right. Maybe it won't. Not for me. Not for them.

Still, as for the here and now...

'Okay, Wendy, lead on, lead on...'

Brrrrrb, brrrrrb.

Hmm, my phone's vibrating.

Oh yeah; left it on silent.

Don't tell me, it's Nigel wanting to know why I've still got my own phone?

Nope, no number I recognise.

Don't think I'll bother answering it any more.

Ever.

The dog

Mm-hmm.

These benches in Berkeley Square never have been very comfortable.

And particularly not when lying along the full length gazing up at the sky through the tree canopies and having to ignore the frequent tutting of disgruntled lunchtime seat-seekers.

Zen escapism meets numb-bum-ism, on this the auspicious occasion of my last ever lunch in the employ of Middleton Lyons.

If, technically, as of this second, I'm even employed there any more?

But, yes, I suppose I must be if I haven't resigned or signed whatever it is that Nigel wants me to sign.

The last rites for my career before I'm sent off to endure daytime tv with every other useless, hopeless, futureless person in Britain.

Well, some of them anyway.

Except perhaps during the World Cup, of course; or the Olympics; the European Championships even.

A month off in high summer would have been perfect then.

If I could have gotten the year of my sacking right.

Humph.

And assuming I even have a home and tv I can face going to;

one that doesn't have the utterly lovely but forever traitorous and lost Samantha in it, tormenting me.

Oh, blimey, this same tutterer's back again.

'Alright lady, alright, I give in.'

'Sorry...'

'Yep, I'm sitting up, legs gone, there you go.'

I suppose it was inevitable I'd have to return to a life vertical eventually, even if there is no single facet of life worth facing.

And if I did want to buy my own place away from the Shaghound, what sensible mortgage adviser would entertain me now?

Mortgage Adviser: 'Well, I'm sorry Sir, but, whilst I understand entirely why you want to leave that arsehole tosser of a flatmate and his fabulous girlfriend, with your having no job, no prospects and absolutely no talents or skills or abilities, I don't see how we can offer you anything... Although I do have a mate looking for a gofer in his estate agency if that could be of interest?'

Hmm.

This grass down here looks quite appealing. Maybe I could camp out with the billionaires in Mayfair for a while?

Actually, there are plenty of other benches still free, so why did Ms Tutterer here want to sit on this particular one?

Just to make a point, maybe? Is this particular bench especially designed to take extra-lly obdurate people or something?

Or is it simply reflective of the prevailing Zeitgeist? And that, in common with the uneasy minds of all the other oppressed of London, she's convinced that, if she doesn't have the same lunch on the same bench at the same time of every day, her world will cave in?

'When it already has lady, don't you know?'

Nope, even my best look of solidarity elicits nothing more than a dismissive, sideways glance up from her lunch box.

I'll doubtless be joining her in psychotherapy before I know it.

On which subject, I wonder how that spy of a spaniel cottoned onto my book as she called it. Was it simply my antics at the photocopier the other day? Did I accidentally print it twice or something? Or has she been watching me for weeks, monitoring my computer like some half-witted cyber spy, just waiting for the opportune moment to stick the knife in?

Crikey, if so, she and Nigel really do deserve each other.

I actually hope they are shagging, the blinkered, stupid so and so; Nigel the fucker in chief, she just another of the unwitting fools who he's got just where he wants us, or them. At least in Wendy's case she could actually do something about it. He's been rogering me whether I like it or not.

And then there's also the fucking principle of it, the fucker saying what he did.

How fucking well dare he?

Humph.

Only, dared he bloody well has.

Regardless of the principle of it, the injustice of his diatribe, there's just no way out of it. Fair or unfair, it makes no difference any more; it's simply a matter of how I go now, not if. I've gone and left my belt undone, and Nigel's perfectly poised and all too ready to bend me over. Either I do what he wants and resign, or give him the additional satisfaction of shafting me. And who would employ me then, having been sacked for what the bastard would doubtless claim was working on my 'book' in company time?

Fuck, how I'd love to stick it down his arrogant, conceited throat.

Me: 'That *book* as you call it is actually a screenplay you ignorant, arrogant twat, and I just sold it to Hollywood for a million quid, so I won't actually be needing your poxy fucking job any longer anyway Nigel.'

Nigel: 'Oh..., really.'

Me: 'Yes, and it's really nice to see how you're so pleased for me, mate, by the way.'

Nigel: 'Oh I am, I am...'

Me: 'And I didn't have to act like a complete tosser all my life, like you, to pull it off either.'

Nigel: 'Hmm, except that you haven't sold your poxy screenplay to Hollywood, have you John? From what I read it's just too crap, really, isn't it? And you're just too much of a wimp, a talentless loser to have pulled something like that off, aren't you?'

Me: 'Well, erm...'

Nigel: 'What's the matter John? Can't you even stand up to me in your imagination?'

'Harrumph.'

As ever, that'll again be a nope then.

Mm-hmm.

Only, what if the reality is that I don't actually want to leave?

What if I don't want never to feel sorry for Gail again, or condescend to Freddy or be baffled by Andrew; even if we are, all of us, completely oppressed, stifled, stiffed, routinely?

Just exactly why don't I ever have the balls to stand up to him, Nigel?

Maybe he's simply right after all, and I am a wimp and no fucking use to anyone, one of life's losers?

And it's just that the truth hurts.

Just what *do* I do? What use have I been? What have I ever done?

I value, market and sell commercial buildings for a twat of a boss in a nowhere company. That's it, no more, no less.

And now I haven't even got that. Fallow in every sense of the word. Five nil down before I'm even twenty-five.

And if I can't even make this job work, what hope have I got with any others?

And after all the time I've put in, all the putting up with Nigel, for what? As much as I'd be perfectly happy never setting eyes on him again, what the hell else am I going to do, really?

God knows what I was thinking trying to write a screenplay, wanting to be a film producer.

How predictable and prosaic was, and is..., that?

There are teenage German backpackers with better English than I've got, written as well as spoken doubtless. The only interesting or successful events in my life take place in my head, and I can't even get all of those right. Now it's just the reality that's comic, or it would be if it wasn't so tragic. The first girl to give me a proper look in months can't swerve me quick enough to jump into bed with my flatmate, I'm outwitted by clipboard obsessives and gimp-gear-clad media executives, and now I've even managed to render myself unemployable. And that's just in the last three days.

Oh, and a ridiculous pavement chaser, can't forget that; in Samantha's eyes at least.

And, really, what would she find interesting, let alone fanciable, in me? I am the court jester, the type that falls on his arse trying to kick a football while fetching the company trifles, the amusement for the girls at the start of the night before the real business of finding a bloke they fancy at the end of it. My name symbolises perfectly who and what I am, in fact. And I don't have to be my flatmate to work out the implications of that.

Hmm.

Yep, time to get out of here and head for the gate, I think.

This place with its tree lined sides and walls and canopy is starting to feel way too like a giant coffin all of a sudden.

If not London generally right now.

If I'm to make a temporary escape, I'll need to pack a bag at the flat first though.

Yep.

Trusting that Simon and Samantha aren't still there?

But even they must be shagged and laughed out by now, yeah?

Even if it's just an interlude before more of the same tonight.

Yep, a quick get-into-flat-and-laptop-to-email-my-resignation-letter-and-out-with-a-bag-of-clothes-to-crash-at-Duff's-for-a-bit has a good ring to it.

Any more drama today really would be the end of me.

One thing Nigel is right about, I'm certainly not cut out for the way he carries on.

You don't have to be like that to get ahead, surely?

No, life's too short, no matter what I'm going to do with the rest of mine. Even if I've got no choice any more, Nigel can stick his job. The likes of Albert Singh will have to look after themselves, look after number one. Like me.

Although, what I certainly must give a monkey's about, or should do if I want to avoid being tracked down with dogs and golf clubs, is remembering to tell Messrs Brodsky and Petrenko that I'm not going to be around to handle their offer for Platinum.

And particularly so on the off chance that Mr Brodsky wants to employ me alongside Vlad the Impaler as his special property investment and golf guru, that is.

Mm-hmm, I could just about tolerate being chauffeured around in one of those limos for a while, no matter what the threat to my lifespan.

Still, they can all look after themselves apart from them.

Yep, if there's no email from Nigel in my inbox when I get back home, my first resignation letter will be clear and straight to the point; no convoluted, pride-saving valediction about what a wanker Nigel is, why what he said is unfair, or about how it's really because I want to spend time with the family.

I hereby resign with immediate effect.

Job done.

Literally.

Oh crap, is that Leanne up ahead?

She's all I need. I'll have to cross the road to avoid her.

Oops, nope, won't make it. I'll have to pause on this traffic-bollard-island-thing for a second or two.

Oh, no, it's not Leanne. This woman's not tall enough.

Only, blimey, that little girl over there is the living embodiment of the waif.

Wow, it's now not only the billboards that are pursuing me but the real thing!

And that's some fancy dog she's stroking. What the hell is it? Some exotic foreign breed no doubt, only found on the distant plains of Guatemala, and in Mayfair.

One thing I certainly won't miss is being reminded there are dogs in the world with better coiffured hair than mine. Not that that's too hard I suppose. This one's almost as well preened as its aloof gentleman owner.

But don't follow it into the road between those parked cars my darlin'.

'Wake up Mum, nanny, lady. What can be more important in that flower stall?'

Fuck, that skip lorry..., rounding the bend..., at speed towards us.

And her.

'Quickly one of you, for fuck's sake.'

No!

'Driver?... Look!!'

Not...

'Watch... ing... No!!'
No choice.
Girl, scoop, staccato, roll.
'Woooaaaarhaaaaaaaarrrrrggghhh, uuuummmmphh.'

Arrggh.

Ahh.

Fucking hell.

But got her.

And, yep, now quickly scramble..., shuffle..., anything, the rest of the way to the kerb.

Blimey, the bumper, the tread on those tyres...
So huge, so heavy, so close.

And this one so light, so fragile.

I'm now gripping her too tightly though.
Need to let go.
Yes.
Stand her upright on the pavement.
Yes.

The young boy's staring now.
The waif's usually more troublesome brother?

His hand held tightly by the woman still obliviously scanning the flower stall.

The waif won't stop staring at me either.

'Oh, now you look Mum, lady...'

No, make that glare.

And as suspiciously as she is intensely.

And who has now grasped the waif's hand and pulled her and her brother away protectively.

Other people are staring and pointing too.

But I just can't...

Not here, not now.

No...

Even the guy in the newspaper kiosk is staring.

Got to get away.

Waif's Mother: 'Did that man hurt or..., *do* anything to you Chloe?'

'Don't-look-back..., ackh. Yes..., just-keep..., walking..., and-nobody..., ackh..., will-know.'

Yes.

Just-turn..., my-face..., to-the-wall.

And-keep..., walking...

Only..., the-pain..., burgeoning..., in-my-knee...?

Yes..., got-to-stop..., if-only..., for-a-moment.

Ackh.

A hole, in my trouser leg..., my knee bloodied behind.

Is that a scar..., across the toe of my shoe?

But..., no..., just..., got-to-keep...

And-my-jacket..., yes..., still-on-my..., forefinger.

Only..., wait..., is-that-a..., tyre-tread..., across..., the-sleave?
Can-it..., is it...

Need-to..., steady-my-path.

Yes..., that lamppost.

Yes.

> *'Look driver!!'*

                              Stop!
        No!
                Stop!!

Why-didn't-he...?!

                    No.

And now...

My-Mum..., Dad,

                    funeral...,
          in-black...
                              my funeral.

But-there-was...,

                                        no-time.

She...,

          ...so-vulnerable...

                    ...so-precious.

                    But..., so-close.

Beeeeeeepppp!!
Stop.

Car horn.

Back onto pavement.

Piccadilly.

Yes, but..., just can't...

                    Nothing left...,

          in my legs...,

                              ...in my head.

Got to sit down.

That..., doorstep?
                         No.

Yes, a bench...,

...in the park.

Green man; can cross.

Yes.

                    Through-the-gate.

There...

                              No.

A-deckchair.

Yes.

No..., why...?

Why..., tears?

None-of-it...,

                    was-real...?

        No?

                              Yes?

But...,

            just..., nothing-left...

Just...,

            emptiness.

Just...,

            nothingness.

Just...,

        tears.

Two and two

Your life really does flash by in front of your eyes then.

An irrefutable split-second staccato montage, even if I was too busy wrecking my new suit to have properly clocked it at the time.

'Probably just best to ignore why it's taken you nearly twenty-five years to put yourself in a position for it to occur though, eh John?'

And, also, why, apart from at least one surprise appearance, I can't seem to remember much of it, precisely; if it didn't feel as bland and predictable as I'd have thought it would be.

Shock maybe?

Yeah, shock maybe.

I wonder if the waif's short life flashed in front of her eyes?

She seemed completely unfazed staring back at me from the kerb.

Oops, the deckchair man.

Deckchair Man: 'That'll be a pound please guv'nor...'

And it really was worth every penny, if not its weight in gold. Think he must have just taken pity on me until now.

'Yep, here you go mate.'

And at least I'm no longer getting any more of those concerned-cum-intrigued glances of strangers; hesitating as they pass me by, unsure as to whether to leave me be or not.

Such still being the enigma – or should that be stigma – that is a supposedly grown man utterly spent.

Or just one who ran out of saline.

Mm-hmm.

And make that two suits I've trashed this week: this one irreparably so, given the holes and rips in the knee and jacket.

No wonder nobody has bothered me.

I must look like I've been the lead protagonist in a drunken brawl after an all-night drinking session.

Brrrrrb, brrrrrb.

Hmm.

My phone vibrating again.

And, yep, I suppose I do need to return to the real world eventually. Much as I might like to, I can't sit in this deckchair for the rest of my life, no matter how difficult they are..., ackh...

'Blimey, is there any part of you that isn't painful Johnny Boy?'

...to climb out of.

Oh, and four voicemail messages.

Somebody still wants me then.

I should just delete all of them unheard.

121 ring.

'Come on then, let's hear it.'

Dougie: 'John. It's Douglas Ardern here. Just following up on our conversation on the Lambeth site yesterday. Give me a call with the details. I'll give Nigel a call about it now too.'

Fuck.

Douglas Ardern.

When did he leave the message?

Message left: 8.15am

Hang on, what was it Nigel said?

You just couldn't fucking leave it alone, could you?

Is Douglas Ardern and Lambeth what he meant?

`Bleep.`

Petrenko: 'John, it is Vladimir..., Petrenko. We drive by Old Vauxhall Street this morning, and Mr Brodsky is very interested in it, but we would like to know a little about the permissions, the planning, so we have engaged advisor to investigate it for us. So, all being good, I hope we speak this afternoon.'

`Bleep.`

Simon: 'Hey man, think we need to talk, I need to..., ah..., give me a call...'

Nope.

`Delete.`

`Bleep.`

Albert Singh: 'Err, hello..., Mr Smith? It's Albert Singh here. From Singh Enterprises? I'd like to talk to you about the, err, my sale please, and about our meeting with the solicitors, this afternoon. Could you ring me please? Thank you.'

Our meeting with the solicitors?

Hmm.

I'll need to ring him back to check.

`Bleep.`

Or do I, any more?

Even if he is in an even worse place than I am?

`Message left: 9.31am`

What time is it now?

Oh.

11.06.

But if I can maybe help one of us out of the depths we're in...

`Recall.`

Albert Singh: 'Hello?'

'Hi Mr Singh, it's John here, John Smith, of..., err..., returning your call and message of earlier... Sorry I missed you; I've been out and about I'm afraid and only just got your message.'

Albert Singh: 'Please, not at all, thank you for getting back to me. I had a couple of questions before our meeting, but I've since spoken to Mr Plender about it and it all seems quite straightforward.'

Oh?

'What meeting is that Mr Singh?'

Albert Singh: 'Err, with the solicitors and the purchaser, at one o'clock, to finalise and exchange contracts? Mr Plender said you'd be coming too?'

Blimey, they're looking to exchange contracts today.

That's quick.

'No, change of plan I'm afraid, Mr Singh. But off-market offers can be very lucrative, I assure you. What have you been offered?'

Something approaching four million I should think, to get it off market.

Albert Singh: 'We managed to get the full two million asking price in the end, unconditional. Mr Plender says I should be very pleased, what with the way things are at the moment, with the market, and the need for a quick sale. And it's more than enough to repay my creditors, which is the main thing.'

The full two million...? But that's less than half of what it's worth, isn't it? Unless I'm missing something here...?

'When you say unconditional Mr Singh, has Nigel been through the planning policy context with you, the site's development potential, maybe discussed the possibility of a planning top-up or overage provision?'

Albert Singh: 'Mr Plender recommended that I leave all that to the purchaser, what with my circumstances being what they are.'

Or could there be some freehold title restriction or something else I haven't seen?

'And Nigel hasn't mentioned any specific problems with the title or anything?'

Albert Singh: 'Err..., no, I don't think so, just that the market is poor for development sites at the moment, and particularly given that I need to sell quickly to repay my creditors...'

Hmm.

Did he now...

Albert Singh: 'And in any case I understand the purchaser wants to keep the existing buildings for his distribution business; there aren't too many warehouses around here like this any more of course...'

Uh-huh, of course.

Not.

Blimey, I wonder...?

'Is the buyer Orencap SA, do you know, Mr Singh?'

Albert Singh: 'Err, no, I don't think so. Vauxhall Distribution Limited I think they said.'

'Oh, right. I thought it might be Menachem Kalin of Orencap.'

Albert Singh: 'Oh no, wait a minute, yes..., Mr Kalin..., I made a note, he owns the company, he's who we're meeting this afternoon.'

Gosh.

Fuck.

No wonder Nigel wanted me out of the way; today of all days.

Albert Singh: 'Why, have you come across him before?'

It can only mean one thing, can't it?

What else can Nigel be doing than trying to undersell it for a share of the illicit profit?

When they either develop it out or flip it with planning consent?

Albert Singh: 'Mr Smith?'

'Yes..., yes I'm afraid I have Mr Singh.'

Nigel the lazy, arrogant, good-for-nothing bastard is just not prepared to graft for it. Couldn't resist an illicit opportunistic windfall, me and Mr Singh here completely expendable.

Only, what to do about it though?

I've got to be absolutely sure before I light this particular touchpaper, no matter how tempting the ramifications.

Albert Singh: 'Hello? Mr Smith, are you still there?'

'Yes, err..., sorry Mr Singh, still here.'

Okay, why not?

'I was just thinking it's a big decision for you Mr Singh, and how, if I was you, I'd want to be absolutely sure that it's the right thing to do and that you're getting the very best price and terms. Only, whilst I have indeed come across Mr Kalin before, and I'm sure his money's as real as anybody else's, in all honesty I'm not convinced yet that his offer represents the best way forward for you..., as it stands at least.'

Albert Singh: 'Oh?'

'No, from what you've just told me I really don't think you should commit yourself legally until I've been able to explore a few potential alternatives for you, the price and the detailed terms and so forth. It shouldn't take me more than a day or two though. I think it would definitely be in your best interests.'

Albert Singh: 'Oh, err, oh..., but my solicitor is expecting me today...'

'Don't worry about that Mr Singh; just ring your solicitor and say something important has unexpectedly arisen for you today, and you'd like to meet instead at your warehouse..., in a few days..., say Wednesday next week?'

Albert Singh: 'Well, oh..., err, yes..., alright Mr Smith, if you think I should, I can ring him now.'

'Yes I do, Mr Singh.'

Albert Singh: 'Goodness! But I've already signed the contract to sell to Mr Kalin's company!'

'When you spoke to him, did your solicitor tell you they've formally exchanged?'

Albert Singh: 'No, but isn't...'

'Then signed contract or not, it doesn't matter Mr Singh, you're not committed until you've exchanged. All you need to do is ring him again now and tell him that you don't want to exchange today and that you need a few more days before you make your final decision.'

Albert Singh: 'Oh, right...'

'To be honest, Mr Singh, my strong advice is that you shouldn't presently contemplate selling for a penny less than three million. I really don't know where Nigel's coming from on this, because your site is very valuable, and there will be any number of parties interested in buying it from you for a very good deal more I should think..., even the way the property market is at the moment.'

Albert Singh: 'Oh...'

'Yes...'

Albert Singh: 'Oh, oh right... And you're sure, even though Mr Plender thinks I should be happy with two?'

'Yes, although we can both discuss this with Nigel after I've explored the alternative interest. I should be able to get back to you on this later today or tomorrow, if that'd be okay?'

Albert Singh: 'I suppose I do have two or three weeks yet...'

'And, if Mr Kalin's serious, he'll still want it in a few days in any case. It's only purchasers with hidden motives that play the now-or-never game.'

Albert Singh: 'Oh, right, in that case, thank you Mr Smith. I'll ring my solicitor now to tell him.'

'Oh, and Mr Singh? If any of the other potential parties would like to view inside the property, would they be able to do this later today or tomorrow morning? I can show them round, I'll just need you to open up for me.'

Albert Singh: 'Oh, err... yes, that's fine..., just let me know...'

'Great, I'll see you later today or tomorrow morning then.'

Oh, actually.

'Oh, and it might make sense to just speak to me rather than Nigel until then Mr Singh, if you don't mind. It might just, err..., complicate things for us both if not...'

Albert Singh: 'Oh, err..., yes, of course, if you think that's best...'

'Great, bye then Mr Singh, see you later today or tomorrow.'

Albert Singh: 'Oh, right, yes, cheerio then.'

End.

Right, good.

Assuming Nigel doesn't put two and two together.

Still, now for phase two then.

If I can find Vlad's business card that is.

I parked it in my wallet, didn't I?

Phew, yes, here it is.

Vladimir Petrenko.

Call.

So, let's see what my new Ukrainian friends might be up for.

Petrenko: 'Ahh, John Smith...'

Wow, he must have saved my number on his phone. That's a good sign.

'Err, yes, hello Mr Petrenko. I got your message, sorry I missed your call...'

Petrenko: 'Not at all...'

'I'm really glad you called...'

Petrenko: 'Old Vauxhall Street is very interesting, just as you said...'

'Yes, it really has massive potential doesn't it... And there's been a slight change of events with it...'

The proposition

It's not only the spice you can smell in this place, it's like it's also imbued with the scent of river too, somehow.

Not that it'll be around much longer after one of this assorted bunch of eager developers buys and demolishes it.

It's like Mr Singh – sitting quietly and contemplatively with his solicitor behind their makeshift table over there – will be the only one here likely to be sorry to see it go.

Shame that I won't get to play a role in whatever it's redeveloped into.

Almost.

Blimey!

What the fuck was that? It was like a gun going off.

Oh, it was just that Mr Chomyszak bodyguard of Mr Brodsky's, accidentally pushing open the connecting house door too enthusiastically; the wall taking the impact.

Don't think I was the only one to jump with the nervous tension either.

Even Mr Brodsky, judging by the way he's quietly berating his minion.

'*Yep, okay Mr Brodsky...?*'

Mm-hmm.

Still, yep, at 10.55, just another few minutes for them all to complete their open viewings before Nigel and Menachem Kalin should turn up.

The latter two hopefully still none the wiser that they're now in a crowd for it.

Only, which of all of them will want to buy this place the most, that's the intriguing question?

Douglas Ardern's and Gemma's respective clients will likely be among the stronger contenders for it.

But then there's also Mr Brodsky, and the guys from CWMS still standing watchfully in the corner over there.

And, as humble and unassuming as he is, Mr Singh has played his cards beautifully these past few days, keeping both my erstwhile boss and, by extension, Kalin warm just in case I'm wrong about the whole thing...

Like he's rediscovered his mojo.

Um-hum.

It's all certainly unconventional, but, if this little Dutch auction goes well here today, not only will Mr Singh learn demonstrably the real value of his property and be a darn sight richer, but the look on a darn sight poorer Nigel's face will be something to behold too with any luck.

Even if it is a shame he's not already at Her Majesty's pleasure.

I'll just have to trust that what's left of Nigel's respect for his professional obligation to Mr Singh – in open company like this at least – is more powerful than his urge to challenge what I'm doing here.

Until I've done anyway.

Giving Gail copies of the paperwork Fred and I dug out on the two other deals Vladimir told me about was probably a good idea as insurance though.

Yep.

And, given that's Nigel who's just appeared in the roller shutter doorway, it's too late to do anything else now in any case.

And, mm-hmm, one of those two shadows only a step or two behind him must duly be Menachem Kalin too; the other either a bodyguard or a suitably large and indulgent solicitor possibly.

Blimey, look at Nigel hesitating mid warehouse like that.

This must be the first time he's genuinely stunned at something I've done or said.

Definitely no going back now then.

'Okay, yep, we're on Mr Singh.'

'Right I think we're all here now, everyone – Nigel, Mr Kalin – sorry to keep you all waiting, but if you could all just gather round a little please, I'll explain the process.'

Yep, Kalin's duly looking to Nigel for an explanation, but Nigel's eyes are fixed on me, betraying his confliction, his mind whirring.

'Yes, you should have bought me that mobile phone Nigel...'

This may work yet.

Clipboards and offer forms next then.

'I'm sorry that this is all a little unconventional, but as you know Mr Singh is keen to secure an early, in principle agreement today, so hopefully, if you've all seen and heard what you need to, I'd like you to take and complete one of each of these please...'

'Yep, here you go Gemma..., Douglas..., Mr Brodsky..., yep, Michael..., Mr Kalin...'

Hmm.

The first time I've made eye contact with Nigel since he fired me, but still he's not reacting.

Neither distance nor body language is going to be the reason why we fail to understand each other here and now.

In fact, before even I doubt otherwise, it's like he's more taken aback than I am by the speed of our evolving estimations of each other.

Back to the task at hand though.

'So, as you're all aware, this is a selective off-market offer, so if you can kindly confirm for me on the offer form the name of the bidding entity and your best offer for the site plus any planning overage please, and then I'll come around and collect them...'

At least, in another first in our burgeoning relationship, there's no further pretence between Nigel and me any more.

Pretence from him that he's not a scurrilous scumbag.

Pretence from me that I don't know it.

Not that that's stopping him from sidling over to Mr Singh of course – rightly gambling that I haven't told our client yet; assuming Mr Singh hasn't worked out for himself Nigel's malign intent.

Albeit, looking at his feigned casualness from here, whether my hitherto untouchable boss feels embarrassed or defiant, vulnerable even, or just surprised at the turn of events, is still anyone's guess.

Kalin, on the other hand, doesn't know whether to complete the form or throw it across the floor in fury.

Hah!

'Nope, look to him as much as you want Mr Kalin, but I really don't think you'll get any more help from Nigel today...'

And, yes, as well Kalin might surreptitiously view Mr Brodsky et al warily in his consideration of whether to make a scene or not.

'Yep, that's it, just write down your best and final offer like the others Mr Kalin, that's it.'

Mm-hmm.

Looks like the majority have finished.

And, irony of ironies, Nigel's even sharing a smile and whispered exchange with Mr Singh now too.

'Okay, everybody, if you're all done, I'll take the offers from you please...'

And left to right is as good as any way I suppose.

'Thanks Douglas..., Gemma..., Mr Brodsky..., yep..., thanks..., right you are Mr Kalin.'

So, let's see, what offers have we got here then?

Hmm.

Yep, just as I thought – mostly three and a half million and upwards, and a couple with overage too.

Still, yep, I can now just leave these with Mr Singh and his solicitor to run through.

'I think this should clarify things for you Mr Singh. Please let me know if I can further assist in any way; otherwise I think your solicitor can take things from here. Cheerio and best of luck with it.'

And as surprised as Mr Singh looks, that is indeed me out of here.

'Yep, goodbye Nigel.'

Mm-hmm.

'Take it easy Gemma..., Mr Brodsky..., everybody...'

And..., wow.

It may only be because he's terrified by what I've got on him, but was that the first ever vaguely respectful look Nigel gave me then?

Blimey.

And just how the hell am I supposed to react to that?

Just take him literally at face value, and treat it as just another genuine first in a day of them? Belated acknowledgment that Johnny Smith came good eventually?

Or, just, whatever his intention, as too late for either of us?

He must surely know the law will get him and lizard face soon enough, in whichever way it comes about; the now unstoppable wheels that are the freehold transfer and company ownership documents will see to that, closely followed by Messrs Middleton and Lyons and their professional indemnity insurers no doubt.

There must have just come a point when being a bastard oppressor, being crooked, became easier and more lucrative than being supportive and honest.

But, nope, I really don't care any more.

Oops.

Who does this shadow out here belong to?

Ah, but of course, who else but Mr Vladimir Petrenko.

Standing apart by the roller shutter, as if this is exactly what he anticipated.

Oh, and I get a twin finger head salute and knowing smile too.

'Yeah, so long Vladimir, you take it easy too mate.'

The circus moves on pretty fast doesn't he know.

If we don't stop and look around once in a while...

A special kind of lovely

They said we'd be boarding in five minutes at least fifteen minutes ago, didn't they?

Even a broadsheet newspaper pulled up in front of your face doesn't shorten the wait or improve the view in this monstrosity of an edifice. It may be an airport, but couldn't they have made even a small effort with the architecture of it, or apply just a little bit of aesthetic design ethos?

Then again, the view this end seat is affording me of this air hostess slinking her way into my eye-line might start to dispose me just a little more to its merits.

Samantha: 'Don't let me stop you...'

Oops, caught.

It really didn't take her long to grab that take-out coffee and sandwich then.

And bang goes my theory that recent events are going to make me mature anytime soon.

Not that I shouldn't make the most of my immaturity while I've still got it obviously.

'I'm just reading my newspaper, so I have absolutely no idea about what..., or who..., you're on about.'

Yikes.

Oof...

And, no, I suppose a newspaper is no barrier to a flying sandwich wrap.

'Mmm, chicken and sweetcorn, perfect, thanks.'

Samantha: 'Here, I also bought you a city guide, so you won't get lost without me.'

'Oh, right, wow, thanks.'

A native New Yorker's guide indeed.

Good job she didn't throw this through my newspaper.

Samantha: 'You're going to love it...'

'Thanks, but you do realise I'm only going with you because I've got nothing better to do this next couple of weeks, yeah?'

Samantha: 'Sure. It was nothing to do with your mom threatening to come down to sort your life out for you then?'

Hmm.

'Nope, that actually had nothing to do with it Yanks, trust me.'

Samantha: 'And, if you don't behave yourself, I might accidentally leave you alone with mine...'

'Now you suggest it, I suppose I could just about force myself to see your MOMA at some point or other...'

Hah.

'Go on, laugh at my terrible joke, I know you want to.'

Or, actually, was it technically a pun?

Samantha: 'Hmm. But I do actually want to introduce you to that particular M.O.M.A. You can get *yourself* to the Guggenheim, where you can get all those nerdy Frank Lloyd-Wright-y inclinations out of your system.'

And here was me thinking I'm interesting in an unpredictable kind of way...

'Thanks, very generous of you.'

'It's not those particular inclinations I'm hoping you'll give me a hand with though Yanks.'

314

Samantha: 'You're welcome, don't mention it.'

'And I thought American's didn't do sarcasm.'

Samantha: 'The British side of me.'

'Right; keep forgetting.'

Samantha: 'Hey, look at that on the tv... Isn't that the street a couple of blocks along from the office?'

Blimey, it is as well.

'Berkeley Street...'

TV Newscaster: 'And finally, amazing CCTV footage has emerged of an incredible act of bravery in London's West End...'

'Fuck, you've got to be kidding me...'

The waif.

And me.

TV Newscaster: 'A so far anonymous, real-life hero – seen here on the right – making a seemingly death-defying lunge to save a young girl from the wheels of a skip lorry...'

Christ, that really fucking well really actually was as close as I thought then.

Fuck.

And, ouch.

No fucking wonder I was staggering away like that.

And, yikes, make that me in reasonable close-up on full tv screen too now.

Oops.

Samantha.

And that quizzical look on her face again.

'Hmm, what?'

Nope, she's turned back to the tv again.

Oh, and of course.

The waif's mum now as well.

Madam Negligent there should be hiding her head in shame rather than giving tv interviews.

'*That reminds me lady: you owe me a new Paul Smith suit.*'

Actually, don't I recognise the man she's with too?

He wasn't there was he?

TV Newscaster: 'And in a remarkable twist it has emerged that the little girl so spectacularly saved in the footage is the daughter of reclusive media tycoon Richard Forbes, who's been trying for more than a week now to track down the elusive hero.'

Blimey.

Actually, looking at that I should feel quite pleased with myself, shouldn't I?

Yep, even the fearless Tommy-I-do-my-own-stunts himself would be impressed.

Tom: 'Not bad, John! Not bad at all...'

Samantha: 'That is fucking unbelievable....'

Me: 'Thanks, Tom. I just did what came naturally.'

Tom: 'Wow, that is some naturally, I'll tell you that. That would've taken me at least two takes to get that close to the lorry. Phewy!'

Me: 'It was actually real-life Tom...'

Tom: 'Eh? What...?'

Yeah, that makes two of us baffled and uncomprehending at my stupidity matey.

Oops.

Samantha: 'Are you watching this...?'

'*Eh..., I dunno..., watching what?*'

TV Newscaster: 'Are you the hero of Berkeley Street? Or do you know who he is? If so, we'd very much like to hear from you.'

Woah, where the hell did they get that close-up still of me from?!

Lucky it's a bit blurry.

But, yikes, Samantha's done a double take.

TV Newscaster: 'A truly remarkable story, I think you'll agree. But now over to the weather...'

I'll need to pick the newspaper up again. To stop anybody else thinking they can put two and two together.

Samantha: 'What the fuck...?!'

Crap.

'Eh? What the fuck what?'

Samantha: 'That is, that's you, isn't it?'

'Crikey Samantha, can you keep your voice down?!'

'What is? That? Hah, yeah, right.'

Why won't the leaves of this bloody paper stand up properly any more?

And now she's gone and slumped back in her chair in thought.

It's too late, she knows.

She just can't think of the words.

Any second now though...

Yikes.

And, yep, there goes what's left of my newspaper protection.

'Terrific, thanks for this Samantha.'

Has anybody else in eyeshot noticed, that's the question?

'I wouldn't be too rough with this newspaper. It's a long flight and we might run out of conversation.'

But, nope, the only one paying us any attention is that bloke on his phone over there.

And with any luck he's just been drawn to Samantha tearing my newspaper down and just thinks we're having a domestic.

Samantha: 'Was that the same morning as...?'

Hmm.

'...as you and..., harrumph..., you mean...?'

Mm-hmm.

'That was then, this is now though.'

Samantha: 'That..., was amazing...'

Tom: 'Oh yeah, tell me about it...'

Me: 'Okay, that'll do now thanks Tom.'

317

'It didn't feel like that at the time, trust me. Although I'm glad the wee waif's okay.'

Oops, did I say that last bit out loud?

Samantha: 'The wee what?!'

'Err, it's nothing..., the..., err, wee waif...'

'*What?!*'

'...the young girl...'

Blimey.

I've made her slump back in her chair in thought again.

Samantha: 'You've got to stay, make the most of it...'

Eh?

'Oh yeah, and do what exactly?'

'*Hmm?*'

'In fact, New York is probably the best place for me to go right now...'

Yep.

'*Not that you're now even listening to me, though, eh?*'

Samantha: 'You'd be famous..., I dunno...., earn thousands from the newspapers..., or something...'

'*Oh, now you look back at me.*'

Samantha: 'And that guy, the father, he must be a billionaire for Pete's sake!'

Wow, the dancing light in those eyes of hers, just when I thought she couldn't get any lovelier.

Hold-ups will have to relinquish her crown – if she ever had it in the first place.

Samantha: 'Well?!'

'Well, what?'

Samantha: 'What?!'

'*Nothing, wow...*'

Samantha: 'Come on, what?!'

Hmm.

'If I learnt anything from it, it's not what, but who..., and with maybe a little bit of when...'

Samantha: 'Can you please just listen to me and talk sense for a few seconds....'

Hah!

Oh, the irony.

'Okay then, Miss Lovely...'

Let's really see where this..., us..., is going.

'In the moment..., I had a staccato..., you know, a life-flash..., and you were in it. So, tell me, what does that say? That I want to stay and make the most of it? Or that I just want to go to New York..., with you...'

'And, well, yep, there it is Yanks.'

Oops.

There's that hard-assed New Yorker stare again.

As a prelude to what I've actually gone and succeeded in doing: namely making her look down into her lap.

Or worse, upsetting her even?

'So, well, there it is. Okay?'

Mmm.

'Fabulous John, well done, even better.'

Yep.

'Ben Keady, you've got a lot to answer for...'

Samantha: 'What?'

Oops.

Samantha: 'Who?'

'Nobody... Err, well, somebody, obviously..., just nobody you...'

Know.

'And I mean, come on, what could an extremely grateful, mega-influential media billionaire possibly, really, do for me, anyhow?'

319

'Come on Ms Sexy Lips, show me a flicker, please...'

'And Freddy's been trying to out me for years on something or other, so how could I deny him a gilt-edged opportunity like this?'

Samantha: 'And that's your attempt at talking sense for a few seconds?'

'Well..., there are also the bars full of sexy American girls you've promised me too, of course...'

'Come on, you can do it pursed lips, all I need from you is just a flicker...'

Yep?

Nope?

'Sorry..., if I...'

Samantha: 'Okay, you can stop talking now...'

Blimey, what's she...

Yikes, there goes what's left of the newspaper then.

But, oh..., wow...

Mmm.

So, I did get to kiss her.

And, mmm..., wow.

The taste...

Her smell...

Wow.

Is there anything about her that isn't fabulous?

Wow.

And she's even giving me the arms-wrapped-around-the-neck treatment too.

Mmm.

But, yet, at the same time so tenderly, lingeringly.

Mm-hmm.

I've said it before and I'll say it again, I should throw myself, or a cake, on the ground more often.

Bing bong.

What..., really..., now?!

Tanoy Announcer: 'Would all passengers for flight BA3126 to New York please proceed to boarding gate 24. Please ensure that you have your passports and boarding cards ready for inspection.'

Typical.

'No, don't let go...'

We can maybe just stay here and do that a bit longer, can't we?

Gosh, even her corneas are a special kind of lovely.

Samantha: 'Well, I don't suppose you were ever going to get round to kissing me first, were you?'

'Oh, I dunno..., looking at that I seem to be able to scoop up the occasional girl in my arms when the mood takes me...'

Otherwise engaged

Umm? Yes...? Err..., eh?

Oh..., Samantha.

Mmm, must have dozed off.

Maybe long-haul plane seats aren't so uncomfortable after all.

And, for once, nope, I didn't dream the whole thing then.

'And what are you looking at me so closely for, Ms Palin?'

'That's not actually a Rom-com you've started reading while I've not been keeping an eye on you, is it?'

Samantha: 'Oh, this is just homework, a bit of essential reading.'

'Yeah, right.'

Samantha: 'No, really. Fifi suggested it. It's a story about a cool girl tolerating a plonker of a guy on a travel trip, apparently. Can't think why she thought of me though...'

'Hah, hah.'

Samantha: 'Come on..., as a long-haul debutante..., it's important we stretch our legs...'

Debutante?

Me...?

Pah.

What?

Blimey, where's she leading us now?

It's near pitch black in here and almost everybody else is trying to catch some shuteye; can't I just doze off again too for a bit?

Oops.

This annoyed professional-flier type certainly thinks I should have stayed where I was in my seat and doze for a bit longer.

'Sorry..., excuse me..., err..., sorry...'

Actually, I suppose it is good to stand up and stretch our legs.

And, yes, maybe now would be a good, quiet time to use the loo.

'Okay, I know how...'
Whooaahhh!

Yikes.

Blimey.

That'll be yanked – in both senses of the word – into the loo by my own T shirt and the lock deftly slid to engaged behind us all in one motion then.

And..., gosh...

Wow, the taste of her lips again...

'Mmmm...'

They should..., carry-a..., heart-warning...

Ooh.

Hang on, is she...?
Noh...
Samantha: 'What?'

Wow, she really is...

Samantha: 'And I don't suppose you were going to get round to this, first, either, were you?'

'Well, I...'

Samantha: 'No...?'

Blimey.

Samantha: 'What's up, lost the power of speech all of a sudden?'

'Well..., ahh...'

And if she can reach for my belt buc...

'Ooh...'

Maybe her T shirt will...?

'Ahhh...'

Samantha: 'Don't tell me – When Harry met Sally?'

Crikey, she really doesn't wear a...

Samantha: 'Mm-hmm?'

Oh gosh, these lips again...

'Mmmm...'

Blimey.

'Ooh...'

Her hands..., too...

'Wow, can we really?'

Samantha: 'Oh yeah...'

Wow.

So this is what she meant by stretching our...